Three Long Days
The Unspoken Truth

Michael Cantwell

KSM Publishing

ISBN: 0615640028
ISBN-13: 978-0615640020

DEDICATION

This book is dedicated to all who have volunteered their time and energies in the service of others. It is also dedicated to my family and friends who have shaped me in more ways than I care to admit.

1

*T*he three days I had to spend sitting in a federal prison cell were the toughest on me. What crime? Loving my country and attempting to end corruption and wasteful spending that runs rampant in our nation's capital. I realize that many in my situation, while sitting in prison, all want to believe they are innocent of the crimes for which that are charged but in reality many are liars and will not repent their sins. I am not untruthful nor do I have sins to repent for while representing my district. I was a member of the House of Representatives in the United States Congress representing the 22nd district from south Florida. I was given the daunting task of proving my innocence and clear my name.

My name is George Thomas McAdams and I think the truth should be more than a passing thought. One of my favorite quotes comes from President Abraham Lincoln which states, "No man has a good enough memory to make a successful liar." I will fall on the truth every time even if it means sitting in a prison watching my mother wipe the tears from her eyes for a vicious crime I did not commit.

It all started for me in my youth, my aversion for telling non truths. One day when I was eleven years young a group of us kids were hanging out at a friend's house. Despite a stern warning we were tossing around a ball in the main room of the home. Inevitably a nice lamp was broken and we all knew who threw the ball that hit it. I had been sitting off to the side not participating in the ball tossing. When my friend's mom returned home from shopping, the game of twenty questions ensued. When I was quizzed, like the others before me, I clammed up not wanting to sell out my friends. Every one of us acted as if some total stranger had entered the place while we were all doing our math homework quietly in the corner and we didn't know a thing. Well that cost each of us over five dollars to replace the broken lamp. Try going home and asking your dad for five dollars for a broken lamp and again explain how you didn't see a thing because you were merely an innocent bystander and see how quickly you get your requested funds. You don't, not easily. I had to work it off in my grandmother's yard one long hot afternoon to earn back the small bill buried in my father's wallet.

As if that one incident was not bad enough, the second big lie hurt me more than the time spent cleaning up my grandmother's yard. I enjoyed my time on weekends playing board games with my granddad. We had played checkers and chess along with other games for years. I was new to the game of chess so my granddad would beat me on a regular basis. He was not one to "let me win" and would always tell me "you earn it if you want to enjoy the fruits of success". So even though I enjoyed our games together, I was a competitive kid who found my name too often in the loss column. One day while playing chess I was actually about even in a game that was nearly half way completed. It was the best I had ever done in holding my own after approximately twenty moves. My granddad left the table for a few moments, which allowed me just enough time to move my knight one space to the left, which made it much easier to attack my opponent's queen. Now that I am older I know how easy it was for an experienced player like my granddad to notice but back then it never entered my mind. When he returned he took notice of the one space shift almost immediately. "Is that board set up exactly the same way as when I left?" he asked me. I am sure my muscles tightened up all over before I very sheepishly replied "sure, why do you ask?" He looked at me knowing for the first time ever I was not only a cheat but a liar, he knew it and I knew it. I didn't back down from my lie and despite what was I am sure the guilt written all over my face and my slumping shoulders, I grabbed up his queen anyway. I don't remember who won the game but I do remember that was the day I lost the trust and respect of my granddad, something I never completely restored. I can't be sure if that was my last lie but I know from that day forward I made a pledge to never do it again. What seemed like such a small thing at the time hit me hard when my granddad refused to play chess with me for several weekends after my one misstep. It was never the same after that day between us. Occasions like that are not easily forgotten.

We all have our vices and things we wish we could "do over" since we are mere mortals trying to live life but for me telling the truth is something I strive to do every waking moment no matter how hard the truth might affect me or others. I made a pledge to my grandfather the last time I saw him before his passing that I would do everything in my power never to cheat or lie again. I did all I could to make it right between us. I want to believe I succeeded even as I sat in a solitary prison cell branded as someone I knew I was not.

I grew up in a small ocean community on the east coast of Florida called Boca Breezes. You could barely breathe without someone else knowing about it in this town. In the early days there was only one grocery store, one movie theater, one insurance office, one accountant and so on. They all operated out of buildings along a mile long street. It stretched from City Hall to the bridge that connected the main section of town and across the intra coastal waterway to a smaller strip of land and the Atlantic Ocean. The ocean was the east border of town and City Hall was to the west at the opposite side of Boca Lakes Avenue. The sleepy town was developed in the early 1920's by citizens invading from the northeast parts of the United States and a few settlers from Europe. We did have one older gentleman, Mr. Joe from Iron City, Michigan who made sure we all knew how much snow was on the ground in his former home town as opposed to sunny southern sections of his adopted town. I imagine every small town has a Mr. Joe.

My parents were both successful with my dad a lawyer and my mom a veterinarian. I was an only child who was always busy after school socializing or playing sports. There was not much reason to head home before dinner time since both parents were rarely at home before seven in the evening. I would end up at the beach on weekends if I was not at sports practices or a game. Despite my constant socializing I never had a steady girlfriend till later in life. I was usually too busy and maybe too selfish to want to worry about having a steady date on weekends. I grew up with a permanent tan and a lean body from all the beach parties and work outs from sports. I attended a small private high school which made it easy to participate in athletics if you had a shred of ability and showed any desire to compete. I was a better than average athlete so I usually played a fair amount during basketball and baseball season. I ran with the cross country team my freshman year but I really did not see the point with all the running. Maybe I was too lazy to want to be in the top shape you need to be in to be a top runner, who knows? I know I didn't like coming in around 20th place and running more than a few miles each day in the baking Florida sun. So I mostly stuck to basketball and baseball along with the chess club. My parents were mindful of my grades so I worked just hard enough to keep them in the upper ten percent of my class. That kept my parents from snooping into my business too much. I knew as long as I stayed out of trouble and kept top grades I could do pretty much anything I wanted most evenings and weekends without too much interference from them. Besides they were usually not home to know if I was around or not.

Our next door neighbor growing up was an aging but still regal looking gentleman with silver hair and as legend had it was once quite the ladies man. Everyone suspected he started the legend but I didn't care about such things. To me he was the guy who was always staring into space out of his back window. People stayed away from him and he for the most part stayed away from others in the neighborhood. I asked my mother about Dr. Carter a few times and she would tell me "he's a grumpy old man who does not like people so it is best to leave him alone." Dr. Carter would sit for hours staring at the sky or so it seemed to others. Sometimes I would sit on our back porch and I would watch him and try to figure out what he was always watching or what he was trying to accomplish with all his staring. Every now and again he would leave his porch and move closer to the water line and bring with him what looked to be a large camera on three legs. He would disappear under a cloth for several minutes. He would within a few minutes emerge from under the black cover and move everything back inside. Doc would sit for hours but the ritual with the camera would last for only a few minutes until he would again disappear back inside his house. As I got older, I grew more curious but no one else in the neighborhood seemed to care what the old doc was up to under that cover.

One fall day in my sophomore year in high school we had a teachers work day or some lame excuse for an off day, but I didn't care. It meant we had a day off with no sports practice and no homework during what should have been a normal school day. I was sitting on my porch deciding between hanging at the beach or playing tennis when I noticed Dr. Carter and his three pronged camera being placed carefully looking at the reflections of the sky bouncing off the water. The sun was peeking through the clouds in an early position of the day so it had an almost mysterious quality about it. I decided to finally go over and check out what was going on under that cloth of his. "What'cha doing over there Doc" I yelled from about ten feet. No response. I cautiously moved a few feet closer. Again I ask, "Is anyone under that hood with you?" No response again. Finally he pops his head from under the black cloth that was surrounding most of his frame and seemed shocked that I was attempting to speak with him. His response was not one I was expecting, "Do you realize that the sun is only in that exact spot one day each year and at one time? I have waited a full year to get that exact image and I was lucky to have a similar cloud and shadows that I had this exact time last year when I missed it and now you have interrupted my day!" I could now see why most didn't attempt to engage the good Doctor with banter. What did I know about sun positions other than its frigging hot in the summer and almost bearable the remainder of the year? I apologized but told him that I thought he was rather rude since I was only attempting to be polite with a short conversation. You see part of not telling lies also lent me to not always being as tactful as maybe I should be from time to time. Also since my attorney dad was always drilling in me to give direct responses to questions I was usually that way no matter what the situation. It was maybe not the best way to live but it is who I am even to this day.

After a few moments Dr. Carter apologized for yelling at me. He showed me his journal that he had kept for more than a few years now of where the sun would hit the water at certain times of the day during the year as well as other things around his back yard. He knew where just about every shadow would be in his yard at any particular time of day on any given day. It was a meticulous journal that at first seemed crazy to me. I mean why go to all this trouble? I think possibly his guilt took over even more when he invited me onto his porch for a glass of iced tea. I felt obligated even though I knew my friends would be calling soon to arrange our schedule for the day. After our initial conflict he seemed to be quite pleasant with me and started to share his passion for photography and why he kept the extensive journal. It turns out that the good doctor was a retired ophthalmologist who had a passion for riding horses in his youth and into his early forties. However when he was forty-three he was thrown from his horse and hurt his back. It got worse over time since he spent much of his day getting up and down from chairs constantly in his profession. He was forced to retire with near constant back pain in his early fifties. So now he sits in his comfortable seat either on his porch or staring out the window spying on shadows as they dance across his yard. Photography was now his passion.

I am not sure if the Doc wanted company for a little while or maybe he enjoyed the fact that I took an interest in his photography but he allowed me into his home to show me all his work hanging on his egg shell colored walls. When I dared to ask why he only took black and white and not any color photos he quickly snapped back "George last I checked shades of gray are colors too." He then made the fatal error of asking me my opinion of his work without understanding my ability to cut straight to the end game. "I think that one is maybe too dark in that area of the photo and well that image over there makes no sense to me at all. I do like the one on the side wall but does it

7

really have to be that large, I mean who are you trying to impress?" Dead silence hit the room as if the eye of a hurricane was over south Florida. "Well George I appreciate your comments but maybe you should learn about composition and fine art printing before offering another opinion." I knew I should have accepted his response and let it all go but for some reason at that moment I could not. "You know Doctor, if you don't like a real critique or my opinion then maybe you should not have asked for it." I really did say it as politely as possible not meaning to be rude or insensitive but he did ask for my true opinion. Doc let out a loud bellow from across the room and said, "You know what kid, I like your style, I did ask a direct question and you gave me a direct answer. If I was afraid of the answer I should have never asked the question. I have gotten so use to people walking in here and telling me how fabulous all my work is you are maybe the first person to give me their honest opinion. Instead of being upset I should thank you for your remarks." Not the response I was expecting but it did seem to offer an insight as to our future relationship.

If Doc Carter was still on this earth I am sure he would have been the first to defend my character the day I faced Judge Hook and a jury of my peers during my trial. He and I had so many talks about how dirty politics can be. Despite that he would constantly tell me that our nation needed men of ethics like me. He was however also worried that one day I would be swallowed up by the same people I would later try to eliminate from serving our great land. He always thought I was wise beyond my years but now I wonder if I should have listened to my mother when she would tell me "find a nice desk job and go raise my grandchildren without me worrying for your safety so much." I may have been wise beyond my years but nothing could prepare me for what was to come in later life.

I was never one who wanted to be seen as the leader but it seemed I was always making decisions for my circle of friends and even teammates. I was named co-captain of our school baseball team as a junior as well as being in student government. I was a bit uneasy with the small amount of attention for being seen as leader but it was better than letting some knucklehead attempt to use up quality meeting time by suggesting that the student government should try to get no homework days twice a week. I mean how could a small student group be taken seriously if all we did was debate what flavors of soda should be dispensed in the cafeteria? Or better yet, our other team co-captain wanted me to go with him to the athletic director's office to let him know that we wanted new uniforms each year since our team had new members. Somehow I missed that meeting and left my dignity in place. I wanted to be taken seriously when it came to ideas and it seemed the more I voiced that publically the more I was being put on committees to fill my days and weekends. I am not sure my ideas were often adopted but I was not afraid to offer some. I was gaining valuable experience in public speaking but at that time in my young life I never gave serving our community at large a second thought.

The remainder of my high school experience was a good one. I know sometimes people look back and think how horrible it was or how out of touch most teachers seemed but I really enjoyed my time in high school. I participated in many events including community clean up the beach days or monitoring sea turtle eggs. During the summers I worked odd jobs to make spending money. In school I enjoyed subjects like history as well as my economics and accounting classes. From that I made a decision to be a financial analyst as a future career or possibly a tax attorney. I enjoyed finances and understood it very well so I wanted to pursue something using those abilities. I finished with a grade point average that put me near the top of the class but I knew I didn't really work hard enough to be class valedictorian. I wanted to do other things in school and I didn't have the mental ability to be at the very top unless I put in more of an effort. Besides the brains of the class Linda Nicole, spent her off times in the library just for fun. She only missed one question on the SAT college prep tests. She was the complete package, beauty and the brains of the class. I knew my limits.

The one thing that did occupy my free time when not in school or with friends was my growing interest in photography. I started to spend parts of my weekends with my neighbor Dr. Carter who had this fantastic dark room hidden away in the back of his home. He took the time to teach me the finer elements of fine art printing. One day when we were waiting for a print to wash I asked him why he decided to be an eye doctor. He told me "The eyes are the path to someone's soul and I wanted to see what was in everyone's soul." When I first heard that remark I took him as a bit of an old tired quack doctor who had lived alone far too long. Years later I developed that same ability to look deep into another's soul through their eyes. It was the Doc who was wise beyond his years, not me. It is now something I rely on heavily and will now request my accusers to look deeply into my eyes to discover the truth.

One thing that you learn if you study photography is to see things that others don't see as easily. It makes you more aware of your surroundings. I realize that many people would think that you are only being observant but I believe it's more than that. Sometimes it's a carefully hidden osprey in a tree or a shadow or a shape that maybe you would not have noticed before learning the concepts of composition. Dr. Carter told me that it takes ten years to learn how to be a photographer. I suspect it takes longer. It did make me take closer notice of the people around me and how they dressed at times and how that fit their personalities. I don't say that in a demeaning way at all.

Here again, it made me more aware of many things in my life. Over the course of a few short years Dr. Carter taught me how to respect a brief moment in time and space using light as the source. I think it also taught me that everything was not always black and white but there is color in a shade of grey. I will let you think on that one.

 In politics everyone wants to look for the grey and not solve the black and white issues in front of them. I grew so impatient with the process and the concept of being reelected as opposed to doing the job I was sent there to do in the first place. It all seemed so ugly to me and when I voiced my opinion I was only banished farther down the hallways to a smaller office or being asked to serve on committees that had no real economic issues to solve. That was my downfall. Most in Congress knew I could help solve the budget crisis with sound decisions. I grew to learn it was the self inflicted conflict between them all that led to more reelections and not real problem solving. When it was clear to others that I did not want to "kick the can down the road", I had become a problem that had to be dealt with before I took my questions public.

2

When it came time for college I was really torn in my decision. Both my parents and Dr. Carter thought I should go to a big city away from Florida. This was one of the first major decisions I had to make in my life. I decided first on leaving the state then chose the city of Philadelphia and finally LaSalle College. I think at the time New York City was maybe too intense for me but I wanted to be in the north east area of the United States. I also considered Boston, and I know this is not a good reason, but growing up I was a National League fan when it came to baseball and Philly was a National league town, Boston was not. I know, I know, but when it almost comes down to a coin flip and being eighteen years young we sometimes make choices based on odd things. Besides Boston was about a five hour drive and Washington was a three hour trek in the opposite direction. So I could visit both towns over time as well as New York. Philly seemed like a good place to experience the range of the north east section of our beautiful country. Besides I knew from history that Philadelphia was chosen as the nation's first capital based on demographics and because it was centrally located at that time in our history.

So there I was leaving sunny south Florida for the colder and darker skies of the north east regions of Philadelphia not knowing a soul. My dad was working on a big murder case and my mom, well she was just busy as always, so I loaded up the Chevy Camaro they bought me as a graduation gift and went alone. I had not really been outside of Florida often since we rarely took family vacations so driving up the coast alone was a bit scary. My mother made me stop and find a pay phone at least every four hours until I reached my dorm room except for the time I slept. I think however it helped me grow up even faster than my age would suggest. Upon arrival I noticed that even though everyone was still speaking English there were accents to which I was unaccustomed. I also noticed my bright colored clothes and sandals gave way to dark tee shirts and Converse sneakers. Many of the girls had big hair that was hard to explain and many of the guys were named Anthony and the girls Marie. It was all a bit of a culture shock to me but it didn't take me too long to ditch the Hawaiian shirts for the flannel ones that seemed to be the uniform of choice in that part of the country. Once fall hit, the flip flops were no longer good foot wear so I bought a few pairs of boots and sneakers. The entire dress code and new hair styles were all foreign to me. I mean I wore jeans and polo shirts all during high school and had shorts and muscle shirts on five minutes after the school bell rang. I was not used to having to wear sweaters in October. My wardrobe needed a quick makeover.

I was assigned a room with yet another "Tony" as a roommate. Tony Montero was from across the Delaware River outside of Trenton, New Jersey. He went to St. Anthony's High School and had a long standing girl friend named Marie Mancini who he had known since they were both seven years old. Marie attended St. Joe's University across town. Tony told me that they decided "they both needed to have some space to see if their love was true or not." Oh yuk. Tony was a good guy but the gold chains were at times a bit much especially during pickup basketball games when I got hit more than once in the face going up for rebounds at the same time as Tony. He meant well but we were from different worlds. I soon found out that he grew up a New York Jets football fan that made me ill being a Miami Dolphins fan. We had to sit at opposite ends of our dorm rooms at least twice a year when they played each other. He too was an accounting major so we shared a few classes as well as other common interests. Overall he was a good roommate despite his poor judgment on who to root for with his football team.

His girlfriend Marie would come to visit on weekends or Tony would make the trek to St. Joe's. It was about a twenty minute trip by car so they kept in close contact. Marie was majoring in making Tony jealous so that he didn't let her slip too far away from her control. She wanted the four years to be over so that they could both move back to Trenton get married and start having children. She had long black flowing hair and a very attractive figure. But make no mistake about it she was the boss over Tony. He put up a front like he was in charge but everyone knew within moments of meeting Marie and seeing them interact who wore the pants in the family. Don't think I didn't tease him every chance I got. However, I never teased Tony while Marie was in ear shot since she would protect him like a mother gator over her eggs. She could be very sweet most times but her temper was something I did my best to avoid.

Freshman year was quite the experience all around. I took Tony with me on spring break back home to Florida. I think it was as much of a culture shock for him heading in my direction as it was for me living in Philly. He had to call Marie every day at exactly five in the afternoon or she would assume he was up to no good. Since I don't think she could hear all the way from Palm Beach County to Trenton I let him have it a few times with my best teasing. Before you think I am being too harsh the few times he took me to Trenton for a home cooked meal his family would let me have it about being a soft Floridian with a football team with no defense. Through it all I managed to keep good grades and left my freshman year with a new friend in Tony and a grade point average high enough to keep my dad and mom paying for me to return the following fall.

Before you think Tony and I never spoke after college, he was the first person to visit me after landing in prison. He never once asked me if I was guilty or innocent he only asked what he could do to get me back in the open community where I belonged. It did not hurt that his grandfather was a former federal prosecutor who I have met several times over the years who also was willing to offer assistance.

Sophomore year was spent taking more of my core classes like marketing and finance as well as upper level accounting classes. One of our class assignments was to find and analyze a minimum of three companies trading on the New York Stock Exchange of our choosing with an allocation in an imaginary bank account of ten thousand dollars to start the project. The winner would be given a summer intern position with a law firm in New York which handled finances for celebrities as well as other things. I won the assignment by taking the original amount and turning it into more than three times that number in just over six months. My instructor was very impressed. Second place in the class made just over two thousand dollars, most lost a partial amount. So I was highly recommended to an agent and attorney to the rich and famous. Carl Peterson was just taking over the investment and agent side of his law firm. He was a good friend of my economics professor.

Working in an office in New York City analyzing stocks was a mental challenge. I was given the chore to find "hidden gems" as Mr. Peterson called them for him to recommend to his clients. I thought it all a bit odd that a law office would recommend stocks but Carl had this idea of offering high powered clients an all inclusive firm that would handle their finances as well as their contracts. It was a good experience for me. I was a good analyst even at a young age. I was in the hub of the world's finances but you would never know it since they stuck me in a converted supply closet with no view of the downtown Manhattan skyline. I realize that everyone has to pay their dues but I was so spoiled growing up with bright sunshine all around me that the one light bulb made me depressed at times. I wanted to prove to the world and to Mr. Peterson I deserved a window. Funny how small things can motivate a person.

One day while minding my own business in my dark cramped office a fellow with holes in his jeans and in need of a shave and a hair cut came barging in and barked at me "Why would you suggest to Carl that I invest in startup companies like Apple and Microsoft? Don't you know computers have many years before they are relevant in this world and you are wasting my hard earned dollars!" "Excuse me but who are you and why do you feel you have a right to speak to me in that tone" I responded. "I am Dylan James, Carl's most important client and you are offering bad advice with my money."

At this point I really did not know who this guy was in front of me nor did I care I only wanted to know why he thought I was offering bad advice. I tried to collect my composure and asked "Please sir, explain to me why I would offer bad advice and still think I could continue to work here or anywhere else for that matter?" He brushed the locks from his eyes and said "I don't like computers so I don't need any other reason."

"Well as long as it's based on a well thought out business plan Mr. James I will reconsider all my analysis. However in case you have not noticed they have already appreciated in value since you purchased them. But maybe I can find a company selling horse trailers for cross country travels since you obviously are stuck in the last century with your opinions on all things to do with computers."

When you are just twenty years old you don't always think ahead to the consequences of your actions, this was one of those times. Moments later Mr. Peterson called me into his office for a scolding about rising above the prima donna attitudes some have in life and that I should never forget that I was the professional. He was right, I had lost my cool and it was a good learning experience for me. He did profess to me that Mr. James was not always appreciative of others and that he was going through some tough times so he understood why I could have lost my composure with him. "However next time be the professional" he repeated.

Junior year was a time to start getting serious about future endeavors. Marie was visiting campus almost every weekend now and I think Tony was starting to feel the pressure of marriage after graduation. I would watch her rub the ring finger on her left hand every time she broached the topic. He would try to dismiss it as quickly as possible but she was making sure he didn't think beyond graduation, a job, her wedding and maybe not in that exact order. I dated occasionally in college but I was still focused on keeping my grades up and occasionally would snap a roll or two of film. I had become involved with the college radio station which allowed me to spin records on weekends. Some of my campus friends thought the station was a play toy and tried to enter the studio during my scheduled times but only once did I slip up and allow them inside for the mayhem to occur.

It was a Saturday afternoon session when I allowed two friends in and even allowed one on air for a few moments. Mind you it was about four in the afternoon and his opening was "Hello all you night owls this is your good friend Mike Cameron speaking to you live on the radio." From over my shoulder my other friend screams out "It's the middle of the day you f***ing idiot, are you that drunk?" I was fairly certain my shift would be taken from me but since only a few hall mates and Tony ever listened to me I was safe. However that experiment didn't last much longer than that brief interlude. Everyone back in the dorms got a big chuckle from the episode but it was my name attached to it and I was not happy.

After my junior year I was offered a summer position with Mr. Peterson again but foolishly I refused the offer. I was a Florida boy and even though the summers can be beyond warm I missed home. I spent most of the summer working in the dark room with Doc Carter and catching up with my pals. My parents convinced me that this was likely to be the last extended free time I would possibly have till retirement so they really wanted to me to enjoy my last summer before college graduation.

During the summer Doc Carter taught me about when making an image in the dark room to discard any prints that are not good enough to be hung on a wall. "You only show your best in life that goes for an image as well." He would ask me every time I brought him an image for his critique "Is that the best you can do?" Mind you I don't think he was telling me it was not my best work, I think the point was more that if I was not satisfied with my effort why should someone else be happy with it. He had very subtle and sometimes not so subtle ways of getting his points across to me but I think he liked the fact that I was a sponge when it came to his advice and experience. He really encouraged me to do my best even when tired or no one was watching. He also taught me how to keep an extensive journal about dates and time, place and even the chemicals used to produce my images. Every small detail was recorded.

The summer came to a close with my future in doubt other than my more determined attitude to do my best work in my senior year. I realize some use it as a time to have one last hurrah and party in college but I was a border line honors student and was determined to get my grade point average into the upper regions of my graduating class. I took all the required core classes like my advanced finance and accounting classes and filled it in with law classes and what I thought was a pop history class. Well the write up on the class was "History of the Beatles" but a few days into the class I realized it was a song writing class. Not something I thought was the best use of my time. I did enjoy the law classes both semesters and even received the highest grade in the class the second semester. So here I was within reach of my goals of graduating with honors but I was very much struggling with the song writing class.

Then as if someone above was watching over me I received a call from Mr. Peterson again asking me if I would be interested in working with his firm after graduation. It seems four out of the five stocks I had recommended earlier had doubled since the time I had suggested them. Plus Mr. Peterson and I had kept in touch and the other stocks that we talked about in later months were doing well too. He knew I had an ability to read balance sheets and see into the future with industries. It did not matter to him that I was not even out of college he knew talent and didn't want me to get away. He made a very lucrative offer and I had to give it serious consideration despite the fact that I really didn't want to live in New York City. I know most would jump at the opportunity but I really had my heart set on returning to the laid back life style of Florida as opposed to Manhattan.

The kicker to the entire conversation was that he told me that none other than Mr. Dylan James was pressing him to hire me since he was the recipient of my abilities. I was told Mr. James "was in a much better frame of mind now and wanted to make it up to me somehow." One phone call later and none other than Dylan James was giving me song writing tips to write a quality song for my class final. Like my dad always tells me, "It's not always what you know but who you know in life." Boy did that statement ever ring true for me that semester.

Tony and Marie announced their engagement in the spring of our senior year which was possibly the worst kept secret in history. Tony tried to keep the date open ended until he had secured a job but it seems not only did Marie have a date all picked out but Marie's father offered Tony a job as a loan officer in his bank. We all knew Marie's family was well off but we didn't realize he was the majority stockholder in one of the largest regional banks in the

Delaware Valley area. I am sure Tony knew his future father in law had clout in the bank but I am not sure until that day just how much clout he did have. As much as Tony pretended otherwise, we all knew that was his destiny. I only wish he had a few weeks to kick around Florida with me after graduation but he had to start his new job two weeks after graduation. He promised Marie he would go with her to Wildwood, New Jersey with her family for their traditional summer vacation. Her dad had a summer home there and the family would spend two weeks there as a family unit then weekends the rest of the summer.

I finished my senior year with straight A's including my song writing class thanks to Dylan James who made a few calls to see how I was doing from his home in North Carolina. My parents came to the graduation which was the first time they had stepped foot on campus. We had a lovely dinner in downtown Philly with Tony and Marie and their parents the night before graduation which I suspected would possibly be the last time I would see Tony before he was a father, other than his wedding day. I assumed after I went to the wedding in November of that year it would not be long before she really would start to press to be a mother. I am not sure why she bothered to attend college other than to be closer to Tony on weekends and make sure he had no designs on anyone else. She didn't even talk about finding work after college in the short term. She was going to be a wife and mother and that would be it. Here again Tony acted like he was being forced into it but he was not fooling me. He loved Marie as much as she did him. I was happy for him but that was not me. I wanted to be free and find a path in my life before becoming serious with anyone. Marriage was not on my radar at all. That seemed to be a huge repellent to most women I met in college.

3

After graduation I came to an agreement with Carl Peterson and his firm that suited us both. He had an old college friend who resided up the road from me who was a stock broker on the island of Palm Beach. Tom Darcy grew up in Chicago and attended school in New York with Carl. After graduation he moved to Palm Beach with a family member to start their brokerage. Tom and Carl made an arrangement where Carl would pay part of my expenses if I would also work for Carl and his firm from the Palm Beach office. It seemed to be a good fit for everyone since I really didn't want to be a full time, cold calling broker and my strength was really in evaluating companies. So just when I thought I had a break from schooling here I was studying for my Series 7 license. It was not an easy test by any means but before the start of the following year I was fully employed and licensed in an office that was a short walk to the beach. No more one light bulb broom closet for this boy or so I thought. A few years later I would once again find myself in a room all alone with no window only this time with nothing to occupy my time other than contempt for the people responsible for putting in my quiet cell.

After gaining the confidence of my boss Mr. Darcy he started to pass along a few of his clients to make recommendations regarding investments. The other two days of the week I was to only work exclusively for Mr. Peterson to look for startup companies or companies that I thought had potential for growth in the near future. I was starting to see that Mr. Peterson wanted to offer a big splash at first with his new clients then move them to more stable investments once he made a good early impression. However he did always like to keep an eye open for maybe a more risky investment with a larger upside which is where I came in. I also started to take my left over cash at the end of my pay checks and invest in my own stock picks. I was living at home for the time being so other than my new car and insurance I had few bills. I also was not making as large a salary had I moved to New York and worked for Mr. Peterson exclusively but it was enough for me at the time. The way I looked at it I didn't have the living expenses either like I would have had living in New York City so it really should have worked out about the same in the long run. I was more about getting experience than banking large sums of cash for now and being stuck later in a dead end job. I didn't know what my future would hold but leaning up against the power brokers in town didn't hurt me. Some of the people that Mr. Darcy started to send my way were mostly retired men who were at one time leaders of large companies or people who had done well over time and were savvy investors. Not that I would ever try but these people could sniff out a phony broker and that I promised myself I would never be. If I thought it was a bad investment I would express my thoughts even if Mr. Darcy thought it was a safe play. I am not really sure if he respected me for going against his choices now and again but I had to stay true to my beliefs on how to analyze a company.

About a year later one of my clients was the long time mayor of my home town. He wanted to know if I would be interested in applying for the position of town finance director. The town was flailing away with a golf course that never seemed to be profitable, a utilities company that was bleeding cash and a beach project that never could get off the ground. Mayor Henry Jacobson had been in

charge of the town for over thirty years and I think he knew almost
every citizen by their first name. So in that regard it would be near
impossible to vote him out of office even though I had no intentions
of trying such a suicidal mission. There were five members who sat
on the town council with the mayor being one of the five. The other
four ranged from almost anarchistic in their views to wanting to
control every time someone wanted to paint their home something
other than white. It was truly a town of residents who were varied
in interests, economic well being and cultures. In my opinion it was
a town with no identity only a sleepy ocean side town that didn't
like major changes. So I really had to think about whether that was
something I wanted to get involved with as a career change.

I went to my parents and Doc Carter for their advice. They all told
me to look deep inside and I would know the answer. Besides the
job was not promised to me, there were several applicants but I
suspected the mayor would push them into giving me strong
consideration. Here again, sometimes it's not what you know but
who you know. Up to that point in my life I had never really
considered working in municipal government. I had always seen
myself running a large company or doing analysis for another who
was in that position. Yet, maybe in reality my corporation could be
a town of citizens as opposed to stock holders or clients seeking to
improve their wealth. Maybe I could impact more lives working for
a town than I could for one company and a limited number of
clients.

The first step was to fill out a resume. Up to this point, I had never
had to create one, since my connections with Mr. Peterson got me
my first position and Mr. Darcy hired me solely on Carl Peterson's
advice. My mom and dad had no real experience in creating a
resume so I asked the office secretary for some help. She was a
twenty three year old, very attractive woman who had started to
work in the office after one year of junior college. She knew how to
run all the office applications and her soft smile and pretty voice

was enough to charm the clients who would visit the office sometimes I suspect just to see her. Nicole Hunter knew she could use her good looks and charm to get more than smiles but despite that I was mostly immune to her efforts. She had been married when she was a mere eighteen years young and I was told it didn't last much more than a year. I needed help so I offered to pay for her computer abilities. She told me that she would do it if I took her out to her favorite restaurant for dinner on the ocean in Palm Beach. Like I said, I was mostly immune to her charm so I accepted the proposal. We had a nice dinner and during the evening she told me her background then later I told her mine so she could take notes and prepare my resume for my interview later in the week.

I showed up for my interview with a clean shirt, new tie and pressed suit. I mostly dressed in a suit and tie for my current job so I was a bit taken back when I noticed many of the town employees were in jeans and polo shirts. I know this was Florida but I was not expecting such a laid back attitude in the office that controlled the city. The lady who was interviewing me told me it was "dress down Friday" after I asked about the dress code in the interview.

I thought I was doing quite well in my interview which had already gone on for about thirty minutes when my interviewer started to ask what I thought were inappropriate questions. "Let me ask you about our mayor, what is your opinion of having one for over thirty years Mr. McAdams sir?" At first I was really taken back and not expecting that type of question at all and all I could think to say was "it really does not matter what I think as long as the voters keep electing him."

She didn't want to let me off the hook with such an easy response and continued to attack me, "But do you think it is healthy for a town to have one person be such a driving force for so many years in one town?"

My response was now "I am not running for mayor or any other elected office but to be the town's financial advisor and bill collector. I really don't see how that is a relevant question on your part."

She stared me down one more time and I was now seeing why Mrs. Anne Des Darte had the reputation she did in the town for being good at her job. "Mr. McAdams you are dodging my question and I can assure you if you have any designs on this job you will give me a direct answer to my question, so try one more time."

At that point I was not sure I wanted the opportunity to work there any longer so I let it out. "No, unless he is the best manager of a town that has ever come along I do not think it is healthy for any town, city or national office holder who has that type of power over others to stay in office that long. That is not a personal reflection on Mayor Jacobson because I do think he is a fine man who wants only the best for this town but this town needs new ideas and new leadership."

After a few seconds I noticed a bit of a smirk in the left corner of Anne's mouth until she looked down at her notes again. "I have one last question for you Mr. McAdams, what is your relationship with Mrs. Hunter?"

Here again I was very taken back with her question, "Excuse me, but I again don't understand how that is relevant to my interview?"

"Well let me tell you how it is Mr. McAdams you were spotted out having dinner with a married woman in Palm Beach and we will not hire anyone who runs around with a married woman, that's how it's my business."

Again I was really shocked thinking that possibly being this visible in the public eye was not something I was ready for no matter how it might look on my future resume. "How do you know I was even having dinner with MISS Hunter and why don't you ask me what you really want to ask me?" Now this interview had taken a very wrong turn but she looked at me again and would only say "I happened to be in the same restaurant the same evening as you were so I was asking about it because her husband is my husband's cousin. Now please answer me, what is your relationship with her?"

 I really didn't want to give in but I finally did and told her the truth which was that "She helped me with my resume and in return she asked for me to buy her dinner, so I obliged. It was nothing more and nothing less and I have been told for over a year in knowing her that she was divorced and never once have I seen her with her ex husband."

 Dead silence till my interviewer again looked down and muttered "You might want to make sure she gives you all the facts since she does live apart but has never divorced. And for the record she is not one to only go out for dinner unless there is more involved. Let's just say she has a reputation of knowing how to use her charm get what she wants with men."

 Now I am getting hot under the collar being accused of something I am totally innocent of and let out "If you are asking me did I have sex with that woman, no I did not have sex with that woman and now I do believe my time here is up." I promptly got up and shook her hand, thanked her for her time and as I turned I could see a silhouette of a person who was likely standing behind a partially open door that was to my back. I really didn't pay it much more attention. Here again my photographic nature took notice of the shadows, something that came very natural now. I didn't storm from the room but I did leave the room before Mrs. D could finish her last words. I think whoever was standing behind the door was caught off guard with my early exit. I didn't take notice of who it was since my eyes were clearly focused on the exit signs.

 As soon as I got in the front seat of my car I could hear Mr. Peterson scolding me in my head for once again failing the keep my cool under pressure. It was starting to enter my mind that I really needed to work on handling my words and actions when being pressured about my ethics. I sat for several minutes with the car running knowing I could no longer let my quick temper destroy my opportunities in the future.

I went home and sat in the pool trying to prevent the sting of my botched interview from ruining my weekend. However I spent almost my entire waking hours for the next two days going over every single question and my responses till I realized that was really the first time I had an interview with something at stake or the outcome not being determined before the start of the process. My interview with Mr. Darcy was never in jeopardy as long as I didn't insult the man or call his wife a bad name. Maybe I was being too hard on myself since I really had never been through that process before. But even so it was imperative I got better at it when pressured.

I went to my job at the brokerage house on Monday resigned to the idea that I would be there longer since I had failed my interview. A few hours later Mrs. D from the town office was calling me to set up another interview. This time I would be sitting with the Mayor and another council member. I was not sure how I really felt about moving forward again but since I was not a quitter I wanted to play it all out and keep my options open. I spoke with Mr. Darcy about it and he took me to lunch and told me about his father's brief career in politics back in Chicago. It seemed all so dirty to me after hearing some of his stories and even though Boca Breezes was a far cry from Chicago he wanted to make sure I held firm to my convictions and not let anyone change me over a job. I was wise enough to understand his not so hidden messages but not experienced enough to really know how to control the interview. I also had spoken with Nicole about her marital situation and she claimed that the only reason she was not divorced was because her husband had refused to sign the papers but she was now going to press him or talk with a judge to push it along. Her marital situation was not really that big of a concern to me other than to know the truth in case it came up as an issue in the next interview.

I went to Doc Carter for some advice about the interview, his only recommendation was to quote Lincoln "'Tis better to be silent and be thought a fool, than to speak and remove all doubt." I was not completely sure what he meant, was he calling me a fool or telling me not to make up an answer to a question I didn't really know the answer? I just assumed the good Doc was sniffing too many photo chemicals in the dark room that day without the proper ventilation.

When I arrived for the interview not only was the Mayor there with another council member but Mrs. D was sitting behind me with another person who was never introduced to me. I later found out it was the town attorney, Scott Sharlay. I really didn't like that they sat in the back of the room where I could not see them. Right away I was starting to feel uncomfortable so I focused on Mr. Peterson's directive to keep my cool. The Honorable Mr. Jacobson our mayor introduced me to Mrs. Kara Jones the town council woman who would also be asking questions. After the introductions they sat me in a chair slightly below their level on the other side of the table. I am not sure if this was an intentional move on their part but I did notice it was a seat that had a fixed position, not one that could be raised. Maybe I was starting to look for conspiracies that didn't exist but they clearly seemed to take pleasure in looking down at me during the interview. The Mayor started out with what now seemed the usual question of "tell us about yourself, George" and Mrs. Jones followed with "What experiences can you bring to this position being so young?"

I thought the way she phrased it was maybe a bit out of line but I only responded with what I thought I did bring and ended it with "Not too bad for a young guy like me" and a small smirk. I know I should have let it go but I had made up my mind going into the interview I was not going to allow them to treat me as somehow a lesser candidate because of my age or their presumption of my lack of ability or experience. Maybe I was on guard from all the stories of politicians thinking they are above others from Mr. Darcy and a few from my dad so I had to temper my remarks and give these people the benefit of the doubt with their off colored remarks and questions.

The interview was moving along until Mrs. Jones asked "So tell us why you want this position." The problem was I was not sure I did and it quickly came spilling out of my mouth, "I am really not sure I do." I reached into the air desperately trying to catch my words before they hit their ears but it was too late. They both sat back in their chairs and I knew I had to define those words and quickly.

"I was under the impression that the hiring process is a two way street and until I have time to ask some questions of you I have not reached a conclusion that this position would be a good fit for your town or for me." I was so proud believing I had been able to control the situation when they both spoke up "So then ask whatever questions you might have the floor is yours." Now I was stuck because I really had not prepared any questions which meant I was poorly prepared for this interview. There would not be a third interview or a job offer unless I thought of some questions and fast. "Would I have autonomy in running my staff as I see fit as well as being able to make decisions or does everything have to run upstairs to someone else?" After a bit of stammering from the Mayor he gave me a political answer which is to say that he said a lot of words and I have no clue if he answered me or not. I proceeded to ask a few more questions and each time even though they were all very direct questions I was getting not so direct responses.

I was becoming less interested in the position by the minute. It was all a mystery to me how they could expect a direct answer from me when they went nowhere near offering a full response. It was frustrating yet gave me a much clearer picture of running a town, even a small one. I was yet to be convinced I wanted to participate. Then the questions from the past interview started to come out again. The Mayor looked me directly in the eye and asked me "Do you think I have been Mayor of this town too long?"

I responded with "Would you like me to answer that question the way you all do or would you like me to really answer it?" Now granted I knew I was hanging myself and was even bordering on being rude to the town Mayor but after the past fifteen minutes and the two of them not giving me a real answer to any of my questions, even ones that should have been simple like what is the benefit package being offered, I was staying cool. However my patience was being tested since I think they thought they could get away with being unresponsive.

The Mayor laughed and I am not sure whether this was at me or with me but states "I want your answer, not what you think I want to hear." "Well Mr. Mayor since I really don't know what you think my answer should be I can only tell you the truth, which is, I think you have done a wonderful job over the years but I do believe it is time for new ideas." Mrs. Jones then looks at me and asks "Who would be your first choice to replace him?" I decided to resort to their responses and stated "Whoever the voting public decides" and I looked away from her direction. Assuming I would be ushered out the door after that response she asked one more set of questions. "Tell me Mr. McAdams, what is your greatest asset?" Without a moment's hesitation "The truth" I let out quickly followed with her next question, "And your greatest weakness", "The lack of patience for others who do not possess the same asset." With that, we all parted but I left feeling far more comfortable this time even though they might not have always liked my answers. I didn't try to be someone I was not.

I thought back on that interview when it was time to speak to a judge who held my fate in his hands during my arraignment. I did not want to be rude or not answer the questions directly but I also didn't want to leave open the chance of him not understanding my inner thoughts. It's not always an easy proposition to give direct answers and not come across as rude or insulting.

When I got home from my town interview, Doc Carter was in his usual position of watching the sun fade across his back yard while casting shadows across the lake. I was in my usual position of lounging in the back yard pool. He called me over and asked me how the interview went and I did my best to relive what to me was my last visit to city hall for the foreseeable future. Doc starts laughing as loudly as I have ever heard him and tells me "Those people had no idea what to do with a guy like you George." When I quizzed him why he thought that, his only response was "We need guys like you in politics George but the powers in charge will do everything they can to keep you out, after all you tell the truth." I guess I was still too young and naive to fully understand his point but I was starting to see what he meant once I went over in my mind how the two of them in the interview never really answered any of my questions but made sure they pressed me until I offered completed thoughts.

I woke up Saturday morning with not a care in the world assuming my life would continue on as a financial consultant in my Palm Beach office when two calls came to the house, neither of which I was expecting. The first was from Nicole Hunter wanting to know what my plans were for the evening and the other was from Mayor Jacobson wanting to know if I could meet him for lunch in a not so discreet café on the main street in town. I accepted the Mayor's offer for lunch quickly but danced around with Nicole on the phone for several minutes trying to decide what she was really up to in the call. "Look George if you are really so blind that you can't see I am trying to get to know you better and I am asking you out on a date then put your head back in the sand. I never understand men who can be so book smart yet when it comes to socializing can be so darn stupid." At first I was taken aback with her comments since I had never been accused of being anti-social in the past but I would admit to being distant when it came to relationships with women. So after her scolding we decided to have dinner later that evening.

I met with Mayor Jacobson in the busiest lunch location in town. I knew him well enough now to know that was the very reason he picked that spot. What I was not sure of was why he wanted to meet. He was still my client when it came to some of his financial choices so I assumed he wanted to review them.

It was not uncommon for my clients to meet for lunch but this time the timing was suspect. When I arrived he was standing at the front entrance of the restaurant holding court with several residents who enjoyed the fact that "their mayor" was easily visible in town. I stood listening as he rattled off answer after answer to me not saying a thing yet somehow satisfying them with his responses. Maybe it was me but I wanted more than clichés and happy words to a question. But then again in my line of work I had to be very precise and detailed so maybe I was looking too deeply for answers from the town leader.

I was starting to see now that being mayor had a mystique about it that had to be respected on some level. I remembered that back in the 5th grade we were learning about our national and local governments when my friend Tommy Tanner told me that the mayor lived in a huge mansion with guard dogs on a giant hill. First of all, I didn't remember any giant hills in south Florida and secondly maybe he was not the same mayor who lived a few blocks in a very middle class home around the corner from my house. I mean what did I know maybe one was his real house and maybe the other was the official house where the mayor lived while being mayor? Tommy swore he had been in the mayor's house before but then again Tommy had a way making many things seem real that maybe were not. It was not until the next year when my parents took me to a holiday party at the mayor's house around the corner from us that my dad assured me that was the only place the mayor lived full or part time.

Once the Mayor was finished assuring the few on the corner who hung on every non descript word that the town was in great shape and I was done day dreaming of the big house on a hill that didn't exist, we moved inside for our lunch.

"So George, I have to start by telling you how impressed I was with your interview. There were no ifs, ands or buts with you, not even a maybe. You answered every question directly and it took guts to tell me that it was time for me to retire. You were confident in who you are as a person and really didn't care if you knew we would not like your answers. You were thoughtful, honest and came across as very sincere. Now if I can get you to be that confident yet not answer so directly maybe I can make a town leader out of you just yet."

I leaned back in the seat not sure how to respond other than to say "Thanks sir, I will try not to be so direct in the future" and smiled. "George it is not common knowledge but I have no intentions of running for mayor again. I know I stayed too long but there really was no one I thought could do a better job so I kept running. Maybe that's my ego talking but I do agree it's long past due that someone else steps in and runs this town. As you have already seen we have such a diverse group on the town council which is why most votes, even ones that should be easy, end up being a 3-2 vote with my vote usually the deciding factor. It's rare I am in the minority of votes. So this is where you come in my boy. I need someone I can trust that will stand up to the new mayor and make sure they don't do anything silly in the near term. I would push you for mayor but you don't have the political skills to be a leader yet. When your time comes you will know." I stopped him there and asked if I should take that as a compliment that I didn't have the skills to be a politician. I realized then how quickly I could be out of his good graces with his long stare across the table so I buttoned up the lip rather quickly.

The Mayor and I sat for over two hours and as he reminisced about his thirty years in power. He did everything in his power to convince me that he truly did have the town's best interest at heart. He loved living here and wanted to do everything to make it a better place to live. He loved the town's people and had a nurturing style that was not evident to me until I could speak with him in a setting like this one. What I was not aware of was that he was a successful insurance agent as well. I guess I had never really paid attention to the fact that being mayor, though being a full time position, was not his full time job. He had run a very successful insurance agency in town for over forty years. He was not only retiring as mayor but also selling his agency to one of his agents. I guess I should have known it since I saw some of the financial trades in our office but I never really looked into a person more than numbers on a page. I knew in that afternoon chat that I needed to open my mind up to more than seeing people as a balance sheet.

Mayor Jacobson saw people as people not voters and I now knew why he was elected ten times as leader of our town. "George, I was the one behind the door during your first interview. I didn't want to hear about your interview second hand, so I listened behind the door. I wanted to hear it for myself and yes I asked Mrs. D to ask everyone if I was mayor too long. You were the only one who said yes. I knew instantly you were the guy we needed to clean up our financial mess. I had to disclose to our council and legal department that you work for my investment brokerage but that will not be an issue for me or you. This is a small town and things like that happen but as long as we are open about it we can work past it. Now I want you to really think long and hard about being our financial guru and tax collector. You would be serving your community and it is an honor to do so even if you might not see that yet. I was so blessed and honored that your neighbors and mine put that faith in me for decades. I don't take that lightly and neither should you. So you take the weekend and think long and hard about the position but it is yours if you would like it."

At that point I was caught off guard and I am sure he could see my mouth drop to the floor with the offer. It was not about the money since it was not for any more than I was currently making but the idea that he had that much confidence in me or so he made it seem. He made me feel like it was a privilege to work for the town and maybe I had never looked at it that way until our lunch. I was left with a lot to think about.

Later that evening I had my dinner date with Nicole. I told her about my lunch and her first response was "If you accept the job I won't see you in the office, I am not sure I like that idea." I guess I really was clueless since her mood around me seemed to have changed since the time we went to dinner where she helped with my resume. She gave me those sad eyes that only women and puppy dogs seem to be able to do but she went on to say "I have been falling all over you since our first date and you act like I am not even in the room, are you blind or stupid?" I was having quite an eye opening day to say the least.

"Nicole I will admit that my mind has been occupied with other things right now but I was also warned to stay away from you since technically you are married." For an instant I thought maybe she had eaten a spicy piece of her dinner when her eyes lit up and her face became beet red but it was only to let me know that she had been living apart for years from her ex and that he had several girl friends all over town. He was refusing to sign the divorce papers because the bank would not change the mortgage to reflect she would no longer be on the hook for the loan. He does not have enough income to be the only signature on the note and that she saved up enough money now to get an attorney to petition a judge to move it along. I got the point. "I don't care what you have heard about me, I rarely date or have any social life because my ex husband has people all over town claiming I am something that I can assure you I am not and that people need to stay away from me. This is about my ex husband not having to sell our little house that we bought when we first married."

Here again my day was full of surprises and I for sure was not expecting her to tell me that she had been "dressing up and trying to get your attention for weeks." I assumed Mr. Darcy changed the office dress code and she had new perfume. I started to think I needed to take a vacation after my long Saturday.

After a couple of days of soul searching I accepted the position with the town and gave my notice to Mr. Darcy and Mr. Peterson. Carl Peterson offered me a full time position with his firm in New York again trying to convince me that my skills would be better served with him but the slower pace of Florida and the warmer climate was more my style than the hustle and bustle of New York City. I was flattered with his generous offer but we did agree to try to come up with an agreement down the road where I could still offer stock advice to his firm. Over the course of the past year and more, I was still way ahead in stocks I recommended to his firm. For whatever reason even at a young age and barely out of college I had a real knack for discovering stocks on the upside being publically traded. I would miss on one now and again but I had a proven track record even if it was only over a few short years. I did have Mr. Peterson negotiate my contract with the town for me.

My first day on the job was a real eye opener. I was placed on the lowest floor in our town hall that was built in 1923. That is to say that the building did not have central air conditioning only a few noisy wall units that seemed to push out as much dust and mold as it did circulate cooler air. I had one assistant who had moved here from the Mediterranean Sea area. She was ballerina thin and later told me she was in fact a former dancer in her youth. Mali Rubin had a quick wit and did not like having to deal with a new boss in her department. She made it known to me quickly that she had her "own way of keeping track of things around here." I quickly informed her that "together we would find ways to improve the department but her attitude was only going to find her the exit."

I guess she saw some young kid walk in and thought she could set the tone in the office. It took a few days but we eventually came to a happy middle ground. I was the boss, she was not. It was the first time I had anyone answer to me directly and I was not ready for her desire to put me in my place. It was a good thing that my first day on the job I had no clue how much I would have suffered without her knowledge of the department. She might have won the battle of wills from the early stages. I think once she realized I knew my way around numbers as well as she did and got over the fact that I was offered the position and not her we settled into a good working relationship.

I made the mistake of telling Nicole that I had a former dancer who reported to me in my office. She showed up in our moldy cramped office to surprise me with lunch the very next day. I think she wanted to meet Mali for herself and let it be known that she was not going to allow any other woman have designs on me. Mali and I were strictly co-workers but Nicole wanted to make sure everyone knew the rules in the world of Nicole Hunter. Later that afternoon Mali said "Next time you are too busy to get out of here for lunch tell Nicole that I am wearing a short skirt, and that you want roast beef." I knew after that comment that we would work well together.

I immediately contacted the city manager and the Mayor for some clarity about my autonomy to collect back taxes and much to my surprise their only comments were that I needed to pick up the pace in setting up a system. The upcoming budget debate was about to begin soon and they needed a projected revenue number. Mali offered little consolation as well only telling me that "In my country our homes have bombs swirling overhead in the dead of the night, get over your out dated index card issue and be a man." I thought about contacting the town attorney to see if I could sue for sexual harassment for her comments but then again in this place they likely would have taken me seriously.

Our town manager, Jon Nelson was a crusty old veteran, who claimed to have stormed the beaches of Normandy in World War II. I think really he was in the civil war. Every time I took a suggestion to the guy to improve our collection system he would shoot it down quicker than our Jacobson shot down clay pigeons west of town. Mr. Nelson was not going to change a darn thing nor was he going to attempt to add anything to my minuscule budget. When I suggested the town should start to look into computerizing our records his only comment was "computers are a waste of money and will not be here in the next century." Just another example of why I think he fought in the civil war not one a century later. When I took the idea of getting a computer in the office to the mayor he would only say "Talk with Nelson, he knows if we can afford it or not." I realized this was not a top law office in New York City like Mr. Peterson's, this was a small south Florida town of about twenty five thousand residents but times were changing and this town was being led by people who were stuck in decades long past.

This was the first real time in my life I was being challenged to rise above my emotions when it came to my career since everything had been made fairly easy for me in the past. Neither my parents nor Doc Carter had any sympathy for me only telling me "You are in the real world now, deal with it." I knew I could get a minimal amount of sympathy from Nicole since she was the one person I could lean on without being scolded for wanting to run when things got hard. We were starting to spend more time together since she had officially filed for divorce. Mr. Darcy made a call to the local bank president and got her name off the mortgage on her home she had shared with her soon to be ex husband. It was the only thing of any value they owned jointly any longer and she didn't want any part of the perceived equity in the house. She only wanted out of the marriage and to move on with her life once and for all. I think it helped that the bank president was Mr. Darcy's Saturday golf partner and somehow they refinanced the house to reduce the ex husbands payments so that he could qualify alone. I understood the concepts behind the refinancing of a loan however what I was still learning was how eighteen holes of golf could make all this happen.

Several months went by with me learning town politics as well as having Mali update her catalogue system. Her system seemed to fit the town's needs less than her need to keep me in the dark for her own job security. I think once Mali realized her job was not in jeopardy as long as she did what I asked of her and I got her a small raise she started to adjust to me being in control. I still had my almost daily fights with the town manager to update not only our system but some of the others around town but to no avail. For example in visiting our town owned golf course I found out that there was little or no system in place to keep track of how many golfers really did play the course each day. I have no doubts this was done so that some of the town residents could get a free round of golf from the good graces of either the starter on the first tee or the golf course manager. I know the mayor and town council members handed passes out like candy too. When I dared to attempt to install a time stamp machine with numbered invoices and then compare that to the starters paper list I knew instantly how many free rounds were being handed out. There was too much of a pushback not only from the golf course people but from the town officials as well. No, this was not what I had signed up for at all. I had to decide how to navigate the waters yet still keep my job. I knew the more I attempted to rid the town of small town politics and border line corruption the more my job would be on the line.

One day I had lunch with the town attorney. He was not much older than me and was not an employee of the town. Scott worked for the law offices across the street from city hall and in reality was assigned the job because the managing partner of the law firm was good friends with Mayor Jacobson. Scott would sit in on town council meetings and handle any legal issues the town had but they were few and far between. He had graduated from Rutgers Law School about the time I graduated college and it turns out we both ended up in Florida about the same time. When I asked him why he moved to Florida he told me that while in undergraduate school he made a trip to Ft. Lauderdale over Christmas break with some college friends and "Seeing good looking ladies in bikinis in January was not the worst thing in the world." I agreed.

 The reason I wanted to meet with Scott was to see if he had any advice on how to get the town to move into the late 1980's like the rest of the world. He too was frustrated with what he had seen but admitted the town had its own charm and was successful in the way it had been run for years. He did hint to me that he was giving some thoughts about running for mayor since it was starting to become common knowledge that our current mayor was not seeking reelection. We both knew he had a large uphill battle to win the mayor's seat but he was considering it.

4

What type of person runs for public office and why do they do it? I am sure some do it for ego, some have a burning desire to serve others and for most I guess it's a combination of multiple reasons. At that point in my life I had little desire to run for even dog catcher but had I run, I believed it would have been because I wanted to make a difference in helping the less fortunate. That is such an easy statement to make until you are put in position of power as I would later find out. Even with small town politics, I quickly found out how entrenched people on both sides of the political spectrum are in their fundamental beliefs. I also know that the word "change" is only a word used to get elected. So many use it, yet people rarely ask, change too what? Years later I would discover just how right my perceptions were about political leaders. I would learn to what ends they would go to fulfill their own personal crusades but for now I was still working in a small town. However, what I was discovering was what many politicians were capable of when they perceived you as an adversary and they possess the power you eventually crave.

During the course of my work I ran across my first issue where I had to dance around politicians while keeping my job. I knew people were using the public's assets for private gain and how many of them did not want me to expose it. I was not trying to be a bad guy or ruin lives I was merely doing what I thought was my obligation. It all stemmed from what I considered town leaders who felt entitled to use our local golf course free of charge.

I felt an obligation to fix what I thought were wrongs taking place within the realm of revenue collections for the town. I met with the town manager and told him that if the golf course didn't have some type of system in place soon to track how many players visited the course, I would take my grief to the local newspaper reporter. There was always one sitting in the back of the room during town council meetings. He was looking for a good story and mine would have a bent that the politicians didn't want to track revenues because it was their personal playground. I knew that would not sit well but I had to act. The town needed the real revenue the golf course could generate and not the numbers they wanted to report. I was convinced the town was losing thousands of dollars each month due to free rounds. It was a city owned course and the people deserved their profits. After a few shouting matches behind closed doors he finally gave in to my request. I don't think he was abusing the course, not sure he even played, but I did believe he was protecting the abusers.

By the time I was back in my cramped office the Mayor Jacobson was on the phone inviting me for lunch. It was not a surprise to me that word traveled so quickly. I agreed and attempted to have Mali join us since I knew what was coming but the mayor insisted I come alone. It all seemed so over the top to me but I guess making changes is never easy, even for a small town.

"Thanks for joining me for lunch George. We should have done this long ago. I wanted to see how things were going now that you have been with us a few months." The mayor went on and on acting like he knew nothing about my trip to the golf course earlier in the day only pretending that all of a sudden he cared about my well being. I was not going to give an inch till we were about ready to leave and he could not resist the subject.

"You know George I have always prided myself about not allowing the press to know our internal issues. Am I to understand that you had a hissy fit with Jon Nelson about running the golf course your way or you would take your findings to the reporter who sits in on our council meetings? Is that true?" I offered a slight chuckle and at first would only reply, "I am sure you heard correct but the words hissy fit might not be accurate."

He was not easily amused with my short response and I could tell by the frown coming from behind his wired frame glasses that I needed to expand my answer. "Mr. Mayor, I have little doubt that you want what is best for this town but there is, in my opinion, a waste of a beautiful resource at our golf course. Too many are using it as their personal course and not being fair to all the members of the town who pay taxes here and deserve the maximum return on their investment. Would you not agree?" The frown only grew larger for a brief moment till he said, "Are you accusing me of misdeeds with your words George?" Now my inner voice wanted to let it all out but I stepped as close to the line as I could with a simple, "I am only stating Mr. Mayor that I do believe the golf course can generate more revenue than it does now. You hired me to be your tax collector and town financial chief, if you no longer think I am doing that then please remove me based on that fact. However if you believe I am only doing what you hired me to do then please allow me to do my job."

Mayor Jacobson sat back in his seat on the opposite side of our booth overlooking the main avenue in town. I assumed he was reviewing my recent remarks although I guess I will never be sure. Maybe really he was scheming ways to remove me and make it look like I was doing a poor job. Either way I do not think he knew the person he hired a few months back. I thought he saw a young guy not far from college who would sit in the office and not make waves. If that's what he thought, he made a bad choice with his hire.

"George, you got a lot of guts to say what you did to me. I am not sure how to take you now but be aware that there are many in this town that are not going to like the fact that you are shaking things up at the golf course. Be very careful how you proceed with this and any other projects you may find." I then sat back on my side of the booth only to say, "I think that was a veiled threat and I am employed by the entire town not only by golfers like you are Mr. Mayor. With all due respect Sir, I would think you would be applauding me for my efforts and not condemning them."

"Young man, you have so much to learn about politics and small towns. Don't allow yourself to be so naive about our town and how it operates. I don't like everything about our ways and maybe in my younger days I would be more on your side but my time is almost finished here, so I wish you well in what you believe to be the truth." With that he stood up and walked out. I was still not sure if I would be fired soon but I really no longer cared. I could not sit in good conscience in my office knowing what I suspected was going on at the golf course. I was not sure either side was pleased with our conversation but the fact that he stuck me with bill was my first clue.

It was such an odd feeling trying to do what I thought was the right thing to do yet be vilified for it. I guess I understood it to a point but I was not trying to raise the rates or close the place. I merely wanted to keep a better track on who was using the course and cut down on free rounds. When I had doubted that I was doing the right thing I would read a quote from a poster on my office wall from George Washington where it read, "Associate with men of good quality, if you esteem your own reputation; for it is better to be alone than in bad company." Mali had some sympathy for my uphill climb but even she didn't really think I would be able to change the hearts and minds of the abusers. I knew someone was cheating the system and I refused to turn a blind eye.

I dropped by on Saturday afternoon to play a round at the course and the starter John Harwood made one big mistake. He claimed that all the spots were taken and I had to wait my turn, so I did. I hit some balls at the driving range and walked around the club house for about ninety minutes while I waited for "my turn". I took notice that the first tee box was full most times so I didn't really think he was making me wait for any reason other than I didn't have a starting time. His mistake however was that under my new system now in place, I could check times and tickets against his logs. There were constant players while I was there yet only three foursomes were listed as having paid for the same time period when I checked on Monday. We now had a new problem. Not only were there far more players but they were not cheating the system as much as it seemed. Because we had annual members, the cashier was not making tickets for the people who didn't pay green fees when they played. So now I had to fix that bug in the system. However in checking John's names against annual paying members not all were the same nor was everyone still accounted for. It was obvious that they were not going to keep track without more pressure. That's when it hit me.

I rushed home and called Nicole about my idea though she didn't think it would work. She didn't think the town would approve it and maybe she was right but the current system was broken even with my attempt to improve it. There was no incentive to make it work. I had to give them a reason to want to make it all work. I took my idea to Nelson on Monday morning and of course he too shot it down right away but I was not going to be deterred. I called Mr. Peterson in New York to get his thoughts and he thought it just might work, as did Mr. Darcy. But then again they were business people not politicians. My dad thought it would be a long uphill battle and my mom wanted me to quit my job and get a "real one" where my talents would be appreciated.

My plan was to offer all the employees of the golf course a modified pension plan. It would be based solely on the merits of the golf course. The plan was that for each person who played the course that the invoice was done correctly with fees collected and they left no complaints about the course then a small percentage of the fee would be put into a fund to be shared equally by anyone employed at the course on that day. Yes it would create some accounting headaches but if the system was set up correctly it would be minimal. The screams from the town commissioners started immediately about the cost. My counter point was that most of the free plays would be eliminated and that the new revenue generated would more than pay for the extra burden with less employee turnover. Every employee at the course had an incentive to cut down on free plays for friends. Besides every other town employee had some sort of pension plan and none of the others came from a revenue producing asset like the golf course. Meaning the fire, police and town workers all had pensions and all came directly from taxes collected not from a place that generated its own revenues. To me it made perfect sense, however the push back was not from residents, but from all the people I suspected were playing for free over many years.

After some back door politics, I had it added to the next agenda for the town council meeting. I made sure all the golf employees attended the meeting for the vote. It did not sit well at all with my boss or Mayor Jacobson but it was something that had to be fixed. The union people were there wanting a boost to their pensions but were quickly dismissed and told to bring it back up when their current contracts expired. I now had to lay low for a while since I had many inside City Hall upset with me but it was the right thing to do. That was my first real struggle with town politics.

Looking back on that day, I can see now how even small things as opposed to trillions of dollars spent on a federal budget effects people's lives. But to this day, I still hold firm with my convictions. I was proven correct when the golf course, over a short period of time, generated over thirty percent more revenues. That more than paid for the fund and it reduced other costs since employee turnover was cut in half.

Later in life I would be put in a position where silence would buy my freedom, not standing up to the leaders who were winning in their battle to buy off my closed mouth. I knew this golf course pension idea was my first real lesson on how to get what you wanted from higher powers within our government. I realized most would not believe that a small group of people can and will destroy the integrity of another human being but it did happen to me. I know now what some are capable of in a short time able to ruin a fine man without a true shred of real evidence. How can men elected to lead other men get away with manufacturing such lies? In the coming years, I would endure days of witnessing highly respected men take an oath to tell only the truth and seconds later turn right around and either lie in court or be so misled with the evidence, they never knew the truth. What I did learn at an early stage of my political career was that there is always a cost to your actions. The key is at what cost should you pay for yours?

After what should have been a common sense solution to an issue with the town golf course, some of the other town leaders attempted to flex their muscle at me and the town. Within a few weeks after our council meeting the chief of police started driving around in a brand new cruiser, which was never included in any budget, or approved by the city manager. He claimed he had the right to do it since under his contract terms he could use resources "in an emergency for the well being of public safety at his discretion". That hardly seemed to fit the criteria in my opinion and after the fire chief attempted to try the same thing I again had to be on the spot to voice my opinion to change policy.

I now had the fire and police upset with me for taking away free plays on the golf course as well as limiting their ability to spend funds not approved by me or the city manager. Here again, it was not popular within the walls of City Hall, but with an election on the horizon the town leaders did not want to face voters responding to questions as to why holding down reckless spending was a bad thing. I was not popular at all with town leaders but some articles were being written in the local paper about how someone was fighting to do what was right, though not politically expedient. I was not looking for media attention. In fact I didn't want to draw any more attention to my perils than necessary since I was already being pulled over to check my registration more than I am sure your average citizen would have to endure. I am also sure the fact that my tires were flat more than once while heading for work was not a coincidence.

At that point most of my friends and parents begged me to walk away from my position and let the town settle back down to the "old way" of doing business. I had learned from my sports playing days that "Winners never quit and quitters never win". I was not a quitter then or now and I did not want to allow others to push me around for what I knew was the right thing to do. No, I was going to be principled no matter the cost. It was not until years later when I spent those three long days in that tiny federal cell all alone with only a few believing in my innocence, I was starting to realize the cost of holding onto your principles.

After the ruckus over the changes with the golf course billing system and changes to the autonomy of department heads, the next election was a disaster for incumbents. The two town council members who were up for reelection, lost in landslides and a new mayor with no political experience took the oath as a town leader. I have no doubt that many pay close attention to elections and the consequences each holds but just as many or more are swayed with a cute slogan. I was one of the latter until that election. My parents always made sure I voted in all elections but never did I really consider how much power one vote really holds. I know now. My father in particular always told me "If you don't vote then don't you dare complain about our town or country." I know now what he meant. Our small town was in turmoil, divided between the older generation who at times abused the system and the younger generation who maybe didn't appreciate all that was previously built. A new generation now had the ability to control power in our small town. I now had more power behind the scenes than I had ever wanted or imagined.

President Lincoln once said "Nearly all men can stand adversity, but if you want to test a man's character, give him power". Our town attorney Scott Sharley won a close election for mayor. The first order of business with him and the new council was to make life so difficult for our town manager that he quickly resigned. I was given full responsibility of the new budget until a new manager could be hired. I was also acting as interim town manager. The local beat writer had written enough damaging reports about the small town politics and corruption that a clean sweep was inevitable. I however was immune from the change since I was the one who was attempting to make the budget free of perks for department heads and politicians. It was beginning to become common knowledge around town that I was attempting to eliminate waste from our ever expanding budget. We had a small town with limited revenues so it had to be watched very carefully.

Our new mayor was out kissing babies and telling everyone who would listen that the town was in good financial shape. It was now my job to prove him right as he stepped back and allowed me to do my job. The other members of the town council were either new or were up for the next election and didn't want to look like they didn't care about wasteful spending. The path was cleared for me to examine every detail in our budget. With Mali's help as well as my new assistant Sue Juran, who was brought in to manage the golf course revenues as well as work in our department, we reviewed every item line by line. I was learning how to truly prepare a municipal budget. Looking back, it was the time in my life that is the reason I would later be set up for a crime in later years. I could not in the future let even one line item get away without an explanation, no matter how hard my party leader pressed me to move past it. But back then for our town budget, a five hundred thousand dollar line item was a big deal, in our nation's budget, not so much. It was the reason why one line item in a federal budget could sit so quietly for many decades with no one really wanting to question it.

The next several months I was burning myself out. I was trying to do what was best for the town until a new city manager could be hired as well as prepare the budget. Not many knew but I was still submitting stock recommendations to Carl. I spent my weekends and some nights researching emerging companies. I was not only doing it for him but I was also still banking most of my money into investments since I was living at home. Many found it very odd I was still living at home with my parents in my now mid twenties but they were rarely at home and my cost of living was small.

Nicole who was now truly divorced wanted me to get a place on my own but I really was not in a mood to do it only to appease her. She wanted more than for me to move into my own place but maybe staying at home was an excuse to not have to make any further commitments to her. I really didn't care that her "maternal clock" was now a clicking time bomb. We got along but there was something holding me back more than my job. The problem was that I could not put my finger on it but maybe it was that she seemed to live way beyond her pay scale and yet was never behind in her bills. It was not like I was responsible for her bills but it was something that did seem to jump out at me. After all my short career was spent looking at numbers, hers didn't add up to me. I am not sure it was a good enough reason to keep a slight distance but my instincts took over with her. I mean, it was quiet possible her family had money and she had inherited it, I never bothered to ask and she never bothered to tell. She never came across as someone who would do something for money from men. She never once asked me for a dime or gifts. She was someone who was attracted to power. She was fun to be with and actually seemed like someone who would be a loyal and dedicated wife but my time for now was all about my career.

After the town council interviewed many promising candidates for town manager, it was decided that I should keep the position. I had no real experience but the council felt I was doing a good job on the interim basis consequently I was offered the position with a three year contract. The one thorn in my side was the newly elected council woman Michele Coonerty. She was a third generation council woman in our town and somehow felt it was her job to let all know who would listen that she was not only a third generation politician but also one of the more successful business leaders in town. I am not sure how accurate all her claims were but she was a constant visitor to my office to "keep tabs on my job performance." She claimed that she knew budgets as well as anyone in town and that she would "make sure the budget was done with great accuracy." I was not sure I was cut out for having to play politics in making a budget but I was willing to put up with some interference in order to keep the town running smoothly.

Mali was elevated to my old position of finance director with my recommendation but the fire and police department heads were not pleased. I did not have an axe to grind with either of them and in fact did all I could to make sure they had a proper budget. Unfortunately, they preferred to hold a grudge. All this was new to me. I had never really experienced all the egos I had to constantly dodge. My mother was after me constantly to leave the town behind and go back to number crunching for Mr. Peterson and Mr. Darcy. However I had to admit my own ego was now being fueled with the limited power I was now being afforded. It was the first time in my life I actually considered a move into a higher level of politics at a later date.

5

*E*gos are a fragile thing. Stunt the growth of one and you likely stunt the growth of its owner. Let it flourish too much and it likely hurts its owner just as much. It's a delicate balance to keep it in the proper check depending on how much you need it survive in your position. I don't think I had ever fed mine or felt a need to until I had real power with my new position. When I became more conscience of ego I did everything in my power not to let it expose itself too often but there were times it was necessary. I was surrounded by huge egos even in a small town politics and if I was not careful theirs would destroy me and mine. As large as those egos were with the local leaders, it was a mere training ground for things to come later in life.

Years later far removed from being town manager I had time to reflect plenty from a cold and dreary holding cell on Christmas day when I was a mere thirty three years young. Never once did I ever expect to have to see my parents from the other side of a table inside a government holding cell being charged with a crime. All I can remember is my mother telling me over and over "I warned you to stop trying to be a savior for the people. This was never for you and now you are paying a huge sacrifice for being my sweet boy." My dad sat quietly most of the time and would only say, "I know the truth seems so powerless now but I can assure you that the court room has a way of giving the truth power." I was torn between humiliation and anger that my parents had to endure seeing me this way on Christmas day. I could hear my mother cry as they left me sitting alone waiting for the guard to escort me back to where I was being detained. They even disgraced me by taking my shoe laces claiming I was on suicide watch. They had no idea who they were charging with a baseless crime. No, I was far from suicidal. This was an intentional ploy to lock me up on Christmas day as a warning to shut up. Actions have consequences. My actions led to these circumstances but I refused to look at it as if I was a criminal. I knew someone wanted me to suffer for my actions but doing the right thing was not always easy.

When I was charged I had been in Congress for less than twelve months in my initial elected term that was supposed to extend for twenty four months. Congressional leaders considered me an irritant. They should have seen me as an elected official who took his oath to office as more than words to recite. I felt responsible for the entire budget, not only the lines they wanted me to see. The way I saw it, had they not tried to hide one small line in the budget and tell me what it was for, all this could have possibly gone away. I really don't know if I would have kept objecting or not but the more they tried to hide it, the more I felt I had to know. Someone had been lying to me and it did not sit well. In the end, it really was a small amount of money in relation to the rest of the budget, but still an amount that seemed to be a useless charge for the taxpayers.

Lucky for me my attorney, who is to this day, is still the best litigator in Carl Peterson's firm knows the man I am and of my innocence. Carl knew from the start it was all a set up but proving it to a judge and jury I am told is always a tricky proposition. My real concern was to prove my innocence and at the same time not upset the fine people back home who had entrusted me with their votes. Even still, I could affect national elections and possibly save myself but I was not convinced I wanted to hurt our great land to save myself. I wanted to prove my innocence and keep hold of promises I had made to the President only a few months previous to me sitting in front of a judge being charged with a crime.

Who do I answer to, me, my God or the country I was elected to represent? Is it better for everyone to know the truth or let them think poorly of only one off the rails politician? It is not an easy task to decide between years in prison or total freedom and having to remain quiet about a small part of American history that maybe was better left unsaid. Besides I am sure at that point any mention of it had been erased from all Congressional records during the holiday weekend while I spent three long days of my life waiting for my arraignment. I was sure that was the goal in picking that particular time to send me to prison. After all, since I knew what some were capable of, making a small part of American history disappear overnight should be an easy task.

William N. Pruitt III is a third generation attorney from Staten Island, New York. He has been practicing law for over forty years and claims the "N" in his name stands for "never loses". He is as elegant looking as he is good at his profession. His silver hair and tall lean body fit perfectly in his Armani suits and Italian silk ties. He is as confident in his abilities as any attorney as he is upset every time he sees an abuse of power by politicians.

I first met Mr. Pruitt while working for Carl Peterson that summer in college when I worked for the law firm. Mr. Pruitt's grandfather was one of the founding members of the firm in 1910. Growing up he wanted to play centerfield for the Brooklyn Dodgers but Duke Snider already had that position so he was pushed into law like his father was, as is his son William N. Pruitt the fourth. He may look regal but is really a street fighter from the inner streets of New York. Despite his early child hood that many would consider privileged, he led a checkered past until it was time to shape up or be tossed from the family business. Not only did Carl Peterson not have to call in a favor to represent me, Mr. Pruitt practically insisted he get the case for only travel expenses and office costs. I know Carl didn't object since I had made his firm a lot of money for his clients with my ability to pick stocks. It was a big draw for him as an agent and this was his way of thanking me. I also think Mr. Pruitt felt bad since that entire summer he would walk past my converted broom closet they called my office and would stop and ask "Can I borrow a mop?", it got old but he was the boss. However at the end of that summer he was the first one to call me into his office and let me know what a good job I did. He told me "The door will always be open for your return". My fate would later be in his hands.

I was scheduled to appear in court for my arraignment early one morning not far from my tiny office in the Rayburn building. While expecting my attorney that morning I had time to decide how far I wanted to protect myself from prosecution or expose what I did know about our nation's history as well as change others lives forever.

I was led into the court room for my arraignment. I was warned by my attorney that the judge assigned to my case was very hard on politicians or anyone accused of a crime like the one I was being accused. Mr. Pruitt was convinced it was not a coincidence that Judge Charles Hook was assigned my case. His name fit his judicial record in being very hard on defendants. He was a no nonsense judge looking for any excuse to give law breakers the maximum sentences. I was told by Mr. Pruitt to utter two words and two words only, "Not guilty".

Since they held me in prison over Christmas day we were all hoping that the ones behind this travesty would come to their senses and drop all the charges before the arraignment. Maybe it was only a message to show the power in Washington. It was not to be. There I was being led down a long grey corridor with Mr. Pruitt by my side assuring me I would be released very soon. As I entered the courtroom all I could think about was how it should be others in my place and not me. My second thought was for all the people who had elected me to Congress, allowing me, George McAdams, to become the youngest representative ever from my district. I know my constituents were all distracted with the holidays but these people had taken my stock advice or went to school with me or lived in my neighborhood. What were they thinking of me now? Worse yet, what would the American public think if I exposed all that I knew? Would they even care? I mean I didn't have a secret like the President was not really the President but it was something neither party wanted exposed. Had our electorate become so jaded that in the end they really would not care what I knew? Was I seeing myself as a martyr for no reason? Mr. Pruitt kept telling me all the way down the hallway no matter how upset I was to merely state "not guilty" and say nothing more for now.

We were first on the docket on that overcast morning. I shuddered as the words "All rise, court is now in session, the honorable Judge Charles Hook presiding." For the first time it really started to become real to me. I mean I sat in prison for three days due to the timing of my arrest and it falling before Christmas breaking the rule that my arraignment be within forty eight hours not seventy two. For some reason all the rules were not applying to me in this case. It was not a coincidence. I was being sent a message and that was that others could control my fate, even if unjustified.

Sitting back and watching my attorney huddle with the prosecutor and the judge at the bench before a word was spoken in open court, still offered hope it would all go away. It didn't. Next thing I can remember is the judge asking me to rise from my seat. "Mr. McAdams you are being charged under Title blah, blah, blah", I heard nothing more until he finished with, "how do you plead Sir?" I have to admit not only did a lump run up my throat, anger started to thump the temples on my forehead. I wanted to blast out what I knew but with a swift kick under the table from my attorney I let out a resounding "NOT GUILTY". It was likely overkill but I wanted to make sure there was no doubt for anyone who would listen. Bail was set at an incredibly high two million dollars, with the excuse I was likely to run. That time I knew it was not a coincidence. I had exhibited no will to leave the country. However just like that it was over. I now had to wait four months for the trial to begin. The prosecution asked for eight months to prepare its case but our side asked for a speedy trial and one was granted. Maybe the judge wanted this trial away from his docket as quickly as I did. I was released but as I rode past the Rayburn building, and gazing into the rear view mirror, I could only reflect back on how I got into the mess years earlier.

6

*A*fter knowing my job was secure as town manager it was time to be an adult in other ways. I found a condo on the beach and went into debt for an asset for the first time in my life. I could have paid cash for it. However I also knew that it's always better to use other people's money if you can invest your money for more than you can borrow it. It was a time in our history when interest rates were very high and in most circumstances maybe it would have been better to pay cash but I was still doing well with my personal investments. I wanted my cash to be fluid. The bank president also told me, "You will get a better rate since all of the town business accounts are in our branch." I didn't bother to take the time to understand what all that meant. I only knew I needed a loan and the bank provided one for me. I asked for no special treatment.

What that did mean however was that Nicole now wanted more of a commitment from me. We had been dating off and on for several years and she wanted to be a mother maybe even more than a wife. I didn't want to be a husband let alone a father. I know that many my age were starting families but my heart was in running the town not changing diapers. It created a lot of tension between us and we, well in truth, she decided that she "needed more and was going to find it." We still dated but I could tell it was not going to be the same after she let me know, "I am going to be a mother with or without you before I am thirty."

One of the benefits of my new found position was that on certain evenings I was asked to attend political events. I was registered as an independent so both main political parties courted me. I was a popular leader amongst the people who knew what was really going on, so local politicians wanted to discover where my heart and true philosophies existed. I had never really given it great thought since I really voted for whoever I considered the best candidate each election cycle. I really didn't want to get all caught up in playing party politics so up to that point in my life I didn't have to choose one party over the other.

It was during one of those events that I first met then Senator Jeff Morrison from the great state of New Jersey who was running for President. Palm Beach had become not only a place for national politicians to stop off for an infusion of cash but Florida was now on the big map for electoral support.

He was a very polished politician who was treated more like a rock star than a political figure. He was a former pro athlete who was in his second term as Senator from Jersey. He married his college sweetheart and they had three children. He was tall with just a hint of grey around the edges of his hair and knew how to charm a crowd. He certainly knew how to charm my date Nicole who draped herself all over his designer suit and no doubt capped white teeth. I found her a few times capturing him in a corner of the room. She barely spoke to me at the party or for the entire evening. All I got from her was "Now that's a real leader who knows how to grab your attention." Our twenty minute ride back to her apartment seemed like an eternity. I think it was because my earlier comment to her was "Yes, I noticed what he was trying to grab and do you need a tissue for all the drool on your face?" I dropped her off at the front door and left quickly at her insistence. She gave me that same cold stare the judge would offer me a few years later right after he asked how I wanted to plead in my arraignment. It is a stare I can live without in the future.

Besides meeting a Presidential front runner in the upcoming election that evening, I met a fellow by the name of Robert Lentz. The guy was near my side for thirty excruciating minutes letting me know that he was "The Palm Beach king maker and if you ever want to have any real success in politics you need to know me". I think I gave him that same stare I never liked when I replied "Well Mr. Lentz, that's all well and good but I was not aware we had elections for kings in Florida." He seemed to be much larger in his words than his height. I suspected he had a Napoleonic complex going on but I would later find out that he had a soft side as well. He helped many out of jams with either cash or places to stay over the years. However, there was no mistaking that he came across at first glance as someone who thrived on power, either his or others.

I had never met him before and didn't realize he in fact was a very powerful contact for politicians in town. I only knew of his place of business which was the best night club and restaurant in the area. "Well kid if you ever lose that smart ass attitude and want to make it in politics here one day you come by my place for a drink and I will make you a real player, not some half ass town manager. Do you think it was only a coincidence the Senator came over to my table the moment he arrived at the party? Don't be so foolish to think these guys don't know what rings to kiss in each town they visit. When they come to the Palm Beach area they kiss mine and don't you forget that you smart ass punk kid". At that point I wanted the fire marshal to inspect his restaurant or have the county health inspector pay him a visit to see who he needs to call in my town but I was more interested in prying my date off of the Senator's perfectly fitted suit. She was leaving marks.

The next day I called the Mayor who I was now very close with personally as a friend and golf partner and he confirmed that Bobby Lentz was the guy to see if you ever wanted to be elected from this area. "I had to pay homage to him even if it did turn my stomach. It is something you might not ever get used to but it's something every politician learns to live with or get out of politics. And besides George don't think that others are not paying attention to the job you are doing in this town. They all want you to know what political party you intend to affiliate with should you ever decide to move along in your political career." At first I was taken back some with Scott's comments. Yes, it had crossed my mind that I didn't want to be town manager forever and possibly a higher office would be in the cards but not to the point as to who's rings I had to kiss.

The next few days I tried to make up with Nicole but she was not around and when I called her office. I was told she called in and said she was "taking a few vacation days". I had a feeling I knew where her "vacation time" was taking her but in truth at that point it was no longer my business where she was on her time off. I had budgets to prepare and Carl Peterson was spending a week in Manalapan at the Ritz Carlton and wanted to catch up in person, so my week was booked.

I met Carl Peterson one evening and I was surprised with his request. "George, I am not sure you are aware or not but I have a small company that invests in real estate with Dylan James and a few others. We would like to expand it here with some commercial buildings and I would like your help to find us a solid investment. We like small shopping centers but are open for suggestions as long as it gives us the cash flow we are looking for as a return. We would also like for you to manage the properties for us for a fee or a small ownership stake. That will be your choice. However we feel that Florida is about to explode and we want to be in this market. Is it possible you can show me around town sometime in the next few days while I am here and maybe find an agent who can scout out a building or two to give me an idea of prices and rents? What do you say?" Well what could I say? My investments to that point were all in stocks and a small amount in cash, it made sense to diversify. I called a guy who I played golf with now and again who was one of the best commercial guys in the area, Frank Camille. He gave us a good idea of rents and prices for a good commercial property. I, of course, was aware of the values based on the tax records but I had never looked at them based on rents versus values. It was another good lesson for me. We gave Frank an idea of what we wanted and he started to keep an eye out for us. Later in the week Dylan James came to town for a few days and I joined Dylan, Mr. Peterson and Mr. Darcy in a round of golf. I made sure we paid full fees even though Dylan thought he should get a free round since he signed a few autographs before we set out to play. That's all I needed was to bring a group to the home course and not pay. I didn't think Dylan's autograph was worth a round of golf anyway.

The next few weeks were rough since I had to negotiate contracts with the police and fire unions. They of course walk in telling me all their demands and my job is to keep it at a minimum increase. It usually is a dance that can take months to complete but I really had no desire to see those people in my office on an almost daily basis for any longer than need be. The fire union rep and I had an agreement with what I thought was a fair increase within a few weeks but the police union was being a bit more difficult. I decided to take the negations to the golf course one day and by coincidence at the end of the fifteenth hole I mentioned you could see the shopping center that I was in the process of purchasing with a group of investors. I asked the rep if he was interested in joining us in that property as an investor or one in the future. I didn't give it a second thought when he quickly declined. We went on with our previous conversation and after a few more days we hammered out our deal. Both contracts were ratified at the next council meeting.

For the first time in my job I felt I had a few days to relax. I called Nicole to see if she wanted to go to the Bahamas for a few days but she told me "I am sorry George but I am seeing someone else now and I don't think it would be a good idea if you and I saw each other any longer." Well, ok then. It was not really a surprise to me since I didn't give her an engagement ring thirty seconds after I had moved into my own place. Our relationship had become strained but from my perspective it was mostly from her end. I tried to see her but for months she kept giving me excuses with an occasional date. I knew then it was time to move in another direction with any potential love life. I was still not really ready to settle down immediately but my life was starting to come into view so I was starting to see a future with a wife and family one day.

I spent a few days in Nassau in the Bahamas. I went alone and one night while playing black jack who sat next to me but Bob Lentz. He was over there trying to negotiate a contract to start a night club in one of the casinos they were building on Paradise Island. "Kid, I heard how you negotiated that deal with the fire union and I really think you should move on from being town manager. The time has come for you to run for state office. I can make that happen. I can see you as the governor of Florida one day. I heard you are a whiz with numbers and in picking stocks, go back to that and become a state legislator. Cut your teeth at the state level then move to the Governor's office or Washington. You are young, smart and you don't seem to be intimidated by these local guys. Your only problem, from what I have heard, is that you don't let's just say ah, know how to bend the truth when the time is right." We moved away from the black jack tables since I was a bit of a card counter and he was messing up my concentration. It was either that or the playboy model they had posing as a dealer was catching my attention. But we did move to the bar for a more focused chat.

"Mr. Lentz, this is now the second time you approached me about becoming a politician and I don't know why? Please explain." He sat back and chuckled before explaining. "Kid, do you think it's even remotely possible for me to get a night club in this town without influence from elsewhere? The company that owns the casino going up across the street is a huge international company. Do you have any idea who is on the board of directors, no I am sure not. You are some punk ass kid who thinks owning a small stake in some broken down shopping center and a few internet stocks is power. Yes, I know all about the center you guys purchased, so what. That's nothing kid. Senator Morrison, our future President sat on the board of directors for the company that's now building the casino out that front door. I gave him a call and he told me if I would raise him one million dollars for his election campaign, I would get my night club. That's power kid! You sit all day long in some cramped office hoping they don't fire your sorry ass while I talk with future Presidents who make my deals happen with one phone call. This is not common knowledge but I own stakes in night clubs all over the country. I do that with connections. I need a zoning change, I make one call. I need the hours expanded for an hour, I make a phone call. It's called influence. Now, I will make you a star but when I call you, I want you to take my call and make things happen for me like the good Senator did."

I was not sure I had ever crossed paths with a guy so brash. I had to take a moment to collect my thoughts. Once I did my only comment was, "If I ever do run for office it will be on my terms and I refuse to be bought."

"Yeah, you keep telling yourself that kid but when you want that legislators seat in the Florida House of Representatives you let me know and I will make it happen for you." I excused myself for the evening.

Upon arriving back to Florida I had realized that I was not the only one who had worked hard over the past few months. I tweaked the budget to get Mali, Sue and a few others a raise for the coming year. I also took Mali and Sue out for a nice lunch at Jackie J's restaurant that overlooked the ocean. I knew it was not only bad form but also against town policy for me to date town employees but I was becoming attracted to Sue. I know Mali was starting to see it as well since during lunch I heard her mutter, "Hey Romeo, dial it down or I will get the waitress to throw some ice on your head." I guess I didn't realize how much I was openly flirting with Sue but I was in a good mood with the town running smoothly and negotiations with the unions complete for another five years. The town council was not only happy with my leadership but even Mrs. Coonerty found better things to do with her time rather than harass me.

A few days later while playing golf with the mayor, police and fire chiefs which was not our usual pairings they surrounded me after the 9th hole about a rumor I was leaving the town to run for the state legislature. I was not only shocked but really pissed off. "Where did you ever hear such a thing and "I can assure there is not one shred of truth to it" I barked at them. Scott stepped up and offered, "Let's just say that it is coming from more than one source that you are about to become a serious contender in local politics."

Bill Jackson the police chief was happy with the thought that I was possibly leaving the town leadership since he never got over the time I stopped him from getting his new cruiser. I had done what I thought was best for the town yet still fair to the police and fire employees. They forget that I had changed their pension plans to one that actually paid them more in the long run and increased their salaries even when other towns were starting to make cut backs. None of that seemed to matter since Jackson still had an axe to grind with me and would not have been upset to see me go. I kept at them to tell me who was starting those rumors but I knew where they were coming from.

I stopped by Doc's Downtown Bar and Grill on my way home from the golf course to set Bobby Lentz straight on starting rumors. He denied it all to my face but left it with "You will come to me one day asking for a favor kid and when you do at least you know where to find me." I once again quickly excused myself.

The next week people were all glaring at me with a different look in their eye. One day Mali walked into my office and said, "Well Governor does this mean you will let me visit you at the mansion in Tallahassee after the next election?" All I had done for that woman and she still loved to tease poor old me. It had even hit the local paper that I was filling out paper work to run for the state legislature. I had to call the paper and assure them there was not one shred of truth to the story. If they had called the election office they would have seen I had not filed any papers for any upcoming election. It was starting to hurt me with the commissioners since they did not really believe me. I had to persuade Scott to convince them that it was not true. Whoever was starting all this was making my life difficult and I didn't know the reason for the rumors in the first place. What could be the motive? Was it only to put it in the forefront of my own thought process? Was someone that sly? President Lincoln once said. "Whatever you are, be a good one." Well I was a town manager and I had planned on being a good one for the foreseeable future now. As much as I had given thoughts to a future political office this was starting to suppress my thoughts so that I was proven to be truthful in my deeds.

7

My buddy Doc Carter died suddenly. His body was found sitting in his chair by his maid, overlooking the lake he gazed at daily. I have little doubt he died a content man. He was the one person close to me who thought I should enter the political arena. He did however also warn me over and over that I might not be cut out for the cut throat nature of politics. After I moved into my own condo I had not seen as much of him but he did keep up with my highs and lows as town manager. I knew I could always go to him for unfiltered advice. I put much value in his guidance over the years and he was rarely wrong. He had keen instincts for how the political system worked despite never running for any elected office himself. I guess he just knew people and after all in the end politics is about how to bend and shape people.

The day after Doc's funeral I heard rumors that Nicole was pregnant. I had not spoken to her much in recent months and it was not until I spoke with Mr. Darcy that he confirmed the rumors were true. I heard Mrs. Des Darte mentioning it in the hallways of City Hall a few days earlier but I was not certain she was speaking about Nicole. I didn't really care to ask her to be sure. I will admit to being a bit sad that she and I never tried harder but we each had our own version of what the future should look like. It really was my fault. She wanted to start a family and I was not ready. Mr. Darcy did however tell me that she asked about me frequently and I should "Give her a call one day."

As much as I worked my butt off to be a good town manager I was growing bored with the position. I had held it for almost four years and the town was running smoothly. It helped that we had a good mayor in Scott and overall a town council with the same vision. It's not that I didn't feel challenged because I did but I really felt deep inside I was destined for a higher calling. It's funny but I never really felt that way until I walked in the shoes of a town manager for a couple of years. Looking back I knew I needed to be on a bigger stage. However my problem was that I had no idea how to proceed to the next level. I did not want to feel indebted to anyone for electing me other than my constituents. I spoke with Scott about it and he offered what he knew from having run for mayor but on a national level, it would be far different. I would need people who knew how to shape a campaign as well as find out if I could raise enough money to be competitive in a race. I didn't want to call Bob Lentz for help. I knew that would only be trouble in the future if I leaned on his type. However I also knew it was inevitable that asking people who would want something in return would be a must to raise serious campaign funds. It was just a matter of where to draw the line.

The latest Presidential election came and went in the fall with Senator Morrison winning a close election. He was representing the party not previously in power and had not held the Presidency for the past twelve years so he ran purely with the theme, it was time for a "change of power". He could not run on attempting to change the direction of the country based on specific policies since the country was in pretty good economic shape and the United States was not engaged in any wars throughout the world. He was a handsome man who looked much younger than his real age. He also knew how to get the women to vote for him. I never really saw him as a great leader as much as I did someone who ran a good campaign and knew what it took to win a national election. Maybe I was still upset he caught Nicole's eye at the party we attended earlier that spring, either way he didn't win my vote. I voted for the man representing the Constitution Party because when I saw him on CSPAN he made the most sense to me. I know most would say I "threw away my vote" but I always believed that if you "continue to follow the herd eventually you will get slaughtered". Besides, it was my vote.

Over the next few months there were whispers I would make a good mayor but the current holder of that office was my golf buddy as well as someone I considered a friend. I didn't agree with all of his decisions but I was not going to run against him in an election. I concentrated on running the town and finding more investment buildings for my partnership with Carl Peterson and Dylan James. It was set up so that each individual building had its own corporation and share holders. I encouraged the police and fire chief along with Nicole to participate as owners on one of the buildings we purchased in the area. Nicole and I had become friends again over time. She once again started to rely on my financial advice. Over time she had built an impressive portfolio for someone her age and income level before we parted. I feared it was not doing as well after we parted and I was willing to wager that was part of the reason for her wanting to become friends again.

The father of her child was still a mystery to the public though I had my suspicions, as did others. There was a stock broker who made his home in Palm Beach in the winter and New York during the remainder of the year who she was seen with publically many times. I was not so sure he was the father but that was the conventional wisdom. I never suspected it could be me. She never made even the slightest inference that I was. She would not admit who it was and would only tell people that ,"The father of my child holds an important job that keeps him away from Florida most of the time." I really never pushed the issue since I knew it would only lead to more drama with her and she didn't need that being so close to delivering her first child.

Nicole's child was born on Valentine's Day and was named Michael Thomas. A month before the birth she moved into a beautiful condo with an ocean view. I didn't understand how she could afford such a residence but she told me "The baby's father is taking care of the rent on this place." Whatever, it all seemed a bit odd to me. The guy is never seen yet he pays her rent? I pulled up the tax records on the condo but it was owned by a corporation with only a registered agent as the contact who was an attorney in Florida. I started to wonder if her sugar daddy had a sugar mama I could date.

A week after Nicole gave birth, our local United States Congressman who was elected ten straight times, perished in a skiing accident in Colorado. It was a huge shock to everyone who knew him. He did have a zest for living and was known for exotic trips as well as doing things like swimming with the sharks or snow skiing around the globe. He was a solid representative for our area but was never one who was out front on hot button topics. Maybe that's how he stayed elected. It was assumed the governor who had the ability to appoint someone to fill the seat would leave it open until the next election in November. Since Congress had the better part of three months off in the summer and we were closing in on March it was assumed the seat would remain vacant. That was until there was a vote scheduled concerning how states received and covered health insurance. The vote would be held before the next election in November.

Insurance was very much a hot topic not only around the country but here in Florida. It seems many want health insurance but how it's paid for was another issue. For many Floridians this has always rung true. Because of the demographics of age, and with so many illegal immigrants and migrant workers, this was a huge issue for

Florida due to the costs that could possibly be shifted from the Federal to the State's responsibility.

The Florida Governor at the time was a woman in her first term who didn't want to seem "out to lunch" when it came to such an important issue. Jessica Waters was elected with great support from the Palm Beach County area since she was born and raised about twenty minutes north of my town. She had become very familiar with many of the local politicians. She came from a family who owned a large insurance business but was an attorney by profession. This issue could also have a huge impact on her family's business as well. I had met her briefly a few times at area events and at a fund raiser for her election but I can't say we knew each other well. In fact I doubted she could remember my name if she had to on the spot.

Much to my surprise one day Michele Coonerty arrived in my office to let me know that she spoke with the Governor about possibly appointing me to the open seat. It seems through the insurance business and women council meetings Michele and the Governor we fairly close friends. Who knew after all this time Michele could actually back up some of her bluster? I was at first humbled she would think of me in those terms but I really didn't think, no matter how much perceived clout she had with the Governor, I would ever get the appointment. There were many more qualified people within the Governor's own party who could fill that position better than an unproven person like me.

I was still a registered independent. "George, the Governor wants someone who will vote her way on one specific issue. I assured her that if you agreed with her, people in Washington would never be able to pressure you enough to get you to change your mind. I assured her that once you give someone your word you don't waver from it, even if at your own peril. I have seen it firsthand here George, I know that if you agree with the Governor you won't change your mind at a later date."

As much as I appreciated Michele's words I was not sure how accurate they were. Well, I knew she was right in that I would not lie about my vote but I really had not studied the proposed bill in Congress. I knew a fair amount about the insurance industry since I had to negotiate rates for our town employees but was not an expert. However, much to my surprise, the Governor's office called me and two days later I was off to Tallahassee to meet with her.

I had not met with Governor Waters since she had won the election. I am not sure how to explain it but since the last time I met her she seemed more confident with the tone in her voice. I can't say it was stern now and had not been in the past but maybe more direct. I would imagine she was always on a very tight time schedule, so being direct would be a good thing. We met in the Governor's residence in her private office with her aide also in the room. The Governor sat high in the chair with sunlight coming through the window on her left side. Her stare was one I had seen many times when I was in trouble or about to be lectured.

"George, this is off the record since I cannot tell you how you must vote on certain issues but this insurance issue has me very worried. We need to protect our state from this hideous piece of legislation. The state of Florida receives about ninety four cents back for every dollar in federal tax monies sent to our nation's capital. There are two states that receive over two dollars back for every dollar sent in and neither state has the aged demographics that our state does. If Congress votes to send even a small part of the cost of Medicare Part A back to us and still shorts our state six cents on every dollar sent up there, it could have a devastating effect on our state budget. They are having a terrible time balancing their own budget in Washington and this is way for them to look like they have curbed their spending. I can assure you it is only a paper trick and is not a solution to any real problem. Now I know not only from Michele but from a few others that you are a wiz with numbers and budgets and if you really looked into this you would see I am right.

It is imperative that even if it's only one more vote in our favor to kill this bill it's one we must use in our favor. Here again, I cannot appoint you based on your vote but I can ask you to call the other members from the Florida delegation who have seen the proposed bill and allow you to ask them questions. We have twenty five members in the House of Representatives and I know for certain that nineteen will vote down the bill. The seat from your district needs to be filled within thirty days."

I did not go into this meeting as unprepared as I had been for previous interviews. I had learned by my mistakes and had in fact called Jim Daniels who I had met several times over the past two years. He was the representative from the area just south of the district I lived in. He did the best he could to fill me in and was very much against the bill. He also filled me in on what the other side of the argument was but it seemed mostly to make it look like spending was being cut. It was not.

"Well Governor I have in fact already done some research and unless I am missing some information I don't see how this bill is good for any state, let alone Florida. I will not sit here and tell you I would vote against it for sure but if the information I have is accurate I would indeed vote no. There are other aspects to the bill I would have to study closer but it does seem like Congress is passing on their responsibilities to cut spending or balance a budget."

"So George, off the record, if I were to offer you the appointment if you gave me your word you will vote the bill down what is your answer? Keep in mind George this type of opportunity does not come along often to anyone across our country, let alone in your own district. It's one vote George and from what you have now told me it seems you are likely to vote against it anyways. I don't care how you vote on any other matters, only this one."

I sat back in my chair not wanting to be rude with my response or be stupid and give up a once in a life time chance to be handed a seat in the United States House of Representatives. I didn't have to ask for one cent in contributions for my seat but I would have to guarantee one vote, one lousy but such an important one. I don't remember how long I took to respond. I only know that it was long enough for Governor Waters to peek at the clock behind my head more than once and start to tap her fingers on the huge cherry desk she sat so confidently behind.

"Governor, it would be so easy for me to guarantee you a down vote. I can tell you once again the odds are very much in favor of a vote the way you would like but I would be a liar if I told you that you are assured of my vote. I can only tell you what I know now and that is I would vote against it on the merits I know currently. I know what a great honor it would be for you to appoint me even for a few months. I am sitting here somewhat shaking at my own words knowing what a fool I am being but I also know I have to be honest with myself and to you. So for now my words stand. If you find someone who can assure you of a vote in your favor I would understand. It is a very important vote and one I would take very seriously. Well who am I kidding, I would take all my votes very seriously but I have to know all the information. It is who I am as a person. If that means I don't get the appointment then so be it but I can leave here with my head held high and my mind at rest."

"Wow, Michele was dead on about you George, I am impressed. You are correct in a way it's maybe not the answer I want but in other ways it's the best response I could expect. I know exactly where I stand with you which can be quite rare for a politician." I had to stop her right there and state, "Madame Governor I am a town employee, not a politician."

"Well George I think that might be true for today but who knows what the future has in store for you. I think that statement will change in the very near term. You know I never did ask you if you were even interested in the position. I assumed you were since you made the trip here but who knows maybe it was so you could tell all your friends back home you had lunch in the Governor's mansion." The smile on her face grew very wide so I knew she was teasing me but then again there was some truth in her statement. I did want to see the Governor's residence.

"Governor before I leave I do have one obvious question for you if I may?" "Of course George, I should have given you the chance for questions." Here again I didn't want to sound rude or insulting but it did seem odd I was given a chance for the appointment at all. "Well, why me? I mean there are many qualified people who I am sure are in your ear for this appointment, who will sell their soul for this chance and who are members of your own party. I am sure you realize I am not even in your party." I am not sure my mission was to make the good lady laugh but laugh she did. Even her aide let out a chuckle under his breath.

"That's a fair question George. For one, you are correct I am being lobbied very hard to give the position to Tom Fraser who ran against me for this office but he said some incredibly hurtful and viscous lies about me and my family during the election. I have not forgotten his words. And yes, there are a few who have political experience but they will look me directly in the eye and sell their soul for this position. I am not in the business of collecting souls. I am in the business of running our state and picking the best candidate for this position despite his or her party. I am very confident from what you have told me that you will vote against this bill not because you want the position for personal gain or bad enough that you will sell your soul. But I am very confident in my facts and that you will see it's the right thing to do. If I have learned one thing today it is that you will do what is right for the state of Florida in your vote. What more could I really ask of anyone? Now if you will excuse me my next meeting is starting down the hallway and I have taken much of your time. My office will contact you later in the week. Thank you for your time George." And within a few brief seconds we shook hands and I was escorted off the grounds. I wanted to stay around for a few days and watch the Florida House while in session but I was going to be the Godfather to Nicole's son and the service was the following day.

8

*M*aybe I have watched too many movies or at times I look for
something that is not there but the baptism for Nicole's child
seemed odd to me. After all, all the people you would expect to be
there like Mr. Darcy and his wife and a few of her friends were but
in the corner was Bob Lentz and a guy who was doing his best
impression of a secret service officer. Why would Mr. Lentz be at
the ceremony? When I asked them, Lentz told me it was because
the small luncheon we were having after the baptism was at his
restaurant. Then when I dared to ask where the father was I was
only told "He is out of the country and for now you are the
godfather so appreciate that and stop asking too many questions!"
I did as requested. I really didn't want to ruin a special day. I really
didn't like it when Lentz kissed my godson on the forehead. It
almost seemed like the kiss of death to me, on such a sacred day.

 The following day, in the Sunday's edition of the local paper, ran a
report that I had been offered the Congressional seat.
Unfortunately, no one had taken the time to ask me if the report
was based in truth. Indeed, I had started to get excited about the
possibility of me actually going to Washington and casting a vote
that could potentially change the future of our nation. However I
was still replaying the previous day's Baptism in my head with two

or three people in attendance that seemed out of place to me. But by mid day I no longer had time to think about that since my phone was ringing off the hook with well wishers, inquisitors and a few not so pleasant calls from people who were not pleased with the Governor's choice. I had to take the time to explain to each and every caller that I had indeed spoken with Governor Waters but she had not offered even a hint I would be offered the position. I didn't want the good Governor to think that I had started the story so I called her office and let them know this was not my doing. Her aide took the call and told me "We eat, sleep and live politics on a daily basis. We know you didn't start the story." The weird thing was that by the time my brief call ended I could swear he either knew who did plant the story or the Governor's staff did to get a reaction from the voting public. At that point I felt a bit like a laboratory rat awaiting its fate.

The next day not only were there letters to the editor about me being the choice but an editorial piece explaining why it was a good choice to name me as the "seat warmer for a brief time in history." It went on to say that "someone with his lack of political skill could to do no harm for a few inconsequential votes." I wanted to ask the editors how someone with no political skill could be up to speed on a major piece of legislation who was merely a reader of their paper yet the political editors acted as if they knew nothing of the pending insurance vote. Go figure, but if I was to be the choice I didn't want the paper to be my enemy. I had always gotten favorable press in the past but I had to admit it was mostly from the local writer who covered our council meetings.

I didn't get much sleep for the following nights in anticipation but I also didn't want to get my hopes up only to be let down when I might not be the choice at all. Mali and Sue were no help when they kept staring at the office secretary every time the phone rang as if it was a call from heavens above. I am not sure they would be happy for me or happy for themselves to get rid of me for a few months. I had spoken with the Mayor and the Council about me keeping my job since it was possibly only a few short months appointment and I would be home more than in Washington, D.C. They were a bit skeptical I could handle both jobs even on a short term basis but wanted to rule after they knew the facts. As much as I now wanted the appointment I did fear losing my job. I admit I was bored at times but I still wanted to leave on my terms.

Finally on Thursday I got the call that I was being offered the appointment which I accepted immediately. I could not worry about my current job. This was a huge opportunity even if it turned out to be for less than one year. The Mayor informed me that as much as they appreciated my performance I would be asked to resign. I did.

Within a few short hours I was called by Miss Kristen Candor who was the aide to the previous congressman who held what was now my seat in the House of Representatives. I was busy cleaning out my desk and almost didn't take her call. It was not until my secretary explained to me who she was that I picked up the phone. My head was spinning so any new name floating in my head was not going to register unless someone kicked me. The last call of the day was from Mr. Lentz letting me know that if I needed anything to "just call and ask." Lucky me.

I knew I was going to need someone who knew their way around DC. Why should I not keep the same staff for the time being? I know she was calling to find out my plans about a staff but I assured her that I wanted to reserve judgment till I could meet the entire staff individually. In my mind however I didn't have any plans to change anyone's position. I did enjoy the idea that I now had someone who could make all my travel reservations and pick me up at Regan National Airport in a few days. Kristen seemed like a pleasant person on the phone. I did call her the next day to get filled on what my agenda would be for the following week. She handled everything for me efficiently before I arrived at my new second home.

   The following Monday morning there I was being escorted to my new office in the Rayburn building by Miss Kristen. Kristen was very devoted to her job and loved the power that was Washington, D.C. She grew up in south Florida and worked as a staff person for a state representative before being lured to Washington three years previously. As much as she was far more advanced to the ways of national politics than I was, her sweet inner core was visible in a few short minutes. She introduced me to the remainder of my small staff once we arrived.

   My ability to learn fast was going to be tested. For whatever reason, remembering names was never something I was very good at, but that had to change in a hurry. My staff was now Kristen along with Matthew Perez and Samantha Kaiser. Matthew was born here in the United States but his family migrated here from Mexico just before his birth. He was the first in his family with a formal education. He informed me about his responsibilities then quickly told me that he spent our recess times building homes in Mexico. He let me know that if he could not keep up his tradition he would have to resign. I don't think that was the best way to introduce himself, but what was done was done.

   Samantha, who quickly informed me that she was to be called Sam and not Samantha, was a local volleyball coach at nights, so working late except for emergencies was not an option. Welcome to Washington. Kristen was the only one who it seemed liked I could rely on. There was one other staff person but it seems he moved back home before I had an opportunity to meet him. So at least for now I had three people on my staff. Matthew was in charge of my speeches, my public image, and arranging any public appearances. Samantha's, oh excuse me, Sam's duties would include keeping track of any information that needed to get back to my constituents including our information on the web page, flyers, answering calls and dealing directly with any issues back home in south Florida. Kristen would be my shadow and would be responsible to be at my side at all times. She was also responsible for my daily schedule and making sure I was not late. I also needed to appoint someone who would be responsible for reading all the legislation and keeping an ear for anything that might be coming up for votes.

I am not sure how he knew, fate maybe, but while I was discussing with my staff about ideas to fill the vacant position, my cell phone rang. It was my old roommate Tony Montero. He was really calling to offer his well wishes but as I was telling him about my day and the open vacancy he offered a suggestion. His next door neighbor back in Jersey had a daughter who had a degree in political science from Georgetown University but was having a hard time finding work. Well, it was not really a mere suggestion he was trying to repay a favor to his neighbor. "George if you would, please give her a call and see what you can do for her? I will owe you one big guy." Tony's neighbor gave him a lead that led to his bank getting a very lucrative loan, so Tony wanted to quickly repay the kindness. Kristen arranged for me to meet with Libby Smith later in the week.

Kristen's next job was to find a place for me to live while staying in Washington. For the first night I would stay at the Watergate Hotel but she scheduled a meeting with another congressional member from the state of Maine. He had an open bedroom and was on a street close to the subway system. All the things that I didn't have time to think about, like a place to live, was now Kristen's responsibility.

Later that evening as I peered out of my window of the Watergate Hotel, I could not stop thinking about how my life was about to change. I was not far past the age of thirty yet I was one of only four hundred and thirty five individuals to represent the public in the House of Representatives. I was thrilled yet terrified as to what might be expected of me in the coming days. Who was I compared to the likes of Henry Clay, Abe Lincoln and John Kennedy all who served as members in the house? I was a small town manager from south Florida who had only moved out of his parent's house a few years ago. What could I possibly offer my district or the nation? For a brief time I was now wishing someone else had been chosen to fill this vacancy. It was not until about an hour later that I calmed myself and remembered what President Lincoln once said about his experiences as a leader "Always bear in mind that your own resolution to succeed is more important than any other one thing." I knew, no matter what was now in my future, I had to succeed or go home and going home was not an option. Looking back, I slept about three hours that night.

Before I knew it, the hotel desk was offering a wakeup call only moments before Kristen was calling my cell phone reminding me she would be picking me up out front in forty five minutes. My day was going to start with the swearing in procedure in the office of the Speaker of the House at nine a.m. sharp. From that moment I would be an official member of congress.

My excitement turned to more thoughts that I was in way over my head soon after meeting the Speaker of the House, who was a rather rude man from Kansas. I had to sit outside his office, as if I was waiting at my local dentist office, for over thirty minutes. That was my first lesson that meetings don't always begin on time in Washington, D.C. When I was finally escorted into the inner sanctum with the Speaker, John Corbin, he acted like this was such an imposition of his time rather than having some compassion for my situation. "I would like to say it is my pleasure to meet you Mr. McAdams but unless I am wrong it's not. From what I am told the Governor handpicked you to vote against the insurance bill so let me remind you that your time here is short. I would suggest you keep your head low, don't say much on the house floor, don't make waves and go back to Florida and get back to your life's work. So let's get this over with quickly, take a photo for all your friends back home then you can go hide in your office and pretend like you belong here."

I was stunned. What did I do to deserve such a greeting? I mean I had never met this man and he treated me like a common criminal. At first I looked around for the hidden camera to see if this was some sort of funny ritual they pull on all new members like a fraternity hazing. It was not to be. He glared at me like I stole his last dollar. We did the swearing in and took a few photos and he darn near pushed me from his office. Before I left I could not resist just one, not so subtle, nudge back at him.

"Mr. Speaker one question if I may before I leave? Do my future votes on any bill count any less than yours or any other member of Congress during my time here?"

I knew that would get a stern response but this morning was not what I was expecting at all. I may have been young and ill prepared for this position but being rude to me was not going to stand on day one.

"George, that is your name right, let me offer you some strong advice. You are not a member of either party. I don't know who you will caucus with but I like this insurance bill. I don't appreciate the fact you are here to vote against something I have worked on for many years and this is likely way over your head when it come to the economics of the bill. If you are smart you will spend your time sightseeing, place your vote and go home. Your time here is very short and by next year you will be a tiny blip in our nation's history, a mere footnote in our great countries records. I have been here for over thirty years doing the work of the people. I don't take kindly to people like you who come to this town acting like you could possibly understand what really goes on here. Now please leave my office."

Here again I looked at Kristen and she looked back in amazement at the rude start I was off to here with Mr. Corbin.

"Mr. Speaker, I am not sure if you are aware or not but I made no promises to the Governor about my vote, though you have done a wonderful job in making sure I do vote against it now. And for the record, I would put my knowledge of economics up against most people serving here including yours. Good day Sir."

And just like that I was being pushed out of his office by his aides and shoved to the elevator across the hallway from his office door.

"Well, I now see you know how to make friends and influence people here Mr. Congressman." I was not sure I needed that comment from Kristen as we entered the elevator but maybe that was her way of reminding me I was up against a very powerful man who by all accounts was never going to help me succeed in this town.

Going back to my office I was still in shock. My hands were trembling with the thought that I just had a brief skirmish with the third in line to the President of the United States. However the man treated me poorly and that was uncalled for in my view. Kristen was in almost a full out giggle when I finally asked her what she was so amused about. "Sir, the Speaker is legendary for his abuse of other members of the House but I had never seen it in person. I am sorry it was at your expense but I kind of enjoyed it."

Oh great, here I was sitting up all night thinking I was about to be in the same class as former Presidents and I get a scolding from a overweight grey haired man with a sour attitude wearing a bad suit. And now the only person who I thought was on my side here in this cold town is getting some enjoyment from me being abused by someone who assumes what he does not know to be true. What kind of place is this? Should I call the Governor and inform her there has been a terrible mistake and I am on my way back home?

When I arrived back in my office Sam was all giddy and rushed me to the phone. "Mr. McAdams, I don't know why or how but Dylan James in on the phone for you. He claims he is friends with you, I find that very hard to believe but he wants to speak with you. He has been waiting for a few minutes till you got back here, I knew you were on your way." I picked up the phone and immediately got an earful from Dylan, "What you are now some big shot politician you can't pick up the phone from a lowly guitar player. That's not a good way to get campaign money you know." I could hear him laughing so I figured it was ok to give it back to him. "Well I do have my standards now that I have an office here in Washington, what do you want?"

"Well I wanted to call and wish you luck and let you know that Carl and I were sitting here talking about you and how proud we all are of you. I still remember when you were sitting in his broom closet pretending to know what you were talking about and now look at you. In truth they could not have picked a finer man for the job, George. I know we have had our moments but I am very proud of you and all you have done for me. If you do half as well for your people back home that you have done for me, I know you will be very successful. Good luck and I will talk to with you soon." I bet the man with the bad suit didn't have rock stars calling his office to wish him well on his first day on the job.

As lousy as I had felt on my way to my office, like a light switch it all changed again. Sam still wanted to know how I could possibly know Dylan James and also wanted to know if I could find a way for her to meet Dylan and Sasha. It seems she was a huge fan of The Overture and had seen the band years ago when they were still touring. I told her I would work on it.

Matthew started in immediately with wanting me to do short interviews with the local television and radio stations back in my home town. He also informed me that CSPAN wanted me to come over and take questions on air for twenty minutes the following week. I was a big fan of CSPAN so I agreed to all the requests including the ones back home. That part of the job had not occurred to me until Matthew started to set up all the interviews. Samantha then let me know that a Mrs. Kleinberg was on the phone and wanted to speak with me about her landlord. It seems that her toilet was making horrible noises and her landlord refused to fix it. She was calling her Congressman to get him to fix it. "What, are you kidding me Sam? Can't you handle Mrs. Kleinberg's bathroom issues?"

Then I figured hey why not, it's been quite a day already and its only 10 a.m. "Yes, Mrs. Kleinberg, what can I do for you?"

"Well, Mr. McAdams my former Congress person would never take my calls so at least you have that going for you. My toilet makes noises when I am sleeping and my landlord won't fix it for me. Will you make him fix it?"

"Mrs. Kleinberg, if you are sleeping how do you know it's making noises at all?"

"Something is waking me up and it sure sounds like its coming from the bathroom."

"I will have someone on my staff call and see what we can do for you and let you know what we find."

As soon as I hung up the phone all three of my staff start laughing like they had just seen the best comedy routine in years. Sam in between belly laughs lets out "That poor woman calls here every day with a new problem I can't believe you actually talked with her."

"Well guess what Sam you are now in charge of getting the landlord's name and calling him to see if he will do an inspection of her place. I want a full report as to his findings and maybe she will stop calling."

"That's not fair, we are not here to fix their problems like that" she utters.

"Oh, then tell me what are we here for if not to listen to people's problems?" I really had no idea if she could get the landlord to check her apartment or how many calls like that we really took on a daily basis but I was not going to let a man with an over inflated ego and a bad suit nor my staff members get away with attempting to push me around. Not on this day. I thought back on my first day with Mali and I knew this was the proper course of action.

After calming myself yet again I thought maybe it was time to find my way to the actual floor of the House in the south wing of the Capitol building. I was confident that Kristen knew the path but I wanted to go alone to take in the atmosphere and allow myself to be in awe of what was around me. One of the first things I noticed along the marble floored hallway was the statutes. Each state is allowed two. I wanted to see what my home state of Florida had to offer. I first ran across one of Dr. John Gorrie who not only was a physician but also a scientist. He was aware of the importance of his patients staying cool so he patented what would later be one of the first ice machines as well as air-conditioning. I also stopped for a moment to view the statute of Edmund Kirby Smith who was a soldier and educator. He would later become the President of one of the first telephone companies in the Unites States as well as a professor in mathematics. I was once again questioning my ability to compete with such successful individuals.

As I wandered ever so slowly down the hallway I was stopped more than once by guards assuming I was a lost tourist. I had to prove to the security guards it was fine for me to be in the hallowed hall. Once I made it to my final destination of the House chamber, I thought it would all be larger somehow. I mean being there gave me chills and in one respect, it was larger than life but I assumed the room itself would make me feel smaller in stature not make me feel humbled, but humbled I was.

I sat in the back row of the empty room glazing at the huge American flag behind the podium, imagining me knocking the gavel to bring the session to order. A few moments later I strolled down the aisle and sat in the front row getting a better view of where I too would one day stand to offer words to a great nation. I sat there for maybe five minutes before I was once again discovered and once again asked if I had permission to be sitting in the chamber. Only this time it was not a security guard but a fellow House member. After a brief introduction and friendly chat she told me that she too sat here when she needed inspiration to do what she thought was best for her constituents back home. Tracey Goldstein was a former real estate agent from New York. After a few moments I had remembered seeing her on CSPAN in the past. She was hard to forget with her red hair and manicured style. I think after speaking with her for a few moments she took pity on me and offered a tour around the Capitol building. She was in her third term and had already risen to level of Chairwoman of the House Administration Committee. Being a former real estate agent this made sense but her rise to power took a quicker path than most. I was feeling more relaxed after Tracey made me realize we are all just people trying to do what we think is best despite our personal ideology. At least that's what I was now attempting to convince myself.

My staff was not pleased that I took over two hours to take in the Capitol sights and get my bearings but I really didn't care. If it was all true that my time here was limited I was going to make it all count. Maybe I would be a footnote in the history of the House of Representatives but I would make sure at least personally, my time would not be forgotten.

Once back in my crowded office, Sam was not happy that I reminded her to take care of Mrs. K and all her mysterious sounds. "So what did the landlord say Sam?" She gave me that same stare that Mali gave me the first day as financial manager in Boca Breezes but I was having none of it.

"What do you think Mr. Mc Adams, I am sitting here with nothing to do but call landlords all over Florida because some crazy woman is hearing noises from her toilet? If I did that, I would do nothing but handle silly calls from crazy people. Maybe you should take phone calls for an hour then tell me my job description again!"

Even Matthew and Kristen raised an eye and were waiting to see what my response was going to be on that outburst.

"First of all Samantha, you will now call me Sir, or Congressman when you speak to me. The next time I hear that tone from your mouth it will be the last time I hear it in his office because you can pack up your desk and never return. And lastly, your job description is what I say it is and if you are not comfortable doing as I ask then please, by all means, don't let the door hit your backside on the way out. Is that understood? Did it ever occur to you that quite possibly if you made even one attempt, just one, to make Mrs. K feel like you did something that would stop her calling you for a few days and that would lessen your work here? Or did it ever occur to you that if you did try, she would tell ten of her friends what a wonderful job you did for her? Now you either adjust that attitude immediately or I will have Kristen call whoever she calls in this town to find your replacement."

At that I turned and darn near hit my head on the door trying to find my desk in the small room to my right. The office was completely quiet for maybe five minutes till the phone rang again. I could hear Sam pick up the phone with that same sour tone still in her voice. It was a call from a Congressional staff member attempting to set up a time where we could meet and I would be given instructions on ethics and other things expected of me as a member of Congress.

The remainder of the day was rather mundane since I only did a few brief radio and television interviews for the audience back in south Florida. I also met with my future room mate John Smead, a white haired gent from Maine with an engineering background who, if I described as conservative it would be a slight understatement. He was a deeply religious man and seemed like a straight shooter. Despite our age difference of about thirty years we got along great and it was decided I would live the remainder of my time with John. I had very few clothes with me at on this trip so moving in with John took only a few moments from the Watergate Hotel where I had been staying. I think John wanted the company as well.

The next few days were spent getting my bearings around Washington as well as learning my duties as a member of Congress. I also interviewed Libby Smith at Tony's request and after another call from him almost begging me, I hired her. She was a nice lady without the same tone that Sam wanted to exhibit. She seemed very sincere in wanting to be a member of our new team. Libby would be responsible for reading any future legislation I would be voting on and making sure I knew all the implications of the bill as best as possible. She was not only fresh out of law school but also a newlywed. She assured me however that since her new husband was also just out of law school and studying for the bar exam as well as holding down a job as a waiter till he could find a job with a local law firm, they had little time together. She could work whatever hours were needed. The staff was complete unless Sam didn't take care of Mrs. K's bathroom issues. I think the real reason I was so hard on Sam about Mrs. K was because of the way she handed me the phone as if the staff would play a joke on me. Well the joke was being passed back to her. I did not want anyone to assume because I was the youngest Congressman from my district in history that it meant I didn't know how to handle staff or colleagues. The time spent as town manager working with a small town council offered me much experience dealing with employees and management.

At the end of my first week in town I was going to be given the floor to resound my first words for the official record as a member of the House of Representatives of the Unites States of America. It would be shown live on CSPAN for the entire nation to watch. What would I say? I spoke with Matthew about it and he told me to be brief and thank the Governor for appointing me, maybe mention one or two brief stories of people back home being a home town hero and leave quickly. "What? I am not expected to bring a bill to the floor to change the energy policy of the United States or change how funding for education is handled back to the States? I am only to say a few brief words and get out?" I knew I was joking, well maybe only somewhat with Matthew, but he too gave me a weird look but with a bit more decorum than Sam and would only say, "Yes Congressman, I think it is best for your first appearance to be brief. After all was it not William Shakespeare who stated that brevity is the soul of wit." Libby who overheard the conversation and came from a British family muttered, of course it was Shakespeare who else but a Brit could write something so poetic yet efficient. I could see she had some English literature schooling in her background and planned on keeping Matthew on his toes.

I took Matthew's advice and we worked on a five minute speech thanking Governor Waters as well as letting the people of my district know I would be there if they needed assistance. I wanted to give them Sam's cell phone number but Matthew didn't think that would be the best of ideas. But after careful consideration and driving Matthew crazy for a day or so we finished off my remarks.

The moment had arrived. The house business of the day took longer than anticipated so my time to speak was pushed back until after midnight on Friday so really it was early Saturday morning back home. I could have waited for a better time but I was determined to get to the floor and feel like I belonged. So there I was in my best suit with a carefully chosen red tie and a fresh hair cut and polished look. I looked out over the all the chairs in front of me and to my amazement only two were filled. It was my now room mate John who promised to stay with me for good luck and my aide Kristen. I felt terrible Kristen had to wait so long into the evening and I told her multiple times it was ok for her to go home and get some rest but she "did not want to miss the first of many trips to house floor by a future President." As much as those words were encouraging I was just trying to keep the seat warm until the next election. Being President of these United States was not even something I had thought about before falling asleep at night. No, I wanted to do this despite the near empty chamber. I felt bad for the cameraman from CSPAN who had to wait me out as well but I guess that was his job.

Here I was in a near empty room knowing that possibly my mother and father were still awake and watching and maybe a few political junkies with nothing better to do past midnight but I was scared to death. I had stood in front of my high school classmates many times offering remarks but this was historic. I always assumed if I could do that or talk before the public in a council meeting that talking in front of the public was a skill I had long mastered. Yet, here I was, likely white as a ghost giving praise to two I had never met and thanking someone who appointed me in this position. More people watched me give out the trophies at the local little league championship games than were watching me deliver my first words on the house floor yet the pressure was immense. I could barely let the words drip from my mouth as I stared at the camera and the person running it yawning back at me. I spoke my four minutes and twelve seconds for the record and immediately after a man walked to the podium behind me, struck the gavel and that day's session was officially over.

9

The following days and weeks were filled with meetings with other house members attempting to get to know me but I think more to maybe sway my vote on the next pending vote. I also discovered how persuasive lobbyists attempt to be. I was being offered everything from hockey and basketball tickets to overnight stays in beautiful hotels. Since I was new to it all and not sure what was even legal to accept, I turned down every offer that headed my way. I made sure Kristen was sitting in the room when the offers came in and documented all that was offered and that I refused it all and on what day. One thing I learned over time was to document anything that could impact me financially or because of my position. I learned that years ago when I was trying to clean up the free golf course plays. I did not like to accuse innocent people nor would I be accused later in life of falling into the same trap.

There were two other things that happened that really bothered me. The first was that everyone I met assumed I was only "keeping the seat warm until the next election." Even my own staff would occasionally make a comment about my time being short apart from Libby. She sounded just the opposite in that she assumed I would keep my position. I had never thought what the process was to run and win the seat in an election but I had Kristen start to work on that for me. I also made sure Sam made all the material being posted sound as if I was long term. I wanted to keep all my options open.

The other thing that was irritating me, though there was not much I could do about it, was that my assignment for a committee was given out and I was put on the Financial Services Committee which was fine but the subcommittee was a very small group having to deal with insurance, housing and community opportunity. I was told by both party leaders that unless I picked a party affiliation I would be placed on small committees with little to do. Also, since I was the "newbie" in town I had to "earn my stripes to be put on any committee of any substance." I was more than a little upset over this since I had in fact sat in on house debates over the appropriations for the budget as well as going to listen to committee meetings and I knew my experience could have been valuable to anyone who cared to listen. It seemed however that my help or expertise was not wanted. I spoke with John and Tracey who were really the only two I trusted for advice and both advised me to be "calm and wait your turn." I really respected the place I was in but I was becoming so frustrated with the process of it all. I had come there without any real expectations but I had not anticipated to be treated as I was somehow not a fully fledged member.

After a three week whirl wind of learning experiences both good and bad we were released for a two week break to go back to our districts for Easter break. I was happy to go home for two weeks but Matt had my schedule filled with meeting people at Chamber of Commerce breakfasts, Realtor events, town hall meetings and anywhere people could have access and say hello. I accepted them all before realizing I had at least one event for every day I was home. I am not sure how I had to stay so busy while Matthew was able to head to Mexico for a week, and while Sam went to coach a pre Olympics volleyball tournament. Kristen came back to Florida and shadowed me at many of the events. I think Libby spent some time with her new husband but she was very dedicated to her job and I was very pleased that Tony had recommended her to me.

After a few days back home, for the first time people started to actually treat me as if I really was their Congressman. Maybe I had to go home to get some respect. I mean there were a few back in Washington who I had gotten along with very well like John, Tracey and one or two others but it was not the same. Here in my own backyard, people treated me if my vote mattered and it did. I was now really thinking I could continue representing them in Congress. I had Kristen fill out any paperwork needed to assume I would be in the race to retain my seat and open up any accounts needed for campaign funds. I also had her update Sue Juran, my former coworker, on all paperwork and accounts.

What convinced me that I may have a chance at reelection, despite the Republican and Democrat parties spending big dollars to elect their candidates, came from an unexpected source. After giving a brief talk at a retirement community, Mrs. Kleinberg who I had no idea lived in the complex, came up to offer a formal introduction.

"Congressman I have been meaning to call you but I have been so busy with all the work being done to my apartment as well as my friend's apartments. But when I heard you were going to be here I had to come and thank you. After you called the landlord he finally sent someone out to my apartment. They discovered there were rats in the ceilings of many of the apartments. The rats were getting in through a hole behind my bathroom wall. They had to completely replace the wall from all the damage and now I sleep so much better at night. Not only do I sleep better, many of the other residents who were having the same terrible noises, are getting rest too. The owner of the apartment complex lives in Texas and it was mighty difficult to get him to understand our concerns. So thank you very much. Our last guy in Washington and that girl who answers your phone never took any of our issues serious. You did, you are the best! I have told all the people who live here they all need to vote for you in the next election. You are the only person who not only would listen to me but now you are here speaking with us in our complex. You are the first person from Washington since I have lived here to ever come and visit with us. We ordered a special cake for you from our local bakery bake to show you our gratitude."

I didn't know what to say other than "You are welcome Mrs. Kleinberg but the truth is that Samantha who answers the phone made the calls and got the landlord to do this for you all."

"Maybe so, but I know you made her do it so eat your cake and hush." I made Kristen send Samantha a photo of Mrs. K. enjoying a piece of cake with me and let her see what can happen with one well placed phone call. I later found out from Kristen that Matthew knew that was Mrs. Kleinberg's complex and they had requested the visit to thank me. No wonder they didn't ask me how I was going to vote on the insurance bill. I was however not pleased that it seemed my staff enjoyed playing "gotcha" on me now and again even after a stern warning.

The next thing that gave me confidence to run was that the local Chamber of Commerce arranged an informal event to meet with local officials not so amazingly at Bob Lentz's restaurant. I was invited along with the two candidates who would be my challengers, along with the Mayor Scott Sharley and the entire Boca Breezes town council. While at the event, as we were being peppered with questions from chamber members, I could tell that I was just as knowledgeable about what needed to be accomplished for our area from a local and federal level. In reality I felt my answers were the best. I picked up an important endorsement because as I was leaving, the President of the chamber let me know he would support me if I chose to defend my seat. My confidence in my abilities had grown exponentially over a few short days. For the first time, not only was I considering very strongly in favor of running, but I also felt like I could win despite the long odds. I had Kristen look it up and the current Congress had two elected as independents out of the four hundred thirty and five current members. Not great odds but at least I would not be the only one attempting it.

Before heading back to Washington I had lunch with Mr. Darcy and Nicole. I told them I was now seriously considering running to retain my seat. Mr. Darcy thought it was a great idea, Nicole was lukewarm at best. "George, I know you think this is a once in a life time opportunity, you have used those exact words with me, but Washington has a way of changing people and I don't want to see you hurt."

"Well Nicole, I do appreciate you looking out for me, but really it can be very thrilling to know you can change the course of history."

"George, you have to trust me on this one, I have seen it change people once they obtain power and many think they have some special calling. They don't have a calling, they have people who can buy them enough media time to smear their opponents and use fancy words to win an election. Fill out your time and come home."

"I am not sure how you know all this Nicole, and I am not so sure I want to know but really I am fine. I appreciate you looking out for me but really, I will be fine."

At that point Mr. Darcy stepped in and added, "George, politics is convincing other people to think like your people and getting enough votes from people who think your people are the right people. Other than that it's all horse manure. Believe me, I would imagine, there are some there with higher I.Q's than you in that town, but none with more common sense or ethics. That place needs leaders, you are a leader. There is a big difference between being book smart and knowing what is right and what is wrong. You know what is right. Now go back up there and be who you are. If you do that, good things will happen." I think Mr. Darcy had become my mentor since the passing of Dr. Carter so his words carried considerable weight with me.

My last stop before heading back up Interstate I-95 to Washington was to see my parents to let them know I was likely going to run to retain my position. My father wanted me to continue, my mother did not. Her concerns were similar to Nicole's so I was started to think it was more a motherly way of seeing things. Maybe I sound gender biased but it seemed the men wanted me to run and the women close to me thought Washington would harm me in some way. I didn't see it that way at all. I never pretended to have a "special calling", I think it was more my ego decided that I was now the best candidate and that's the way it was going to be.

After returning to Washington I took a couple of days and wandered around town. Spring was in full bloom now with the cherry blossoms and tourists were starting to be seen in the streets once again. I took one entire afternoon and sat on the steps of the Lincoln Memorial thinking about all the pros and cons of wanting to run for Congress for a two year term and possibly beyond. I really could not do it only for my own personal gains or it would not work. Then again why does anyone want to run for any public office? Is it really to help others or themselves, maybe both? I was not coming up with a good answer and that was holding me back but in the end it just felt like the best choice. I thought about those people who didn't know where to turn to fix the pest issues in their apartments and my office made a difference with one phone call. If I was Mrs. K's son and made that same call would anyone have checked it out? Likely not, I had to be honest with myself, that the power that came from helping so many people with one simple task started to consume me. Was Nicole right that this town would change me? I am a spiritual man and as I sat there I asked God to give me a sign that should the power start to consume me to the point of no return, I would know to step down. I also stared at Lincoln seated in front of me, hovering his shadow over me, reminding me of how small I was in this town. Every time I wanted to jump up and run out to change the course of our nation I felt humbled, as being like the Speaker told me, but a "blip in history". But just because some grumpy old man in a poorly fitted suit says what my fate is does not make it true, does it?

Later in the evening I spoke with John about why he wanted to run for public office and he told me "It was purely to leave this world a better place than when I entered it, for my children and future generations." With most people I would have considered that to be something you would say to voters but with John I had come to know him well enough to know to his core he believed in those words. We sat for a few hours really thinking about what it meant to serve the public. I really did not want to make this commitment if it was purely to build a resume. I could not do that. However, during the evening of reminiscing about my brief career one thought had come to mind.

Only a few years previous to that, I was asked to attend a job fair at the local high school. After hours of speaking with students at the event, I barged into the principal's office, demanding he personally return our hard earned tax dollars for the lousy job his school had done preparing the students for the job market and college. Now granted I had no right to act as belligerently as I had, however I was so upset over the past three hours I had spent in the gymnasium that something had to be said. The principal sat very stoic behind his desk which was far too large for his small office and asked me "So tell me then George, what are your plans to try and help us fix what you see as a mess. I mean you live in this community, you have a nice place to live, a good job and apparently a large mouth, help me repair as what you see as broken."

I remember taking a moment to think about what the man had just thrown back on me and I came back at him with, "I have a job, I am the town manager. You are the principal. I do my job very well. Maybe you should consider doing yours as well as I do mine." Not my finest moment no doubt, but I was still steaming from sitting with an endless parade of teenagers with no hope of a future if they maintained the attitudes on display that morning in the gym.

"George, before you leave my office with me thinking you are an arrogant ass, who does not see beyond his own boxed in world, I want you to give some thought to using your obvious passion and direct it at the students and not me. I have over four thousand students enrolled in this school, for some English is not even their native language. Some came to us without being able to read at a third year level when they should be graduating, but because of natural disasters in other countries, we take them in for humanitarian reasons. Some are already involved with gangs, selling drugs to fellow students, because they don't see a way out. Some do their very best and need extra help but we are so under staffed now we can't afford to offer them the extra assistance they cry out for. I get here ever day at 7 a.m. and go home many nights after the last game is played in our gym. Many nights that's not until after 9 p.m. I refuse to allow you to stroll in here after three hours and determine what type of job our staff is doing based on what you saw at a job fair. If you had any guts at all you would enter a classroom and attempt to make a difference in even one student's life before you accuse me of not doing my job ever again. Now go back to your quiet office, but tonight think about what I said and get back to me."

Maybe I deserved some of that and maybe he was being overzealous in protecting his reputation as the leader of the school, but he made his point. I was only seeing a small sample but what I did see I was not happy about. I phoned him back the next day and for the last few weeks of the school year I did go to classrooms to speak about career opportunities as well as my own personal career path. I knew it was only a small ripple in the students' brains but anything at that point was better than doing nothing in my estimation. But I also wanted to let the Principal know I would have his back rather than scold him for not doing his job.

As I sat with John and we discussed those few short weeks, maybe I could use experiences like that to prove to myself that I could make a difference for others. I didn't want to return on a white horse as some kind of savior, I surely knew that was not the case. But maybe I did have more to offer than I was giving myself credit for.

The morning after speaking with John, I woke up with our chat again on my mind. I called the Principal, who I had not seen in over a year or more, and made a donation from my own finances to upgrade the new computer lab they were building on campus. I called and matched the same amount to my own high school that was only a few miles away. I knew it was not much but I felt I needed to continue to find a way to help out.

Later that day, I took my staff to lunch to inform them I intended to run for office. Kristen and Libby were pleased but Samantha in particular was torn. She wanted to continue on but was now in line to be one of the potential coaches for the ladies Olympic volleyball team. I told her that she needed to do what was best for her and I would understand. The choice was not going to be made for a few months but she was letting me know it was possible she would be leaving before the next election cycle. Matthew as well was starting to be drawn elsewhere with his heart. He knew long term he wanted to make a difference in making people's lives better but was not sure how. His goal was to make sure everyone had a roof to sleep under but that was a lofty goal for a media person. So for now he would continue on, but he too left it open that he might not return should I win the election.

There was a press conference called for the next day where the official announcement was made. At first, people were surprised, but the people who knew me best told me later they were not surprised at all. My friend and mayor back home, Scott, told me after he heard the news, "I knew it would bug you not to leave until you balanced that budget like you did here." Others had similar reactions about me "being driven".

I also made the political calculation to caucus with the political party in power hoping it would get me a better committee to serve on and maybe not so much spending would be given to the person running against me in the election. The seat I was holding was held by the party in power before I was assigned the seat. So my thought was that maybe they would back off some, but that didn't happen. I was not going to be moved from the insurance and housing committee I was assigned to earlier. I went to the Speakers office and asked to be moved to the education committee when I informed him of my decision to caucus with his party. His only response was "Since you have chosen not to be a full member of our party, I chose to sit you on the lowest rung I can find. Now earn your way up and maybe one day I will put you on the committees you want to be on, but not before." I had no idea what I had done to get that guy so irritated at me but Kristen kept trying to assure me, "He was that way with anyone he perceived not on his side of important pieces of legislation." I still had not come out on either side on my pending insurance vote, so he kept denigrating me over something that was only his perception.

The next task was to start fundraising. Much to my shock, Dylan James offered to play two shows in south Florida at the outdoor amphitheater with former members of his band along with nationally known performers he knew personally. He had recently started a record label so he had one of his newly signed bands open up the two shows along with his daughter's band, "Carolina Sky". Dylan no longer played large venues with members of his former band "The Overture" so it was a real surprise he agreed to do this for me. He joked with me that "Hey, I have been looking for an excuse to play a larger show with Debby and Duke for years, so this will be as much a treat for me as a favor for you George. Besides, like I told you many times, you have done well by me and members of the band who Carl invested for over the years, it's the least we can do for you."

I was having a bit of a hard time getting Sam on board with putting in some extra hours to help me with my fundraising activities. I needed her to assist me with nightly phone calls. However, once she caught wind of the pending concert, I promised her back stage tickets to see both shows in south Florida and to meet Dylan. Those two shows would not only go a long way to filling the campaign account but it would not hurt to have almost thirty thousand people over two nights hear a rock star tell them he sure would appreciate it if they would vote for me and tell all their friends to do the same. One advantage I had with Dylan was that he had been around for years, so the crowds would be filled with a wide range of demographics.

Sam also set up a web site where they could donate small amounts of money. The idea was to promote the web site after each show. We hoped to raise funds from that as well. Carl Peterson arranged a dinner with a few members of New York sports teams to speak at a dinner and sign autographs. That too was designed partly as a fund raiser for me as well. With what I did making calls with Sam at night, we filled up the campaign account rather quickly. It's never enough of course, but I did have enough to run television as well as newspaper advertisements. It was enough to at least get better name recognition against my two opponents. My biggest weakness was asking people for money. I despised it with all my heart, so having the shows planned as well as the dinner, really helped me a great deal in not having to ask too many people for money and expecting something in return.

After settling into the Washington scene for a couple of months I was amazed at how many members of Congress would not give me the time of day until it came time to vote on something. I was then promised the world if I would vote with them on this "one small matter". Even the Speaker had his whip come to me with the promise of a better committee assignment should I win reelection. However, I would have to side with him on a crucial budget vote. I was going to vote with him anyway, but I was learning to play the game quickly when I had Sam issue a press release that I was still considering my options. I have no doubt the Speaker's words were hollow since he gave me little chance to win reelection. I am not sure he was aware of how quickly I came up with a political war chest of cash to compete, but I was starting to relish the idea of being the underdog in many minds in Washington. That one press release got me the promise of being on the education committee in the future. I kept my word and voted their way but I had every intention of doing so before their supposed arm twisting. Welcome to politics 101 I thought to myself.

10

*R*ight before summer break I discovered something very odd in the upcoming appropriations bill. There was a small fund set up for the Secret Service Department. Why would the Secret Service be getting funding from the Insurance, Housing and Community Opportunity Committee? It really did not make sense to me since their budget came from a different appropriations bill that had already been approved. This committee was to oversee the last parts of the budget that had yet to be approved and from what I was told was a simple task. Most of this part of the budget was a yearly offering that was raised a few percentage points each year with few exceptions. I know some on Capitol Hill knew of my stubbornness to closely examine each line of a budget but I didn't think they expected me to transfer that skill to this endeavor.

When I inquired to my committee chairperson, he would only remark, "George this is a massive undertaking each year, if we took the time to examine each and every line of each appropriation each year, we would never pass a budget. I know that particular line item has been in place for many years if not decades, it is a pittance compared to many other parts of what is spent, let it go. I know I already have more than enough votes to come out of committee as is, so don't make waves here. Besides George, the more you aggravate the leadership here the more likely they are to ensure you lose your reelection bid. Keep your mouth closed, raise your hand politely and say yes when asked if you approve this tiny section of the overall budget."

Once again I felt like I was being treated like a child in this town. It was like all the grownups had assigned me to the kids table to drink my milk and eat my veggies. I was conflicted as to whether I should listen to his advice or should I take my oath of office as more than words I recited, only to leave them behind before I could utter the last syllable.

"Mr. Chairman, with all due respect Sir, if we don't take the time to examine each line are we not negligent in our duties?"

"George, do us all a big favor and let it go. As you can see we put less than one million dollars in that fund each year, it's a blip on the budget."

Well now, this was the second time something in Washington was a mere "blip", me and now this fund that for some reason no one seemed to know what it was or why we should just shut up and approve it. The committee vote was scheduled for later that afternoon, so I had time to hunt down Tracey to get her opinion over our lunch break. After all, she was a committee chairperson as well.

"George, he is right in that we really don't look over each and every line item from year to year, the budget process is far too arduous of an undertaking to look at each line, each year. I would think it was something to help some former secret service member from years ago that still sits on the books. It was likely a political payoff that is now used for other things. I would not be too concerned. Besides, you have a big fight in your reelection, place your vote and go home for the summer break."

It seems everyone was more concerned about the next election than they were in doing what they were elected to do in the first place. I know I was new and yes I really did want to win reelection, though there were days I had to ask myself did I really want to do this or no? So now I had to make a choice of letting what everyone thought was a mere "blip" in recorded history remain just that and focus on my election, or go against the grain and do more research on this line item.

That afternoon I sat in on the vote and abstained. So the vote was twelve to approve with my abstention. When asked with a stern look from the committee chair about my in essence non vote, my only comment was "I do not have enough information to place a proper vote." I assumed it would blow over quickly. Wrong again, it seemed I had much to learn about this town.

Later at dinner, my roommate John who was leaving the next morning for home and didn't really want to bring this topic up was asking me about my vote, or lack thereof.

"George, there are times to stand on principle here, find a good one. It could easily be your last."

"John, you are possibly the most principled man I have met here, why would you want me to go against mine?"

"George, consider this advice an act of friendship. I was approached from leadership this afternoon after what you did and was asked to talk to you. Now, you can dismiss this conversation like it never happened but heed my warning, go home and forget about budgets. There are so many larger battles to be won about ideology as well as yes, standing on principle. In a committee vote when it's unanimous, is not that time."

I was sure John really did have my best interest at heart in coming to me. However, I was such a hard headed jerk at times that it was not my nature to question something, not get an appropriate answer, only to walk away. No, it was not me. Most members of Congress left town the next day but I decided to linger behind and do a bit of research. I let my staff go home on break.

The next morning I paid a visit to the Secret Service Department over at Murray Drive, not far from where I was staying with John. I tried to speak with the head of the Procurement Department to see where these funds went after appropriated. I was met by a nice young lady Paula Green. Her name matched her experience with the Service. It seems she had only been employed there for a few days and could barely find the ladies room, let alone how things were funded. I asked to speak with someone with more seniority but as I did my cell phone rang.

"George, I have no clue why you would be bothering the Secret Service but I highly recommend you get your ass on the next flight back home or you will regret your decision for a very long time."

It seemed the Speaker of the House had his minions watching my every step. It was one of his aides calling to threaten me in a not so veiled way. Now this was only going to fuel my curiosity. What was the big deal about me wanting to know about some small line item in the budget? None the less, I thanked Miss Green for her time and asked her to let me know if she discovered where the funds were allocated and to give me a call. I could now see other eyes staring at her and I was not looking to get her fired before she even got past her probation period. It was time to go home despite my curiosity.

After arriving back home my first call was from Bob Lentz asking me to "drop by the restaurant for lunch we have something to discuss." I could not imagine what he and I had to discuss but since

I had few friends right now, I figured it would not hurt to hear the guy out.

"Congressman I understand you started looking under rocks that have not been turned in many a year. I got a call yesterday telling me that I should assist you in every way to see you are reelected if you will focus on your campaign and stop turning over rocks. However, if you persist in this silly path you are taking I was also informed to do all I could to make sure you don't win. It's your call George."

I knew Lentz had some political clout but why on earth would he care about this line item and who called him? This was all boiling up when there seemed no need to me for everyone to make an issue of it all. I mean just tell me how the funds are spent and even if I don't really like how they are spent at least I would stop asking questions.

"Mr. Lentz, why do you even care? This does not concern you at all and how did you even know about this and who called you?"

"George, listen to me very closely, none of that matters. I was not told what you were investigating nor do I care, I only know it caught the eyes of people you don't want as enemies. The federal deficit is over five trillion dollars now, why do you care about a few hundred thousand?"

"Don't you see Bob? We must care about a few hundred thousand dollars here and there or we can't possibly reduce the trillions we now have now accumulated in debt."

"Here again George, your path to winning an election is having the right backers and right now you don't have them. I don't care how much money you think you can raise by holding rock and roll shows and hitting up the local chamber of commerce for a twenty dollar bill here and there, you need clout behind you and right now, you are the walking dead in this election. Wake up and see that. For once in your life, listen to others around you and let everyone get behind you. Win your election and get a new committee assignment and help get funding for education. People love it when they think you are helping the children. It wins you elections and gets you a power base. Once you are in control you can fight your silly budget battle with some clout but right now you have no leverage, none. This can only go two ways Congressman and one of them has you sitting back selling stocks to retired physicians. Is that really what you want?"

I thanked Bob Lentz for his time and advice and told him I would get back to him.

"Congressman, don't be foolish, you have no clue what you are up against over something this insignificant."

"If, that's true Bob, why would anyone even bother to call you?"

I took two days to sit in my apartment and recharge my personal batteries as well as renewing my acquaintance with the local beach. I also took some time to do my homework about the Secret Service. The U.S Secret Service was formed in July of 1865 to suppress counterfeit currency. A couple of years later the responsibilities were expanded to detect persons perpetrating frauds against the government. It was originally headquartered in New York City. It was not until 1874 that it moved to Washington D.C. In 1901 the Secret Service was called on to protect the President, it happened after the assassination of President William McKinley. In 1951 the powers were expanded to the President's immediate family as well the President elect and the Vice President if they so chose to take protection. It is a big agency with powers to investigate fraud and protect even foreign visitors to our shores. I had no idea why they needed funding from our housing and insurance fund but maybe everyone was right. It was probably something in the budget that was misplaced and no one bothered to really discover why it kept being funded. Around Washington since it's rare to ever have something defunded, it's likely the additional cash is just part of the overall budget for the Secret Service. Maybe I was taking my responsibility too serious. No one else seemed to care about a lousy million bucks, why should I? At least that's what I kept telling myself, but then again I am a very stubborn person to this day.

The following days were filled with meet and greet functions all around my voting district. I even made a brief return visit to Mrs. Kleinberg's complex to make sure all steps were being taken to ensure the complex remained cleaned up and maintained properly. They were all very appreciative of my visit only this time I was starting to get questions about my previous and upcoming voting choices. It never occurred to me but Kristen informed me later that it was likely some of the questions came from people who were not even residents of that community. They were more likely trouble makers put there by one of my competitors in the upcoming election. I guess it is done from time to time to try and stir up controversy and this was an opportune time since the local newspaper was there covering my visit. It only confirmed to me again how dirty politics can be.

I also had a visit with Dylan and Carl so we could scout out a new shopping center in Broward County. Our agent Frank Camille had done an excellent job of finding us good clean properties to invest in over the past year or so. This would be our fourth site. I again spoke with the local fire and police chief about joining in with us since it was a large project. I spoke with Nicole as well but she passed on this one even for a small investment. The baby had drained most of her extra cash. Carl brought in a few of his entertainment clients who had the financial clout to pay cash for the site. Both the local fire and police chief threw in the minimum amounts after Frank showed them the positive cash flow they would be receiving was much higher than any interest they would get from their cash sitting in a bank. We closed on that deal before I left for Washington after summer break.

The remainder of my summer break was spent attempting to get reelected. I had spoken with Bob Lentz and told him I would drop the budget issue for the time being. It obviously was not a good enough answer since the President came to town and actively campaigned to defeat me. I think it was more so he could play golf in Palm Beach since he stayed in town for five days and did some fundraising himself. Of course, it received plenty of media for days so it was hard to combat that type of attention. While he was in Florida, I went back to Washington, to pay a visit to the Congressional Budget Office. If the leadership in Washington was not going to honor its word to stay out of taking sides in my race, I was not going to honor mine. I was even more determined now to examine not only that budget item but as many items like that one I could discover while I still had improved access as a sitting Congressman.

Once again I was hitting brick walls everywhere since no one person really knew the budget in total. I did all I could but the only thing that was clear was that it had been in the budget for many decades. The same line, written exactly the same way without an increase other than whatever the overall increase was given to any standard item in the budget. Maybe no one could tell me what it was, only because no one knew and didn't want to admit they didn't know. Maybe no one wanted to look silly in removing something they didn't know who it would affect. I decided to drop it for the time being and head back to Florida.

When I got home I got a call from Nicole who I had rarely seen in recent months. She wanted to get together and see how things were going for me personally. It was also an excuse to visit with her son, my godson. We went to lunch and I could tell about half way into it she was not very pleased with me but was having a hard time letting me know. It was obvious something was troubling her.

"George despite it all, I still care about you deeply and I don't want to see you hurt with all this political nonsense. Please stop running for reelection and stay home. You are a good man and I don't want to see that place rip your heart out. For me, please stay home."

   Well, to say the least that really caught me off guard. Why now, why would Nicole think I could not handle the politics of it all?

"I appreciate your sentiments Nicole, I really do, but I will be perfectly fine. There is nothing to worry about."

   "Honey, I have already said enough but I know you are in way over your head right now with all this political nonsense, please, I beg you, stay home before you get hurt. These men play for keeps and if you continue to rub others the wrong way, they are going to hurt you."

   "Whoa, first of all I am not in over my head, and why do you think someone is out to get me?"

   "Lentz told me that you are going to get hurt and that you have been making the President upset about something and you won't let it go."

   "The President, what are you even talking about Nicole, this has nothing at all to do with the President. I was only asking why the Secret Service has a small line item in an appropriations bill that seems out of place. But I will admit that since everyone is making a big deal about me looking, it only makes me more curious, and how do you know about all this anyway?"

"George, I have said all I am going to say. I only know that you have upset people over nothing, so please for me, I beg you, let it go. The President assured me, err, I mean Lentz assured me there is nothing to all this, so let it go."

"The President, he spoke with you about this, when? Why would the President speak to you about this and how do you even know him?"

"I misspoke, I meant to say Lentz told me that the President told him, I mean, well I don't know what I mean any more, please, please let it go George."

"Nicole, please tell me why you would be in contact with a guy like Bob Lentz let alone the President of the United States!"

"I have known Lentz for a couple of years now. Don't you remember I worked at his place for a while to make extra cash one summer? He comes over now and again to make sure the baby doesn't need anything, that's all. As far as the President, remember we met him when he was running for office."

"That was years ago, I am talking about now, do you know the President somehow, now?"

"George, I know you are as stubborn as a jack ass at times, right now is one of those times. I can see that you are not going to quit the race but at the very least stop looking at the budget like it's your personal bank account. Be like everyone else up there, get us a new bridge from Boca Breezes to Palm Beach and let all the other issues go. I beg you." The rest of the lunch we sat quietly looking at the ocean until the baby got too fussy needing his afternoon nap.

Labor Day weekend was upon us and I was in a virtual tie with one of the two challengers. The other one was more than twenty points behind and depending on which poll you looked at I was either three points ahead or three behind. They were all within the margin of error.

Saturday and Sunday nights over Labor Day Weekend were the two shows featuring Dylan James and members of the Overture. Dylan managed to call in some favors and brought in a horn section as well as some fantastic musicians from around the country. He failed to inform me that we had to pay for all the hotel and plan rides for his fellow musicians to show up, but we still made enough money to run ads when I needed them most in the coming weeks.

My personal highlight and I think Dylan's as well was when his former violinist Sasha showed up to play the encore with the band on the second night. There was a fashion show going on in Miami that weekend and she managed to find her way to Palm Beach for a brief appearance. I guess I was starting to be aware of just how popular the band was a decade or so before since the crowd went crazy when she walked on stage wearing a Miami Dolphins football jersey. There was also some weird vibe between Debby and Dylan like they were husband and wife but I really didn't want to ask about all of that. I was so appreciative of all he had done for me there was no way I was going to start trouble. Besides, I know Dylan loves his wife.

I headed back to our nation's capital to put the final votes in on what was in essence this past year's budget, since the year begins in earnest in October when the process starts all over again. My only issue was would I be around for the next round of budget talks? However for now, the talk of the town was final passage or not of the insurance reform bill. I had taken the time to study it over the summer and despite the fact that I had aligned with the party fighting for the reform I was going to vote against it. In the end it was a bad bill for my state, despite how they wanted to spin it. I was a representative from Florida and I had to take that into consideration long before my personal political survival.

Once my vote was officially recorded, despite the bill passing by a very narrow margin, and despite my record of voting with the party I had caucused with for months, the party leadership made it very obvious I would be shunned an outcast. I thought long and hard about changing my status to become an official member of their party but after the treatment I had received, my ego would not allow it. I was getting advice from every corner of the political spectrum to forget my idea that I could run as an independent and win. However, I had decided once and for all that I had to do this my way or pack up and go home. If I lost on my terms I could live with that, but had I sold out my values only to have party leadership get off my back, that I could not live with.

I was trying to lay low and not cause any more political waves when out of the blue I got an innocent call from Paula Green from the Secret Service about where the money was being allocated from the item I asked her about. I had assumed she was told to drop it all but it seems she did some investigation on her own assuming it was all done in innocence for a sitting Congressman's request.

"Congressman McAdams, I did some research for you and it seems the funds go to a bank in New Jersey but much of what is allocated remains unspent on our books. The funds have been on our records for decades, but the spending has increased over the past two years. This past year, about three hundred thousand dollars went to a bank in Jersey and from what I can see some is then transferred to a bank in California, some to Kansas and some to Florida. It is withdrawn from the local banks but that is all I know about it. I don't have clearance to get any more information for you. I hope that answers your question?"

"Thanks so much Miss Green, you have been very helpful, now let's keep what you found between you and me and I don't want you to look any deeper. I don't want to draw any attention to the fact that you were looking."

"Why, did I do something wrong?"

"No, no, I just don't want others to know I was still looking into last year's budget. I will tell your boss that I ordered you to look it up for me should anyone inquire, you did great, thank you."

So now what do I do with the information? President Lincoln once stated, "Every man is said to have his peculiar ambition". I had to once again decide to follow my instincts and run down not only that budget item but a few others I had seen that seem to make no sense for some reason. It was really nothing more than my instincts from doing a small town budget that every line has meaning no matter how small or trite something seems on the surface. There was nothing I could about this past budget since it was all passed for the current fiscal year and signed into law by the President. It was time to focus on the upcoming election and stay out of political turmoil.

11

*T*he leaves turned to their autumn splendor around town with the internal polls showing I was trailing by about five points. The negative ads against me were taking a toll on nightly television. It was news to me that I wanted, "Florida's elderly to eat cat food and not receive proper medical care" but there it was night in and night out on local television sets all over my voting district. The politics of it all seemed so vile to me now maybe I really was a fool to want to continue. It is very hard to see yourself presented in a way that you know is not you at all. I even had a call from Mrs. Kleinberg of all people who wanted to know if the ads had truth to them. That was one call I was not expecting, but if she thought that of me for even one moment, what did others who had never met me think? This was a very low time of my life. How do you compete with something that is taken so out of context yet made to look like the truth?

The only thing I could to was attempt to stay positive and even though it has long been proven that negative attack ads work, I refused to do to my opponent what was being tried on me. We even tried an ad with Matt's advice to point out that we were in fact only focusing on the positive aspects of our area and made it well known we were running a positive campaign. Believe me, it is not an easy thing to do when you watch a stereotypical grandmother sitting in a wheelchair eating cat food and some sinister looking person is pushing the chair into an abyss with your name associated with it. As dirty as they wanted to play, I refused to participate. I did all I could to meet with every retirement home in my voting district to stay as positive as possible and not even mention the television ads. When asked about them my only comment would be "I refuse to think you all are not smarter than that" and I would not say any more. I was called by Tracey and John almost daily advising me to speak about the ads head on but if that was the nature of it all then maybe I should be selling stocks to retired doctors.

Congress was on break for a couple of weeks before the November election so members could campaign closer to home. Matt and Kristen were doing all they could to get in front of anyone who would listen to me speak. It was a very exhausting proposition. I was physically and mentally drained to the point where I needed a day off. My throat was sore, my body was tired and with ten days before the election I told them I really didn't care, I was going to the beach for a few hours to relax. After all, I had a nice condo on the beach why not use it for a day? I took the morning to sit in a chair and listen to the waves crack and watch the gulls fly over head. My cell phone would not stop going off with constant text messages from Kristen wanting to arrange a meeting for the next afternoon with the local Kiwanis Club who were having their weekly luncheon. I waited four hours to respond, not to upset anyone but the constant barrage of it all had worn me down. It was not helping that I was running about seven points behind in the internal polls. But I was not a quitter I would take this to the end.

Later that day I decided to visit the local grocery store to treat myself to a nice steak for dinner. I must have picked a time when people were going there from work because the parking lot was almost full. I could only find a spot at the outer reaches of the lot. As I was getting out of my car I could hear a faint call for help behind one of the cars not far from me. As I got closer to the plea I noticed an elderly lady who had been knocked to the ground with two teenaged looking thugs hovering near her. One was rummaging through her pockets and the other holding her purse. My only instinct was to become an All-Pro football linebacker and tackle the guy closest to the woman. As I wrestled the one to the ground I could feel a sharp pain in my leg. I remember as I was rolling around on the ground with the one I tackled, the other kept kicking me over and over. At that point a car drove past us and someone was yelling from the passing car. I assume that one off the attackers ran off after the car passed by and now the sirens were off in the background. I did my best to hang on to the remaining kid but the pain from being kicked several times was starting to affect me. The adrenaline that rushed over me when I first noticed the attack was giving way to the pains in my gut and leg. The woman was crying and screaming for help when I finally let go of the other attacker.

There were a few moments where I had time to gather myself and see to the woman's well being before the police and other shoppers arrived to help. I wish I could have held on to the kid but I failed. One squad car arrived at the scene and I was later told another chased the attackers into the neighborhood behind the shopping center. Neither was found but the woman had a pretty good description of the one who had been kicking me.

I was taken to the hospital with a stab wound in the leg along with the woman who was more frightened than physically hurt. They kept us both overnight for precautionary measures. My wound was not that bad, I only needed a few stitches as it grazed my outer thigh. I did have bruised ribs and a very sore gut for a few days. Just my luck however, right when I needed to campaign hard, I was stuck in a hospital. Not only was I subjected to feeling even more beaten down only this time literally, as I laid in my hospital bed, one of those commercials came on describing me as a hater of the elderly.

Just when I thought the political Gods could not beat me down anymore, the promo for the eleven o'clock news was that local Congressional hopeful Tom Sebring fended off an attacker in a grocery parking lot earlier in the evening. The television station that had been running all the negative ads against me didn't even bother to verify the story as to who the Congressman was that stopped the attack. No one with the station could explain to Matthew how that could possibly happen, but it did. By the time the news report ran at eleven they had the story correct, however it made me wonder since the station knew in advance the ad was running before the promo, did the station put the wrong name in on purpose? A year before I would have told myself now I was being far too cynical but after a few short months in politics, nothing would have shocked me.

I was released from the hospital the next day as was the elderly lady Mrs. Wanda Jackson. Her husband came to thank me as I was being released which was nice of him for sure but I really didn't want the fanfare of it all. I wanted to get to my schedule with only eight days left to the election. Somehow Mrs. Kleinberg got a hold of my cell phone number and she called me after I was released.

"Congressman, I saw what happened on the news and I knew you were a good man. I feel bad about thinking those reports about you were true. I hope you can forgive me."

"Oh, Mrs. K, there is nothing to forgive. As much as I would like to continue to be your representative I can't bring myself to running ads based on half truths and things taken out of context like my opponent. I guess if I want to play on the national stage I have to learn to expect this type of attack, but I assure you I am not out to make the elderly eat cat food and go without medical care. It's an absurd proposition. I only hope now that I can count on your vote."

"Not only can you count on mine I will do everything I can to get all my neighbors to vote. We have a bus that drives us all to the local school where we vote. I will get them on that bus for you!"

"Thanks Mrs. K, I knew in the end I could count on you, now I have to get to my next stop, take care."

I kept my schedule up the remainder of the day despite being very sore and wanting to just go home and rest. During the visits most people only wanted to hear about the attack and not the issues. I was doing all I could to stick with the issues but the women especially wanted to know about the attack. Since I assumed most people would have done the same thing, I was somewhat puzzled by all the attention, maybe I should not have been.

I finally got home around ten that night after a very long day of shaking hands inside retirement homes and with civic groups around town. Much to my amazement the promo to the news was "Was the attack a set up, news at eleven." Despite my very sore ribs, I jumped to my phone to call the television station but before I could dial the number completely, Matthew was calling in.

"Congressman, I will handle this. I cannot believe they would stoop to this level but I guess some people will stop at no lengths to win an election."

At that point, I really didn't care anymore. I wanted to lay my head on my pillow and get some rest before the routine was to start all over again at eight a.m. with the Chamber of Commerce monthly breakfast.

The next morning I was greeted by the local television reporter at the door of the hotel where the chamber meeting was being held. Kristen had not arrived yet, so I was on my own. The reporter was a young looking lady who could not have been more than in her early twenties and likely fresh out of journalism school. I learned over time people like that are looking to make a name in the industry.

"Congressman Sir, if you don't mind please, will you react to the story that you set up this attack because you knew you needed something to recharge your campaign. Was the attack a fake?"

At first I thought about just passing her by but that might only give more credence that the story might have some truth to it. So, I briefly stopped and gave her that same stare I had seen directed at me many times now.

"Miss, I am not the type of person who needs to win an election so badly that I run out and get bruised ribs and a stab wound. It is silly to even have to defend myself here and besides, who is accusing me of faking the attack, you?"

"So by that comment, am I to assume you don't care if you win the election, since you have just admitted you won't go to any length to win?"

At that point my patience had run out with her and the silly notion that I somehow staged an attack for votes. I tried to walk past her when again she started in, "So, which is it, you did stage the attack, or you really don't want to win badly enough?"

I turned slowly and could feel the veins popping in my neck while noticing the small crowd now gathered around us. At that moment all the frustrations of everyone telling me that I could not win, or I needed to change my approach, or pick a particular party, all that rushed through my brain. I knew it was wrong, I knew she was winning by getting me to give her a reaction, I knew all that in advance but I didn't care.

"Young lady, I really don't care what you report or say or do. I know I am an honorable man who only wants to do what is best for my constituents. You and anyone else who wants to believe the idiotic report that I somehow faked an attack is fine with me. Not everyone is smart enough to see through your inane reporting. Now if you will excuse me I have thinking people who I need to speak with, good day to you."

It did not take long for my cell phone to start blowing up with texts and calls from not only my staff but other reporters wanting comments on what had happened on the steps of the hotel. I ignored them all and went about my business of shaking hands and trying to keep people on the relevant issues.

Inside the hotel meeting room, word spread quickly as to what had happened outside. Scott scolded me for "losing my cool" and Bob Lentz walked by to whisper in my ear, "they made you break, learn from it." I knew it was wrong, but I could not take the pressure of it all. I mean I go out and help a lady from a purse snatching and somehow I am the bad guy here? Nothing was making sense to me now.

The following night was a scheduled ninety minute debate with the three of us agreeing to the format that we could each ask each other follow up questions. It was the last real chance to reach voters. It was being televised on one local television station as well as on the radio, so anyone who wanted to listen had a chance to do so.

The first twenty minutes went smoothly with not much happening till the direct question came to me about a possible faked attack. I thought it was really a dumb question at this point but all I could do was hear Lentz whispering in my ear, "Learn from it." I steadied myself and calmly stated, "Once and for all, there is no truth to the reporting that the attack was staged, none at all."

The moderator turned to my two opponents, "Do either of you other gentleman think the attack was staged?"

There were a few seconds of silence before Mr. Sebring spoke up, "Considering his voting record I think it's possible he would stage the event, though I am not saying he did, only that it is possible."

My first internal reaction was to punch the guy in the nose but that was likely not the best approach, even if it might have won me a few votes. Instead I questioned Mr. Sebring, "Mr. Sebring, do you honestly believe that I staged the attack, it's a yes or no question."

"Congressman, they never did find the attackers, and Mrs. Jackson refuses to comment to the media."

"Did it occur to you that maybe she just wants to put this behind her and are you suggesting that every unsolved crime is a fake?"

"I am only saying for something like this to happen, only days before the election, seems a bit fortunate for you don't you think?"

"Fortunate for whom, an elderly lady was assaulted and I am still ailing with sore ribs and a stab wound? Is this really the path you want to take in an election to represent the fine people of south Florida?"

At that point the moderator finally jumped in and let the audience know it was time for a commercial break.

The internal polling showed the race was about dead even again on the eve of the election. Many thought that since my main competitor, Mr. Sebring and I were close on many issues we would split the vote and the other choice Paul Longstreet would sneak by with a narrow victory. That was not playing out at all. Since I was close to thirty years younger than either person, I was getting most of the votes from new voters as well as the woman's vote. I was behind with older voters since the negative ads did hurt but I needed enough of them to see through the lies. I would admit that helping the elderly lady did spike me in the polls despite the desperate attempt to spin it that it was all staged. It seems enough people could see through the fact it was only a smear campaign with no basis.

On election night, I was with some friends at the same hotel where the reporter had quizzed me about the attack. Mr. Sebring was at Bob Lentz's restaurant. My opponent had a much larger crowd at his event but my faith was in the voters, not paid off patrons promising discounted beer on tap.

The initial reports came in with Sebring holding about a ten point lead but it was in areas where he was expected to carry with ease. He was a former town council member from this area and should have won with a twenty point advantage. The fact that he was only ahead by about ten points was a good sign for my campaign.

As the night rolled on, the election was getting tighter and tighter with Sebring at thirty eight percent, me a thirty seven percent and Longstreet at twenty five percent. We still had my old neighborhood left to report as well as a few retirement communities in the southern section of our district.

After all the votes were counted the final tally was McAdams showing 41,213 votes, Sebring with 41,198 votes and Longstreet ending with 21, 298. Because of the close vote it was mandated to be an automatic recount. It would take a few more days for the votes to be official.

Here in Palm Beach we have become accustomed to recounts and looking at paper pin marks. However, since that famous Presidential election, steps were taken to make sure it would never happen that way again. The system has been upgraded so there was no need to look at paper stubs to search for perceived votes. It was only about making sure that all votes were counted and counted only once. There was some question as to the possibility of some votes being counted twice in the western areas where my opponent was from, but the lawyers handled all of that. After the recount, it was made official that I had won by a margin of seventeen votes. It seems the retirement community where Mrs. Kleinberg resided voted for me two hundred and thirty and only fifty to my other two opponents. Who knew doing your job could actually get you reelected? A lesson learned for Samantha and the rest of my staff not to ignore phone calls.

The first call after it was made official was to the Governor who endorsed me despite upsetting her own political party once again. She appreciated me taking the heat for my vote against the insurance bill even though it passed. She endorsed me on the basis she knew I would do what was best for Florida, not my own political future. Something she knew a bit about, no doubt. My second call was to my roommate John making sure I had a place to live after my initial term would expire in January. John had won his race easily and would be returning for another term. My friend Tracey won as well. I think both were happy but quite surprised I was able to win a close election.

I called Mr. Peterson as well as Dylan and thanked them for their support. Without it, there was no way I would have had enough money to compete. My campaign manager, Belinda Krauser did a fine job as well. Now it was time to focus on feeling like I truly belonged as a fully fledged member of the United States House of Representatives representing the good people of the 22nd district from south Florida.

12

*D*espite the win, there was still the "lame duck" session to be completed. The next Congress would be seated in early January but less than twenty percent of the seats changed. When I arrived back in Washington a few started to treat me slightly different, in a positive way, but for most I was still an outcast. There was mounting pressure to pick a political party but for me I wanted to focus on the few remaining votes concerning the budget as well as "finding my voice in Congress" as Matthew would constantly tell me.

Soon after returning I was asked to visit with the Speaker of the House, Mr. John Corbin. "Well, congratulations on a fine win Mr. Congressman. I will admit I was moderately surprised since we did throw a lot at you in that race. We pumped a lot of money to defeat you but you overcame it all. Yes, I am still upset you voted against me on my insurance bill but I would hope that we can move forward from this and now look to the future. I will honor my word and have you appointed to the subcommittee for House appropriations for Labor, Health and Human Services and Education."

"Mr. Speaker, I voted your way in over eighty percent of my votes, is that not good enough for you?"

"George, please tell me which is more, one hundred or eighty? I am a very competitive man, so when you waltz into my office proclaiming I can count on you yet only when it suits you, don't pretend as if I know how you will vote when it's crunch time. I don't like surprises, and you George, well at times are a surprise. Now, all that being said, let us look to a future of friendship and working together. You proved something to me with your election and for that you have earned my respect. Consider that a compliment. Now get out of my office, we both have work to do."

I turned towards the door quickly so that he could not see the huge smile on my face. It was the first time I felt like I had earned the respect from someone who actually mattered in this town. I was maybe two steps from exiting when behind me I could hear a few last words drip from his mouth.

"Oh and Congressman, I will again be running to retain my Speakership, I would like to know I can count on your vote."

I did not even bother to turn around. I quickly gave him a wave only to let him know I heard his words. But I didn't want to give him the consideration of the forgone conclusion of my vote. After all, I was the eighty percent guy, not the one hundred percent guy.

The next morning, I was informed I was likely to be removed from the committee I had been on instead of serving on multiple committees. Many members if they are not chairman of a committee were on multiple committees. I didn't want to give up the one for the other. I wanted to be added to the extra one. When I was told of this I went straight to house member Reggie Lampman, who was instructed to make the announcements. He worked on a small committee who picked who sat on future committees.

"George, everyone thought this was what you wanted, the Speaker wanted to honor his commitment to you. Is this not what you wanted?"

"Come on Reggie, we both know the Speaker is playing games here because he wants me off that other committee more than he wants me on the new one as some kind of honor code on his part."

"I am not sure what you mean George, I am sure the Speaker was pure in his desire to get you on the committee you requested. Was he not?"

"Oh I am sure he was Reggie, but he is doing it to remove me from the other one, I want to be on both."

"Ok George. Let me go back and see what can be arranged and I will get back with you."

"Thanks Reggie, I was always told you were the good one on the selection committee as opposed to Henry Fisher and that I could count on you."

The current Speaker of the House, John Corbin, had finished serving his tenth term in Congress and was a former dentist from the great state of Kansas. He was in his late fifties, had a rounded belly, a bad haircut and an attitude to match. This was his first term as Speaker and quickly made as many enemies as he did friends in his position as Speaker. He was not well liked by many Senators who saw him as difficult to create compromises on bills for the President's signature. He was married at the time with three grown children, one worked for a law firm in the area who seemed to get very high profile cases. I am not sure he ever went back to Kansas expect to collect bags of money and ask for votes.

It was a surprise to many but maybe not a total shock Corbin would have a challenger for Speaker within his own party. Though it is not in the Constitution the Speaker must come from the majority party, it has never happened that the minority party won the position. With so many members annoyed with the Speaker, it was not out of the realm of possibilities he could be defeated. It was still likely going to be either Speaker Corbin or his challenger Dan Taylor, which ever came out of the conference. I knew Dan somewhat since he too was from the Florida delegation. I think the current speaker had made just enough enemies that a challenger could win.

Dan Taylor was in his fourth term and was from the Panhandle area of Florida. He is, to this day, a devout Christian who won with big margins in every election. He was very straight forward back then but many feared he would not have the political will to do what it would really take to unseat the current Speaker. Everyone knew he was taking a big risk in making a run for the position, but it was his right. Many in the background whispered that maybe this was a signal to Corbin not to be so confident that he would steamroll everything he wanted through the House. Many members stuck their political careers on the line over the insurance bill since it was not popular back in home districts. He had strong armed many to vote his way. It may have been the way business had been conducted for decades but Mr. Taylor wanted to show another side in being Speaker of the House.

Christmas time in Washington, people are anxious to go home for the holidays. There are at times posturing going on from both sides of the aisle pretending like they have no place to be but in reality they are being pulled home by their families. Many live in the Virginia area and keep small homes back in their districts but others find a temporary home in Washington and really live in their district. I was one who did not want to make the Washington area a permanent home. Besides I really didn't think at that point in my life that politics would be a career.

After a few last minute deals were cut on the budget many members were leaving the area for the holidays. My flight was not leaving till the following day so I went over to the Library of Congress to investigate my mysterious line item in the budget. Libby was very good at knowing her way around the library and since she lived locally she didn't mind giving up an afternoon to assist her boss.

I don't know why I could not let this all go but my instinct kept telling me that I should get to the bottom of it, even if I was being warned to "let it go" by several people around me. After several hours of research, we did discover that if we connected all the dots properly, we established the initial funding started sometime in 1865. We could not find any real notes other than it changed names in the budget three times but it seemed to get whatever the overall increase was to most budget items from year to year, no more and no less. It was how we were able to continue to trace it back through the records of past budgets. It started out originally as five hundred dollars to the national budget. I asked one of the library volunteers to do more research when she had some time. I was somewhat satisfied in knowing the origin but the mystery as to why it was started and why it continued was still a eating away at me. But for now, it was time to travel home for the holidays.

Not much was going on other than a few appearances over the holidays. I was invited over to the Jackson household without any fanfare for a visit with the lady who was knocked down in the parking lot. She and her family were very hospitable to me. She was fine physically but was still not traveling outside much on her own. It was a shame to see that altered her ability to feel secure going to a store that she had gone to for so many years. However we had a nice visit and both promised to keep in touch.

My parents were happy to have me home for the holidays. I spent Christmas day and dinner with them and a few neighbors my mother coaxed in to joining us. There was also a long time friend of my father who seemed to show up every holiday time to sit in the pool. I had to admit it was nice to spend a day just watching basketball and eating turkey without guarding each and every word you utter.

I tried to find Nicole so that I could see her son and my godson but she was away. I did not know where she was but Mr. Darcy let me know that she had some long overdue vacation time and he thought she went to the Bahamas for the holidays. I was not sure how she could afford such a trip or who she would be traveling with but in the end it really was not my business. I just assumed she was with her child's son, her mystery man, who was paying for it all.

My last order of official business before returning to Washington D.C. was to head to Miami for the official swearing in ceremony. I would be sworn in along with five other House of Representative members and one Senator by the Florida Chief Justice. I lobbied hard to have it done in Palm Beach County but since I had the least amount of seniority and the Senator lived in Miami as well as the judge, I lost that battle. It was really quite an honor no matter where the ceremony was being held. We all met in a high school gym witnessed by over seven hundred students with some invited guests and family. Both of my parents where there as well as Sue who kept all my personal records and Kristen who was going to return as my personal aide and oversee the running of my office. I invited Dylan James and Carl Peterson but Dylan and his daughter had a ceremony concerning a medical building he was donating some money to near his home and Carl was busy negotiating a number of contracts for the upcoming baseball season. It was fine, inviting them both was more because they had helped me so much in the campaign and we were becoming close friends from our real estate deals. There would be another swearing in back in Washington done by the Speaker of the House but some members do this in their home states as well.

The day before leaving, I received a call from Michele Coonerty asking if I would recommend her insurance firm to a few former stock clients as well as some members I had met from the local chamber of commerce. I told her that her connections where much better than any I had developed but she asked as a favor for her recommending me to the Governor. I told her that I would do it out of friendship and not any form of pay back. I made a few calls on her behalf and had lunch with her and Mali to see if I could get Michele some more business from connections within the city. I knew Michele knew Mali well from her time on the commission but it was a parting gesture.

As the calendar turned to a new year a hard fought fight for nomination for Speaker was taking place in conference behind closed doors. I was not privy to it all since I was not a member of the party but John was and kept me somewhat updated. I think it was even more of a bruising battle than John had told me. I tried to get some information from Tracey but she was closed lipped about it all. I don't think anyone will know the final count outside of the room but Corbin prevailed. I have to admit I was hoping Dan would win but my consolation to it all was with that a vote that close Corbin would certainly be looking for my vote in the final tally when all members convened for the official election. It was determined that since the vote would be close, it was a recorded vote. It's usually done with a simple voice vote but since it was only going to take twenty defectors from the majority party, a recorded vote was taken.

The night before the vote for Speaker, I got a call from Reggie Lampman this time wanting to know how I was planning on voting. I assured him if I was given both committee assignments, the Speaker would get my vote. I had not spoken with his opponent but had I been turned down, I might have switched my mind. Despite my differences with Corbin, I still wanted to put forth his agenda, not the minority parties. About an hour later, Lampman called me back and told me I would sit on both committees if I voted for Corbin. That told me they really were not sure if they had all the votes needed to secure his position. I never doubted he would win since history was on his side but the party leaders were not taking any chances. Corbin won in a straight party line vote along with my vote, though the other two independents voted against him which made the winning margin twenty one votes. It is very easy to blow smoke until you have to actually be on record voting against your own party. I don't think anyone really expected twenty members but with thirty new members representing the majority no one was really certain of the outcome. Corbin was not well liked behind closed doors.

13

*I*t was always a struggle to pass anything in Washington with the margins being razor sharp thin in both houses of Congress. President Morrison was starting to whisper about his reelection campaign even though he still had two years remaining on his first term. He was not making it obvious he was in campaign mode but to insiders it was clear. He was also spending time in Colorado vacationing as well as an occasional trip to Palm Beach which was not common for a President who did not have relatives or a home in those states to visit so frequently. Sure, one might take a fundraising trip or two during his term, but this President made several trips there in his first two years in office.

For me, I had ruffled enough feathers with the power people around town and I was making an effort to keep my head out of the line of fire. This made my roommate John happy since I think he was taking some heat from the party bosses. John had become a good friend and confidant and I really did not want to put him in a bad position. Had I been able to find an affordable place on my own, I might have moved away and saved him some grief. However my budget did not allow for such luxuries. The traffic in the area was so bad that I needed to live close to the Capitol building and that type of living space was very limited and expensive.

The one aspect of this life that I don't think I ever got used to was the idea that everything was always about the next election. This meant members would be conveniently away from the Capital when a crucial vote was taking place they didn't want to be on record for or against. Me, I placed every vote possible always keeping in mind my own district and in people like Mrs. K who still believed we had a duty to represent their needs not ours. It was not always easy since in my heart the deficits were mounting to unprecedented levels, yet people were still counting on the assistance our government could provide when needed.

Then again someone has to pay for it all and despite what some believe it's really not free money. Someone is paying the freight. I think that is why I wanted to make a mark in education. I wanted all students to understand how the monetary system and a free society worked. Once you tilt the scales and more people are dependent on aid from a government than are paying for it you have tyranny. It is not always the easiest of battles especially when many are here only to survive their next election.

I realize it was not in the same context but I still find it appropriate that President Lincoln once stated "I fully appreciate the present peril the country is in, and the weight of responsibility on me." I felt that way with many of my votes yet most would never even know why or what I voted for in the first place. The thing that surprised me most about serving was how much each vote tore at the fiber of my soul. I made my staff or I read everything about each vote before I would walk into that building and exercise my place in our Republic. Libby was quite good at reading the text of each bill and looking at it from all angles and offering her opinion. Matthew would try to convince me how each vote would look back home and well, Samantha she would complain she was over worked. I wanted to fire her but she had grown on me and let's face it we all need someone to keep us on our toes.

So many try the balancing act of votes and getting elected but I could not worry myself with all of that. I was not here for a lifetime despite my every growing ego. I needed desperately to keep that in check and vote with my conscious and not for my next election. It sounds easy but far greater men than I have failed to keep it all in its proper place. There were many evenings I would sit alone on the steps of the Lincoln Memorial and ask my God to give me peace of mind with each passing vote. After all if we did not have our integrity and ethics, what did we have?

Spring came early and we were in full bloom arguing over the upcoming budget. Once again the house would come up with one plan, the Senate another and the President sat back acting like he was an innocent bystander. If I were to write a book about what went on people would never believe me.

That being said, the reality was that my days for the next few months were filled with committee meetings, reading prospective bills, the occasional hand shake with a previous donor visiting town or every once in a while talking with constituents on the phone. Samantha had learned to handle calls better but I could tell that Matthew was starting to divide his attention between my office and his future endeavors. I overheard him more than once on the phone talking about future projects not only south of the border but here at home as well. Kristen was still by my side as well as Libby who was making a name for herself around Capitol Hill at being one of the best prepared aides when it came time to discuss a prospective piece of legislation. I know that some tried to hire her away from my office but she was extremely loyal to me for giving her a start in Washington. At least that was the excuse she used, I think she was just a very loyal person at her core.

My Tuesday morning in early June seemed like any other day but then again I should have known this day would arrive. Just as I too was falling into the same trap I accused others of falling into, of looking to the next election cycle, my committee met to work on our section of the budget. Staring me right in the face was one small line item of one million four hundred thousand dollars allocated to the secret service for an undisclosed reason.

Tom Lewis was in his fifth term as a Congressman from North Dakota. He seemed like an honest and straight forward man but other than working with him briefly on this committee last fall, I could not say I knew the man well. He had been elevated to the chairman of the Insurance, Housing and Community Opportunity Committee. It seems he was also now the chairman of the reelection efforts for President Morrison in his home state. So after the meeting when once again it seemed that one item was to be quietly slipped through with no discussion I took a different approach.

"Mr. Lewis, I wanted to get your thoughts on eliminating the item allocating funds to the Secret Service. After all Sir, they do have funds allocated from another section of the budget and this seems unnecessary. I asked the former chairman to look into it but he said we really didn't have the time to look at every item. I realize Sir that removing it won't solve all of our problems but we have to start somewhere, do we not?"

"Well Mr. McAdams, you might have a point. I want to make good decisions and since we are not behind schedule let me make a call over to the Secret Service and see what that line is all about. If I do that will that give you some peace of mind regarding this issue?"

"It would Mr. Chairman. I appreciate you looking into this for me."

With that I was feeling like maybe it really could be done away with unless it was something critical to our national idea of what this country was all about. Maybe I really was making far too much over one line item.

We took a few weeks to finalize the remaining sections of our duties to the committee and a vote was scheduled to come out of committee but I was yet to get my explanation. So before heading in I waited at the door blocking Mr. Lewis's entrance to the committee room.

"Mr. Chairman, were you able to find out anything about that one line in the budget we spoke about a few weeks back?"

"I made the call as I told you I would George. I was told it was classified information. When I pushed harder I was told it had to do with the protection of "high value subjects" and beyond that it was classified. Sometimes even elected officials at our level have to understand maybe there are things we don't want to know. His explanation was good enough for me. I suggest it should be for you as well."

"Well, I will drop it for now since you tried Sir, but the protection of "high value subjects" comes from another part of the budget so that explanation makes no sense."

Ugh. I wanted to believe Chairman Lewis was an honest man, but I also knew he really wanted to get elected again. He was not going to allow this one item derail those efforts. I also didn't want to be so cynical when three days after we passed our budget with the line item still intact Mr. Lewis received Federal funding for a new highway system for his district. It was pushed through by a committee that my friend Tracey sat on. While we were chatting over lunch she made reference to it and that Speaker Corbin entered the meeting room and he pushed hard for the funding even though he had no business on with the committee. Tracey was not telling me because of my skepticism but only that she found it odd the Speaker of the House was making such a fuss. She did not know I had asked Tom Lewis to check with the Secret Service for me.

If no one else seemed to care that we were now trillions of dollars in debt, why should I care about a paltry million bucks or so? I was now at a cross roads of being entrenched like most politicians or putting my ass on the line when I was told by so many to let it all go.

I needed someone I could trust away from Washington to offer me advice and maybe skip out of town for a few days. I headed up to Trenton, New Jersey to visit with my old college buddy Tony and his wife Marie who were about to baptize their second child. Even though it would be a busy weekend for their family, I had not even met their first child, I felt it was time for a long overdue visit.

When I arrived in town I was not even given time to check into the hotel before Tony's mother and father insisted I come over for a big family dinner. I was stuffed with pasta and eggplant to the point of having to unbuckle my every expanding waist line. My sporting days were far and few between now and my waistline was starting to show it. Tony's father seemed very interested in what I knew about the President which was not much. He also informed me that he had some past dealings with "Bobby" Lentz and he acted as if he knew more than he wanted to share with me. But he was for sure fishing for something that I could not answer. I was a very low level person around Washington. I was not invited over to the White House for a beer with the President let alone State dinners.

Later that evening after the ceremony and most guests had departed I had time to speak with Tony privately. It had been over a decade now since we were punks hitting the bar scene during spring break, him sporting his black leather jacket in Florida in March. That visual was still fresh on my mind even as I sat across the sofa looking at him in his tailored suit and hundred dollar hair cut. I was now a Congressman and he was quickly becoming a very influential banker in the state. His life was going exactly as it was laid out for him when we were in college. Mine was nothing close to what I had expected back in the day.

"Tony, I have no idea what to do. This silly line item, for whatever reason I can't let it go until I find out what it all is about, yet if I keep asking questions I really believe it will only lead to trouble. Maybe I should ignore that one and take stabs at real reforms. But this seems so simple to me. It's one small budget item yet no one seems to care or really even wants to know what it is. What is wrong with me that I can't just walk away from it and make a career at being an effective Congressman?"

Tony sat back in the corner of his fine leather Italian sofa in the manicured living room that Marie saw as her personal decorating playground and let out a long belly laugh.

"George, do you remember Mr. Stevens who taught us contract law? There was that time he marked you wrong on one question that stopped you from getting a perfect score. He took the point of view from a then recent case and you went back to the late 1800's and found every case law you could to prove your point. You were so convinced that you were right and so pissed off that he would not change your grade. Do you remember that?"

"I do, so what?"

"Georgie boy, it is who you are. When you believe you are right about something you have never learned to let it go. I guess this is just another example of you being you. Most don't give a darn about doing things the right way anymore. I can't tell you how many times people refuse to give me proper information to obtain a loan as if I won't eventually find the truth. My loan officers do things half assed and my butt is out there trying to cover theirs. It is so frigging hard now George to find people who want to do things ethically and in a proper time frame. Stop beating yourself up over it, I know you to well. If you don't get your answer it will haunt you till the day you leave this earth. I know the truth has always been far more important to you than the actual consequences of knowing the truth. I can tell you to let it go but we both know you never will. And to be honest with you, it's not such a bad thing."

Maybe Tony was right, I had to just accept who I was as a person and not let perceived power corrupt me as the individual I was. The rest of the night we watched the Marlins beat up on the Phillies on his big screen. Our never claimed lunch bets had now included the Marlins versus the Phillies not just the Dolphins versus Jets annual contests. I don't think we kept score who needed to collect but I am sure I was way ahead.

When I returned to my office I had a call from Paula Green from over at the Secret Service but she didn't' leave a message. I stopped by her office later that day but she acted as if she never made the call and had no idea what I was talking about. She even seemed upset that I dared to come to her office so I told her my staff must have confused the message and begged for her forgiveness. I assumed Samantha struck yet again.

Later that evening as I did my now almost nightly trip to sit at the Lincoln Memorial, Paula came and sat next to me. I watched as she walked past me more than once before she sat down.

"I am sorry about this morning Congressman but my boss was listening to our conversation. I did call but please next time, don't come to my office, I will find you. I do not know if this is of any consequence to your line item or not but more and more of that money is being sent to Florida and Colorado with some heading to Kansas. I also overheard one of the agents speaking in a break room that he did not like going to the Bahamas with Potus. I was walking past the room and as soon as he noticed me he stopped talking. I asked a colleague to double check and Sir, our log does now show the President with any activities in the Bahamas. I could have easily taken something out of context since I didn't know they were in the room till I was heading to the ladies room next door."

"Thanks so much Ms. Green but you have to protect your career now. Please don't put yourself in jeopardy over this."

"Mr. McAdams my father was a very successful detective back in Connecticut. I watched him struggle for the truth to the point where it made him drink. He was obsessed with finding the truth. Maybe it is in my blood too but the little I do see and hear about this account, something does not add up. We are not protecting anyone in the areas when and where the money is being transferred. And it is against policy for one agent to be able to walk into a bank and withdraw funds. But it only occurs with one agent and with three banks. That was the same agent who was in the break room. Maybe my imagination is running wild but I have started to follow that account. I have no authority to question anyone about it. I only have access to balance the bank account. My boss has the authority to allow the agent to withdraw funds and how much. I wanted to tell you what I knew because I know I am up for review soon and there are already rumblings that I am going to be assigned to another area. I think my boss is getting suspicious but I have been careful not to overstep my job responsibilities."

"Before you leave Miss Green, I have one last question for you. Is that account or file marked classified?

"Classified Sir, I do not know all the levels of who can view each file but I do know very few have access to the account. One of my job requirements is to balance all of the bank accounts and all of the others are kept in a file in our filing room but that one is stored in my boss's office. He told me it was only because he was in charge of this account personally where all the others were handled by someone else. I do know it shows up on the ledger as any other account in our system but the bank statement and file are stored in a separate location away from all the others. It is not like it is a secret but it is not as open as some of the others."

"Well thanks so much Miss Green if I can ever help you out, let me know. You have been very helpful."

"You are welcome Congressman, I feel conflicted for offering you this information since we are so guarded about what we let out but after you came to my office the first time I could tell my boss was uptight about something. I am not really sure why my boss seems so guarded with that one account but so few seem to know that it even exists. Agent Fenton who was the one in the break room has been with the Service for over thirty years and is close to retiring. I know he is one of our finest and most senior agents. I just don't see him as an agent who would be doing things illegal at this point of his career. I do however believe whatever it is he is doing is with more secrecy within our own ranks than our usual protection of the President, family members or other high profile people we protect. That's all I can tell you."

I sat on the steps staring back at the Georgia white marble statute of "Honest Abe". Who knows why so few really have access to the account? It's very likely just something the Secret Service is doing in their ordinary course of business. After all since the Secret Service was created during Lincoln's Presidency in order to stop counterfeiting, maybe they still do some of that work? I know it's all under the control of the Department of Homeland Security now and no longer run by the Treasury Department but it could easily be an ordinary investigation they don't want many to have access to in order not to jeopardize the investigation. But then again, why has the account been on the books for so long? I stared at Abe asking for answers but he stared back at me like the statute he was not offering any advice.

Congress finished up as much business from the House side as possible before summer recess. Much of what we had passed was now being held up in the Senate. The Senate had not passed a budget in a number of years. I can only assume it was so they did not have to go on record for not wanting to curb spending and talk out of both sides of their collective mouths, but who really knows. I only knew I showed up and voted in over ninety five percent of my votes. It was one of the highest voting rates in the Congress. The only time I missed a vote was if I was stuck in traffic or once my flight was delayed returning from a weekend back at home. I know some of my votes were not popular but I did not want to shirk my responsibility in representing my district.

14

*O*nce home for summer recess, with no election looming in November, I was not in as much of a demand as an invited guest to speak at local events. I was invited on an overseas trip in my official capacity as many members are from time to time but I declined. It was later reported in the local newspaper that I was "a lazy representative" for not taking the trip. Of course had I taken the trip the report would have read "another waste of tax dollars". I was learning that no matter what you do, someone will find a reason to criticize. It was one of the harder lessons to learn. I could be called many things, however lazy was out of bounds. The next day Matthew wrote a letter to the editor of the paper about how few votes I missed compared to others in my position as well as the number of visits I paid locally since being an elected official. It was an almost daily chore to keep the record straight.

 I was invited to the occasional ribbon cutting ceremony for new businesses in my district. I did my best to attend all of them even if it did mean baking in the summer heat with a jacket and tie on while most others were wearing short sleeve shirts and sometimes shorts and sandals. I could not complain however since I looked at it as an honor to be invited and an opportunity to meet some folks I had never met in the past. It also allowed me to answer the question of whether or not I had staged the purse snatching from months earlier. It seemed no matter what I did some were still convinced it was all a set up to obtain precious votes. I guess politicians deserved some of the cynicism but I was doing all I could not to offer a reason for more.

I also met with Tom Darcy who was still trying to convince me to resign and assist him in running the brokerage house. He increased his offer yet again but I really didn't want to take it. I really wanted to at least finish out my current term. I had to admit I was starting to feel torn about returning home yet other days as I would walk through the halls of the Capitol building realizing how privileged I really was to serve, it was hard to walk away. It was also flattering that people looked at me as if I was somehow special in their eyes. I knew I wasn't that way at all. But it was a very hard battle not to feel more self important than you really are at times.

All that came crashing down and reality sunk in one day while I was strolling down the center of town saying hello to a few of the vendors, something I tried to do now and again. I was walking past one of Bob Lentz's restaurants when I was asked to come and speak with Mr. Lentz for a moment.

"George, I hear you are still digging into the Secret Service's business. Is that true?"

"Well, Mr. Lentz, I see it more that I am trying to balance a budget that is trillions of dollars in debt. Since no one can tell me why they are receiving this money, I only want to know why. Once someone can justify it, I will move on to the next item. Until then, I want to know where that money is going. And besides what business is it of yours?"

"To be honest George, It won't affect me in the slightest. I only care because it might affect others that I do know and I will protect friends of mine. I am here to offer you some friendly advice for the last time. I do have a vague idea where some of the money is being spent and it's for a good cause. You would be surprised at how close to home it really does hit and how insignificant it is if you were to know the truth. Now, do us all a favor and trust people when they tell you that it's a necessary expenditure and you really don't want that genie out of the bottle. If you get too close there will be consequences for you and others and from what I am told you are getting way too close. No one is going to allow you to expose the truth and even if you did, no one will believe you since all the trails are covered. Do you think it's a coincidence that no one is giving you the answer? I have friends in high places which have shown you a great deal of patience but it is about to run out. I have been instructed to tell you that if you back off, in your next election cycle you will either run unopposed or your opposition will be so weak that all you have to do is fill out the paper work properly and walk and chew gum at the same time. Take the offer George, if you don't life is about to get very difficult for you and all the people you thought were your friends will not be around to watch you burn."

"Are you threatening a sitting member of the House of Representatives Bob?"

"No, you foolish man, I am offering you a chance to be a Congressman with some real clout in the very near future if you will learn to play within the system. But that chance is quickly slipping away."

"Hell, I won once when few gave me a real chance and if I decide to run again, I will win again."

"No George, not only will you not win the next election, you might not even be on the ballot. Stop being a narrow minded asshole, walk away from your million dollar account and do something that matters in Washington. That is your last warning."

With that I got up, but not as quickly as I wanted since my dress shirt was stuck to the leather chair and it was hindering my exit. I had a lot to think about.

Later that evening I called Tony to see what he thought about it all.

"Nothing has really changed since we spoke a few weeks back Georgie. You are who you are and one day it will get you in trouble. When that day comes make sure it's worth the price. I did do some digging for you and I can tell you this much. My father in law has known and done business with Lentz in the past back when he was centered in Jersey. He has tentacles far and wide across the country with friends in some very high places. But he is the stooge, not the real player. I cannot tell you much more without violating many ethics laws myself but know he does have powerful connections. If he tells you he can more or less fix your next election and get you favorable positions on committees, maybe he can't, but he knows people who can. I would take him at his word. That being said, it is your call just how important you think a million bucks here and there is the federal budget."

"Tony, we both know it's not the money at this point. It's the fact that so many want me to stop looking and turn the other way with no explanations. I took an oath to defend the Constitution and not look the other way."

"Sometimes it's about survival George. It sounds to me like they are offering you a huge life raft. Think hard on this one."

The next day I played a round of golf with my buddy, and still mayor of Boca Breezes, Scott. He pretty much offered up the same advice as Tony. I think my highlight however was not the first birdie I had in several rounds but one of the grounds workers recognized me and told me about how since, his job now had a small profit sharing attached to it, he had saved enough money for a down payment on his first ever home. It was a small townhouse west of town but home ownership was something he has always dreamt of and he wanted to thank me for "helping to make it happen". It once again made me think hard about walking away from searching for the truth and changing my motives to find ways to help people like Oscar. Maybe Lentz could help me win an easy election and get me more clout on committees. If that were true, I could introduce a bill to assist in home ownership or who knows but that would certainly have more effect than finding out where a few dollars were being spent.

My last stop before heading back to Washington was a visit with Nicole and my godson, Michael. She too seemed interested if I would back off my personal crusade and I assured her that "it was likely". I did not stay too long since her boy was fussy and she needed to be mommy.

Back in the nation's Capital things started to become second nature for me. I knew my way to the floor of the House almost blindfolded and even though I still saw it as a great honor every time I had the floor for a speech, I was no longer a nervous wreck. Sitting on the steps of the Lincoln Memorial most evenings was now a habit. I started to take notice of the same people who would stroll in the area about the same time of day as I would. It was becoming common knowledge of my nearly nightly visits, so much so that colleagues who wanted to twist my arm on a vote would now search me out there rather than my office.

One night while sitting alone, a young lady approached me and asked if she could sit for a while and talk. I obliged.

"Are you Congressman McAdams? My associate is Patty Green from the Secret Service. I believe you two have spoken a few times. Is that true?"

At first I was afraid that maybe this was a set up but after I looked closer at her trembling fingers I knew she had to be whom she claimed to be.

"Yes, I am George McAdams, what can I do for you?"

"Well Congressman, Patty feels that it is best that she no longer meets with you directly. She did more research looking back over many years and was able to notice that some years there are not any payments from the account yet other years there were many withdrawals. The spending has increased a great deal since starting only a few months after President Morrison was inaugurated as well as Speaker Corbin gaining power. She has no idea what it all means but she wanted to let you know that before Morrison there were many years without a dime taken from the account. There are the initials of "LDF" attached to some withdraws by our agent. She asked me to pass that information to you."

"Well I do thank you and Patty, but please let her know that I am no longer going to investigate what is going on with that account. It does not seem worth it and I really don't want to see your friend put in jeopardy over some wild goose chase on my part. But let her know I do appreciate her concern and all her help. I wish her all the best."

I guess it was my imagination getting the best of me but I did notice that soon after she left so did a non- descript man who had been standing off in the distance. I noticed him standing there only a few short moments before Patty's associate arrived and was gone soon after her departure. I knew that area so well now and all the people that strolled around that anyone who seemed out of place stuck out to me.

A few days later I was invited for my first official trip to meet with President Morrison. I put on my best suit and tie and took Kristen with me for moral support. We had finished a two minute photo taking session as well as some brief pleasantries when he asked for the room to be cleared.

"George let me be blunt and to the point. I am told we met back in Florida while I was running and I would like to say I remember that meeting but I don't. I met so many it is all a blur to me now. However, that is not to say I don't know about you. I know you are a very energetic and focused man who could have a long storied career here if you know how to play by the rules. I am personally extending my invitation to you to join our party and leave this independent tag as a thing of the past. You have a bright future but independents generally don't last long here."

"Well thank you Mr. President but I like my position."

"Please don't interrupt me Congressman."

"I am sorry Mr. President, please continue."

"As I was saying, there are many advantages to knowing who your friends are in this town. I have been led to believe that the budget is a very important topic to you and that you seem to be good with numbers. Is that true?"

"Yes, Mr. President", I said with my knees about to buckle.

"Well good George, I am putting together a committee with a real opportunity to make a difference. The committee will report back directly to my office with ways we can bring our spending back in line. I am considering you for that committee. I can't tell you how good that would look back home and with a Senate seat opening up in four years, so who knows the possibilities. I am told that Senator Fairport has already stated that he will not seek another term, so it will be an open seat. It might be nice to have the President endorse you and maybe raise some money for you should you decide you want to further your career in politics. However, I can't possibly endorse someone not in my own party."

At that point my mind was racing with multiple possibilities, including becoming a Senator. But there was also the possibility that Morrison could lose the next election and if so whatever promises he was now making would go up in smoke. But for now I had to focus on the fact I was bargaining with the President of the United States and he seemed to be in the mood to deal.

"Well Mr. President, that is a very generous offer on your part and one that I need to consider very carefully. I will give it much thought and I will have my answer for you very soon."

"Corbin warned me that you don't like to be pushed around but let me tell you something about this town, if you want to get anywhere, don't turn down opportunities like the one staring you in the face. Now as a parting gift to you, I am going to tell you the answer to your burning question. Yes George, I am well aware that you have been snooping around the Secret Service. In as much I do admire your fortitude and the idea that you want to do the right thing, sometimes you need to know when it's over. I honestly do not know the origin of the fund but in recent years it has been used to protect visitors from foreign shores who need extra protection. The Secret Service is not commissioned to protect foreign dignitaries. However with security being beefed up since 9/11 we can't afford an international incident on our soil. I would trust that you can see my decision in implementing this idea and the wisdom in it, eh George?"

"Yes, Mr. President but why that fund and why all the secrecy then?"

"Congressman as I have explained we are over stepping our bounds slightly and do not want it known about the extra protection. Now, I have given you the answer to your question as a gesture of friendship and I am offering you the possibility of being on a high profile committee, one that can put your career on the fast track. All I ask in return is that you become part of our team and work on the overall budget reform, not some small line item that could be a problem with our international relationships if exposed. George, the people we are protecting do not know we have added the extra protection when they are on our soil. We don't know who we can trust even within their own entourage. Now, it is time for you to be in the big leagues of politics and make a real difference here. I am sure you will see it my way. I will expect your answer sooner rather than later."

"Yes, Mr. President, as I said it is a very generous offer and you will have my response very soon. Thank you for your time and your confidence in my abilities."

Leaving the White House I knew I was being offered a golden opportunity but I also realized I was being bought off. I didn't know if what the President was telling me was true or not but either way my political career was now at a crossroads. I could now accept the President's offer and become one of the bought and paid for politicians I thought poorly of only a year ago, but start to collect real political clout. Living on an independent political island was like swimming in treacherous waters.

My early evening started like many others had in recent days with me sitting on the steps wishing President Lincoln would whisper in my ear just one time and impart his wisdom. All I could think about was how he was quoted one time as saying "Being elected to Congress, though I am very grateful to our friends, for having done it, has not pleased me as much as I expected." No truer words could have been spoken at that moment.

My cell phone rang and it was my mother. It was a rare occurrence to have her call me but she wanted to know if I had time to research some investment ideas for her. It seemed the sale of her practice was imminent and she needed some thoughts about where to invest her profits. I told her about my trip to the White House and meeting the President and asked for her counsel. Her only advice was, "fill out your term and come home." I asked to speak with my dad and his advice was, "If you really can't let this thing go, either take your mother's advice and come home or take the other route and gain enough political clout that they can't ignore your inquiries." Why didn't I think of that?

I sat with Mr. Lincoln for another hour attempting to persuade myself how if I accepted the President's offer, which really was more of an order than an offer, I was really not selling out. I was having a very hard time justifying it but I was going to accept the offer none the less.

15

I took forty eight hours to let the President and the Speaker know that I would be joining their party only so that I could feel like I took my time to make a good decision. This town was making me into someone I really did not want to be yet I had to admit I was becoming mesmerized with the possibility my voice would have substance among my peers one day. The first person I heard from after the press conference announcing my decision was Dan Taylor who had lost his battle for the Speaker of the House.

"So tell me George, what was the carrot?"

I wanted to give him some wonderful answer about how I was doing this for all the right reasons but I knew he was smarter than that and I would look stupid. I also realized I might need him one day so lying about it all was not an option.

"All I can tell you Dan is that I should have held out for more." We both had a quick laugh in the hallway but we both also knew it was a cynical laugh. We made plans to have lunch one day and quickly darted off to the opposite ends of the hallways.

The leaves were starting to turn autumn colors and the air was crisp. The minority party was having debates to pick their candidate to run against President Morrison in just over thirteen months. The House of Representatives had finalized their version of the budget but it was being held up in the Senate once again. Politics were in full bloom even if there was no election in November. Both sides were already posturing for the next election. Even though I was now a member of the majority party I still had no idea why everything was about the next election and not about fixing the current ills. There are not enough cans to kick down the road. It was one thing I don't think I would ever get used to for the remaining time I would serve. Yes, I did keep an eye out for now for the next election but I also still wanted to finish my business for the current term for which I was elected. If my constituents wanted someone else to fill my position because of my votes or actions then vote me out. But then there was the other side of my brain that kept telling me that Senator McAdams had a nice ring to it.

It was now late October and I received a call from someone I spoke with many months ago about the records of my line item over the Library of Congress. She told me that she ran into a historian who was researching a book and had some questions for me. At first I declined since I did give my word to the party powers that I would drop my inquiry. She called three more times before I finally gave in and accepted an invitation to meet and share notes.

Desmond Danker had made a career of researching and writing about past Presidents. He ate, slept and drank history. He was a regular in the Library of Congress and tried very hard to get the facts right without attempting to alter history for his own political gains. He was a history professor at a local University. When we first met, he had the look you would expect of a historian and college professor. His hair looked like it had not seen a comb in a decade and his brown corduroy pants matched his brown shoes and his egg shell colored shirt that had not seen an iron since it came out of the wrapper. I could see this guy coming a mile away. Funny thing about judging a book by its cover, Mr. Danker was a very polite and an incredibly articulate man who told me his only mission in life was to "report only the truth of our past." I liked him within seconds of our meeting. It made it much easier to speak with him and give away what I knew since I felt a bit uneasy breaking my word to the President. I tried to justify it by telling myself that I was not looking into where the money was going now but maybe find out why the account even exists.

"Congressman, thank you so much for meeting with me. I was told over at the library that you are searching for some information about a budget item that seems to have shown up over and over in the budget for several decades. I understand you were even over at the Secret Service looking for answers. Is that accurate?

"It is, but I have to inform you that I have dropped looking into this matter. I am not sure how much I can assist you, nor do I know why you would even need my help Mr. Danker?"

"Well let's just say that we may be able to assist each other. I don't know if you are a history buff but I do understand that you like to sit on the steps of the Lincoln Memorial. I am not sure you realize how appropriate it is that you take respite with Mr. Lincoln."

"No, I imagine I don't."

"Well Mr. McAdams let me tell you what I do know and what I speculate is true. I am hoping that somehow with what you know I can verify some of what I believe to be true. The bill to create the Secret Service sat on President Lincoln's desk the night he was assassinated. In looking at historical documents it is my opinion that the President took great interest in this new agency and handpicked several of the first agents. I cannot prove it but I do believe he met with several of them in the White House only days before his death. And as you may or not be aware the Secret Service was created to stop counterfeiting after the Civil War. So I do know that the agents had access to a lot of money that few even knew existed since they were counterfeit bills."

"Ok, Mr. Danker but the President was killed. He never saw the Secret Service do its mission. That does not explain why the fund."

"True, but in my research I do believe that one or more of the agents that were handpicked by the President were very loyal to him. After he was murdered, Mrs. Lincoln and her four children had nowhere to live and had little income to pay their bills. It is a fact that in 1870 Congress approved a pension for Mrs. Lincoln for three thousand dollars a year. That was hardly enough to sustain her and her children. What did she survive on for the five years from the time the President was executed till the time Congress approved her pension? And why after five years did they even do such a thing? I mean think about it, Congress waited five years?"

"So Mr. Danker if I understand you correctly, my mystery budget item is the pension started back in 1870 for Mary Todd Lincoln and her children?

"Yes, I do believe it is. I have traced it back in the records then forward and all the dots connect to this pension. Have you ever known Congress to stop funding something once it's enacted? But here again Congressman, why did it take five years for Congress to act?"

"I have no clue but I assume you have your theory Mr. Danker."

"I do and it is this. The agents that were loyal to Lincoln took some of the counterfeit money they found and used it to pay his family's bills. Congress could never allow the public to find out that the first act to stop counterfeiting was actually being used to pay the bills for the President's widow and children. It is my contention that once Congress found out what was going on, they created the pension so the agents would stop paying her bills with counterfeit money. They could not fire the agents and risk the public not only having sympathy for Mrs. Lincoln but also knowing there were rouge agents before the Secret Service had a chance to really start its mission. They did not want to tarnish the reputation of anyone including a Congress who would look silly for not taking care of Mrs. Lincoln and her children in the first place. I am working on this theory and you might be able to help me."

"I don't know that I can Mr. Danker, I really never did find out much information."

"Maybe not, but does the name Fenton mean anything to you?"

"I don't think so, should it?"

"Well, maybe not, however there seems to be a pattern of a surname of Fenton as an agent from the Secret Service that always seems to be associated with that account for some reason. I have had little success getting records from the Secret Service under the Freedom of Information Act. However, the name Fenton seems to pop up. What I can confirm is that one of the original agents hired by the Secret Service was a fellow by the name of Lawrence Dennis Fenton. I can't seem to be able to trace any bloodlines from the late 1860's to current day but the name Fenton is the only name ever associated with your line item Congressman."

"Wait, you may have something Mr. Danker, now that I think about this, I was told by my inside source about an agent Fenton who said something about not wanting to travel to the Bahamas with the President."

"The Bahamas, our President has not been there in years! The last President I remember traveling there was President Kennedy in the early sixties. I know Roosevelt enjoyed going there on fishing trips but Morrison, no he never went there that I know about."

"Well, I agree with you Mr. Danker if the President made a trip to the Bahamas I would think it would have been news. Maybe only whoever this Fenton is went alone? President Morrison told me that the USA is protecting foreign leaders with more security since 9/11. Is it possible that we have an arrangement to allow our agents to follow any who visits here to the Bahamas after they leave?"

"I doubt that Mr. McAdams, why would we care once they leave America?"

"Yeah, I guess you are right, I was talking out loud but this does not make sense why he was talking about the Bahamas then."

"Whoever gave you that information could have taken something out of context and it has nothing to do with our President going to the Bahamas."

"Well if nothing else at least I am pleased I know why there is a budget item that no one seems to want to explain to me. I would bet that most I have asked really don't know where it comes from and since it's such a small amount they could never be bothered to find out. I know when I did there were roadblocks set up over at the Secret Service. Maybe it is just another funding source for them so they don't want it to be removed. Let me look at my notes on my cell phone to see if there is anything else I can help you with Mr. Danker."

As I searched my notes carefully hidden on my cell phone, I noticed that same non-descript man standing in the same place he was standing when I met with Patty Green's friend. I did not want to alarm Mr. Danker so I pretended not to notice and proceeded to pull up my notes.

"Oh, Mr. Danker one last item that might help you out. I was told by someone from inside the Secret Service that the initials on the account were many times "LDF". That could be your Lawrence Dennis Fenton connection. Is it possible it is a code name used for that mission?"

"It seems obvious to me Congressman that whatever the fund has been used for since Mrs. Lincoln and her children passed away, it has continued with the same code names. Agent Fenton seems to have survived many generations along with whatever this funding is being used for present day. And I am sorry but I do not believe it is being used for "extra protection of foreign leaders" when they arrive here."

"I would like to believe the President, but I agree with you Mr. Danker, whatever it is currently funding, it seems to be a closely guarded secret. I am not sure I can help you find out since I have given my word to the President and others that I will back off researching it any longer."

"I understand, but if you do hear of something, please let me know. I have a friend in the Bahamas who I trade information with and if he knows of anything I will follow up with you."

"Thanks, but like I said, it might be best if I stay away from it all now since I know others are watching my every move. But I do thank you for sharing with me how this fund started in the first place. It really had grabbed my imagination since it came to my attention."

With that, Desmond Danker got up, stretched his legs, and slowly departed down the steps. I looked up and I could no longer see the man standing next to the tree off in the distance.

The next few weeks were spent debating items that never seem to go anywhere like new rules for what to do with illegal aliens and talks about what to do with entitlement programs. Coming from a small town that balanced a budget or real cuts would have to be made, I still could not understand how continuing to go in debt would somehow stimulate the economy. I know there is an economic theory that says our continued spending beyond our means is only going to help but no one ever could convince me of that. It is why to this day I believe a basic economics class should be a requirement to graduate college and let students at least have some idea of how an economy works before they can graduate.

While having lunch with Dan Taylor he informed me that he was considering a run for the open seat in the Senate in three years. I didn't want to tell him that I too might consider that office even though three years in the future can be a life time in politics. I was not even convinced I wanted to stay in this town on certain days. Before being appointed the first time my decisions always came easy to me. I would investigate the pros and cons and make a decision. I could still do that with every vote and I don't think I ever regretted one vote. Yet, to be fully convinced that Washington was the place for me was something I would toss back and forth in my brain about once a month. Maybe it was better that way or quiet possibly it was a defense mechanism in case I would be defeated in the next election. Maybe I didn't let myself believe I was somehow entitled to stay here forever. Whatever the reason, it was still something I struggled with so running for a Senate seat three years out was still too much off into the distance for me.

For Dan, it seemed he knew exactly how much money he would need to raise, when he would start, what part of the state he thought he could carry and what parts he would have to work on to get votes. I realized he was weaker in the southern part of the state and I wondered if he was seeking my assistance though he never directly asked me for help during our lunch. Since he and Speaker Corbin were not on the best of terms, I knew the Speaker might possibly want Dan out of the House. Should I decide to run in the future, I knew I would have at least one challenger during the primary since we were now in the same political party.

With fall turning to winter I was no longer visiting the steps of the memorial on a daily basis but one day while sitting there Desmond Danker ran up the steps with such haste so he was out of breath.

"Congressman your office told me that you were here and I had to tell you something. My friend is almost positive that President Morrison has been in the Bahamas more than once this year. He has a friend high up in their government and he has seen firsthand a heavily guarded car pull in and out of a secluded home in Nassau. A small private jet brings whoever it is in and out of the area. He claims the plane arrives after dark and leaves the next morning. It is only for a few hours one time each time he was there. If it is Morrison which I have been assured it is, he goes to a private home owned by a corporation from the state of Delaware. I have tried to figure out the real owners but it only leads me to a law firm in New Jersey as a registered agent. But I have been assured it is in fact President Morrison who has been in and out of the Bahamas. You cannot see anyone or even the house from the road. There is a guard who is very visible at the bottom of the hill. My friend assumes there are more. There has also been a report of a woman and a small child staying in the home as well as a few older looking men who come and go."

"Mr. Danker, as much as I would like to help you, I don't know what you want me to do or what this has to do with your book research?"

"My book is about Lincoln's legacy and all of this is a part of that legacy. I really thought you would be interested in knowing this information."

"I guess I am, sorta, I don't know. I think a year ago I would have been all over this news but now I am trying to do my job and represent my district. However, I do appreciate the information."

"They got to you too huh?"

"What does that mean?"

"You know exactly what it means Congressman. I have done my homework on you too and I know some are talking about you for

166

that open Senate seat and if you continue to dig up dirt you won't have a chance."

"I am not sure I like your tone and I respectfully disagree with your assessment of my situation Mr. Danker. I told the President I would back off my search and I am honoring my word to him."

"No, you are letting him buy you off the hunt for the truth and we both know it! Good luck with your posh Senate seat and your gold star for good behavior. Me, I don't need another gold star. I only seek the truth. I was told you did too so I apologize for my disappointment with your new found political ambitions. There really is a place for an honest leader in this town Congressman. But I won't haunt you any longer, good luck with the gold star collection.

It seems no matter what direction I would take at this point I would disappoint someone. Maybe my youth was starting to become a liability since I had no experience in making many life changing choices. I thought I had in standing up to a few local leaders about some golf fees but try staring down the Speaker of the House and a President. It's really not the same thing at all. Why is it so hard to stick to your values when your ambitions get in the way? Is it even possible to have ambitions yet still hold true to your core values? This town has a way of rationalizing your own belief system. I wanted to know who I was as a person and until I came here I thought I did know.

Thanksgiving break could not have come at a better time for me. I needed time to reflect on what my goals really should be in life no matter where that path led me. I had Thursday dinner with my parents and a few of their friends. I tried to talk to my parents about my dilemma but my mother would always just repeat her mantra of "come home" and my father would only offer his usual, "The truth will always win in the end." What the heck was he talking about, the truth? I only wanted to know if I should honor my word to the President or continue on a chase for something that was likely nothing but a left over budget item.

Since the Friday following Thanksgiving is marketed as the "busiest shopping day of the year", I took a stroll down the center of town in Boca Breezes. The restaurants were filled with hungry shoppers and the shop owners seemed content with the amount of people ringing the cash registers. It was a nice sunny day with a cool breeze which allowed my disposition to be much better than it usually is when surrounded by grey skies and cooler temperatures where I do the people's business.

Just when I thought I would wander back to my beach front condo one of Bobby Lentz's staff asked me to step inside to pay him a visit once again. When I told him I was going to go home and not stop he insisted that "It would be a smart move on your part not to ignore Mr. Lentz."

"George, just when everyone thought you were playing by the rules and being a team player you are off meeting with a burned out historian looking to make a buck who is telling you tales of Lincoln and agents who never existed. Why can't you just leave well enough alone and stop all this investigating when you have already been given your answer. Do you have a death wish son?"

"Lentz, I am starting to get annoyed with you snooping into my business and besides I didn't seek out Danker nor did I tell him anything he did not already know. I told him that I could not help him, much to his dismay, so it seems no matter what I do someone is not happy. Now if you will excuse me I have better things to do with my time than to have you lecture me with things you are wrong about. And stop with the death wish talk, too many heard you threatening a United States Congressman."

"No one heard a thing, you asshole. It seems you are too stupid to know when you are in way over your head. Stay away from that quack professor if you know what is good for you."

On Saturday I spent the day looking at another potential real estate purchase with Mr. Peterson. He was in Orlando with his family for the holiday but we spent a few hours looking at an office building and a retail center just south of Orlando. He now represented several professional athletes who wanted to invest in real estate so he really didn't need my limited funds but he did like my advice. I was still going to toss in a few dollars since we were doing very well with the other properties but unlike the others I was not going to be one of the majority owners on the next purchase.

"George when you get this political nonsense out of your system, I have a few propositions for you. One would be to take over the management side of our real estate investments and become the point man in putting together the financing and managing the sites. It won't keep you busy full time at this point since we only have a handful of properties but we would like to grow the business. Also, Dylan and I have put together a record label and he really does not have the business acumen to run it properly. He thinks he does but his health is not really the best. I have to decide if I am going to sell my shares of the label before he sinks it or have you run it and make something of it. I have discussed it with him but he seems intent on running it himself despite my objections and his wife's. Don't take this the wrong way kid but I never saw you as a politician. We can do very well with this real estate thing and it would also free your time again to get your nose back into finding us some undervalued companies. I have access to a large amount of cash now with my clients. I can't keep them as clients if I can't find ways to invest their money successfully. You are far more valuable using those skills then you will ever be in that bickering cesspool they call politics."

"I thank your Carl, I will consider it and yes there are days that I would agree with you but there is something about the power that over takes you. I know that sounds awful but it's true."

"Here again George, I don't say this to stroke your ego since I can see it has grown tenfold in the past year but you were one of the best I have ever seen at picking stocks for me. You have a gift for that. I fully understand that you have to decide what makes you happy and run with it. However, having power over others does not mean a thing if you don't have power over yourself. In my line of work I have seen what fame and power has done to people George. I saw it almost destroy Dylan and others. Take my advice and learn to live with yourself. Be true to yourself and I promise you that life will get so much easier."

16

Carl and the others were right. I could feel myself starting to change but just maybe I could find that delicate balance between not losing my identity in who I was as a person yet still use my slowly but surely growing power base to grab hold of real power. I headed back to Washington for a couple of weeks before we all broke for the holiday break at Christmas time.

The chairman of the newly started budget committee informed me that we would be staying in town until December 23rd. We had met a few times and given small assignments but he wanted to report back to the President with some initial ideas before we all went home until after the first of the year. I had done all my homework not only from my assignment but on the other members of the committee. I was one of only two sitting House members along with two sitting Senators. There were ten other former members of Congress as well as the top executives from a few major corporations from across the country. I was able to hear side bar information about how other companies handled internal budgets as well as their opinions of where the economy was heading. I knew the tone was not good since they were all concerned about not only the health care that had passed Congress last cycle but also more pending legislation coming up after the first of the year. I was happy I had accepted the President's offer to join this group not only for the insight I was gaining hearing from these top executives but also listening to past members of Congress speak about how to make a final bill palatable for the President's signature. For me, no one could have offered me a better Christmas gift then to be sitting in that room. The one thing that did strike me personally was that I was at least twenty years younger than anyone else who was seated in the room. I didn't notice it at first but after the second meeting I started to question my own ability and experience to really be debating with such heavy weights.

The chairman of the committee was a former four termed Senator from New York, Martin Habib. His family arrived on our shores from Greece when he was a young boy. He had made millions in the family import business. He had a very sharp business mind along with his clear understanding of what it would take to come to a consensus with a large committee. I admired his tenacity in working long hours in actually trying to achieve something and not do a half assed job. He did speak openly that he did not think our suggestions would never see the light of day beyond the President's desk yet we proceeded forward.

He was a true believer that we had a real mission despite his fears this was nothing more than a political stunt by the President to make it appear as if he was actually looking for real solutions to real problems. For the most part I would sit silently unless I was asked a direct question. It was not that I didn't have my opinion but these people had egos even larger than mine and were not happy unless they could be heard. Everyone in the room for the most part wanted to put their stamp on the report. Me, I was happy just to listen and learn. It was by far the most educational experience I had to date in my brief political career.

Since December 23rd fell on a Friday, we broke for the holiday recess at lunch time so that the few members who needed to catch a plane ride home could do so. I was going to drive back starting the next morning since I had been invited to spend Christmas Eve dinner in North Carolina with Dylan James and his family. We had developed a bit of friendship despite him being about twenty years older and with little in common.

When I would tell him that his response was "I guess you have never been a band leader before huh my friend. Run a band for a few months and tell me again how we don't have things in common. I had to negotiate most things we did and convince them it was the right thing to do."

After the meeting broke up, I went to my favorite sitting spot when Danker interrupted my solitude.

"Congressman I am sorry to disturb you but my friend in the Bahamas pulled a few strings and had the passports checked of the few who had been in and out of the private home in Nassau. It turns out that they live in your district I do believe. Do you know a Nicole Hunter and a Robert Lentz?"

"Excuse me?" Did you say Nicole Hunter and Bob Lentz?"

"I take it you do then?"

After reclaiming my composure and disbelief I was now back on the case like a hound dog on the prowl. "Yes, I am in a way sorry to say I do know both people."

"Well, I am fairly certain they have been the two that have been there the most. The other is a fellow by the name of Eduardo Ullrich. Do you know him as well?"

"No, I can't say that name rings a bell with me but the other two, oh yes. What do you suggest all of this means? Are you suggesting to me that they are meeting secretly with the President of the United States in the Bahamas? I mean, I know Lentz knows the President to some extent because he does fundraising for the President. But I can't imagine what Nicole has to do with meeting the President."

"Well, I would hate to suggest this not knowing Ms. Hunter but who is the father of her child?"

"Whoa, hold on here Danker, I don't think Nicole and the President had an affair let alone a child together. I don't think she ever even met the President."

It was in that instant that my flashback hit me like a ton of bricks. She had met the President with me while he was campaigning as a Senator back in Florida. It hit me even harder when I remembered that we had a big fight that night and I dropped her off early. She was not in touch for a few days after that evening. After once again regrouping my thoughts, I was not about to sell her down the proverbial river without some proof and even then it would not be an easy pill to swallow.

"Another thing Congressman, what do you know about a company called Tropical Entertainment?"

"I've never heard of it, should I?"

"Not really Congressman, but the President's brother sits on the Board of Directors as does your friend Lentz. When Morrison became President he obtained stock options in the company at a more than favorable rate and they are attempting to build the largest casino this side of Vegas in Nassau."

"I know Lentz was trying to get a building permit and get cleared of all the other regulations needed to build a night club there. Let me make some calls and see what I can find out. I will be home in a few days. I will give you a call once I find out what I think is going on Mr. Danker."

"Well, he stretched the truth maybe some, it is really a seven hundred room casino and golf course. I guess he has a night club or two in there as well. Thanks Congressman and for the record, gold stars are very much over rated."

Not wanting to give away too much until Danker left I did my best to act casually, like I only knew so much. Of course maybe I did know less than I had ever imagined about Nicole and Lentz now. As soon as he was out of ear shot, I immediately got on my cell phone to Nicole.

"Hello George, are you coming home for Christmas, maybe we can get together?"

"Hello Nicole, Merry Christmas to you. Who is the father of your child?"

"Wow, Merry Christmas to you too and I have told you many times he is an influential business man from the northeast. Other than that, it's not any of your business."

"Is President Morrison the father of your child?

After about ten seconds of dead silence all I got as a response was, "George I have asked you to back off many times and I am going to ask you one last time to let it go. It is my personal business and his father takes very good care of his child. That is all you need to know."

"Nicole, I don't think you understand. There are people asking questions now, not just me. I had backed off it all until I was just now informed that you were in the Bahamas more than once with Lentz and possibly the President. Why on earth would you do that?

Do you realize if it is all true no one even knows that the President was there? Explain what is going on, will you please?"

"Look, I think you already know that Lentz's company is trying to build a night club in the Bahamas. Since I worked for him in the past he had me go with him to take notes a couple of times on weekends when his partners came around. That's all there is to that. Now let it go!"

"Please tell me that Lentz is not the father."

"Are you insane? Do you really think that is what is going on here, really?"

"No, I don't. I am not sure what to believe but I am starting to think it's possible that the President is the father of your son, my godson!"

"That town has got your head spinning now George, you need to come home have a nice holiday and forget all these nasty rumors."

"Baby, I don't think you realize that you now have people tracking you in the Bahamas. It is not me any longer looking for answers. It is others who are attempting to get to the bottom of all of this. I do not know if it's connected to my mysterious budget item but all signs are starting to point that way. Or possibly in the direction of Lentz and this casino in the Bahamas but either way, you need to stay out of the Bahamas and way from Lentz."

"No George, you need to pretend like we never had this conversation, forget about the Bahamas and Lentz and the father of the child. I am perfectly fine. Now have a safe trip home and call me when you get here. The baby is crawling all over the place, you have to see it."

At that point I had no idea what to think. It was still not likely in my mind yet it was now possible that Nicole was the mother of the

Presidents child out of wedlock. The President was married with children of his own and a wife of almost thirty years. I am sure this news if true was not something anyone would want to be made public from with the White House. With an election looming in less than a year it could easily shift enough votes to sway an election in the wrong direction for the incumbent.

Morrison won with very slim margins in many battle ground states in the last election with many like North Carolina and places in the Midwest that would not look favorably on a President with children out of wedlock. Was the fund being used to protect that secret? Was that how Nicole was really able to travel to the Bahamas and live what seemed to be above her income level since the birth of her child? My head was pounding now with the thought that if this were all true I could see why no one wanted me near the truth of that budget item. Was the current President the first to use this fund? Patty Green did say that monies did get released from this fund in years past.

I didn't know what to do now. It seemed that Danker was not going to be closed lipped. Should I now go to the President and let him know what I knew and warn him to close ranks and cover this all up? What if none of this was accurate then I really look foolish to everyone. After all I really didn't care as much about the President's future as much as I did about Nicole and my godson Michael. Should I stay quiet and let Danker do the dirty work and warn Nicole. I assumed Nicole knew the possibility that one day people would learn the identity of the father of her child. I needed time to think.

That evening I didn't make it back to my home until long after three in the morning. I wandered the streets for hours just pacing. I stopped in front of Danker's residence and even came close to knocking on his door more than once. It was in a long row of town homes only a block away from where I was staying. I sat on the steps of his place for close to an hour maybe hoping he would see me and come out. I was very conflicted as to what to do. The only other place I stopped was to have a quick dinner at the local steak restaurant within walking distance of our homes. The rest of the evening and into the night I slowly walked the streets. I must have looked very distraught since I had more than one person stop me and asked if I was ok or needed assistance. Looking back, I guess I was in some sort of trance.

When I finally made it back home I had enough wits about me to turn off the alarm. I originally had planned to leave before six in the morning to make the trip to Dylan's house for Christmas Eve dinner. However I knew I would need a few hours of sleep before making the nearly seven hours trek to his Carolina home.

Who knows exactly the time it all happened but someone was banging on my door with what seemed like a great desire to get me to answer. So after slowly realizing it really was my door they were pounding on I wobbled my way to see what all the fuss was about.

"Congressman McAdams, FBI, open the door please."

What the heck was going on now? I opened the door and three men in dark suits and not looking too pleased to be paying me a visit on Christmas Eve shoved me to the middle of my room and started throwing questions at me before I could even allow my mind to register where I was at that moment.

"Congressman where were you between the hours of midnight and three a.m.? Do you know a man by the name of Desmond Danker? Was he attempting to black mail you for your financial misdeeds?"

"Whoa now hold on here, you guys are way off base. Danker was not black mailing me at all!"

"Sir, you need to put some clothes on and come to our office."

I was then out into a black car with three men still not looking very happy to be working on Christmas Eve and not being particularly careful with how they escorted me to their home office. When I arrived it was more of the same nonsense. I was escorted into a room with several cameras pointed directly at my now very concerned and awakened face and with only two of the same men who made sure I could not even brush my teeth before being rudely shoved to where I was now sitting.

"Congressman, we have had you under investigation for several weeks now concerning your past financial gains and it is our belief that somehow Mr. Danker found out about it and wanted money from you. If you didn't offer what he wanted he was going to report it all to the media. When you refused you murdered him last night in his home."

"Where on earth did you ever get that story? It is not even close to reality. And besides are you telling me that Danker was murdered?"

"That's exactly what we are telling you and we have more than one witness putting you at his home at the exact time of the murder. We also have others seeing you wandering the streets looking very upset. We are running prints from the knife used to slit his throat found on the floor. You better start praying we don't find your prints on that knife. So my suggestion to you would be to jump out in front of all of this before the report comes back and we can get you life in prison in a secure Federal facility, not one where you will have to look over your shoulder on a daily basis. So think hard before you want to tell us you had nothing to do with all of this. We have you on video talking with Mr. Danker yesterday afternoon on the steps of the Lincoln Memorial. We also know you have met him more than once in the same location. We also know that you contacted Agent Fenton about using your political clout to get him a management position if he reported back to you private information about the President of the United States."

"Stop right there! I have never met any Agent Fenton. I have never spoken to anyone about using my political connections to get anyone a higher position in this town. In case you Bureau guys don't realize, I have little clout in this town. So this is all nonsense and I want my lawyer."

"I would suggest one last time you reconsider your plea here McAdams because right now you are the only suspect and we no reason to look harder. Oh and one more thing Congressman, how was it that your own mother knew to buy stock in Royal Cola, Inc. just days before they made a big announcement and the stock jumped ten percent. Do you not sit on a committee with the Chairman of Royal Cola? No, Danker was on to all of this and he was going to make you pay for his silence."

"Agent Tanner, that last statement alone should tell you all you need to know. Does it not seem maybe all of this is a little too convenient and tidy for even you guys to think it can be true? Now let me speak with my lawyer."

I was then led to a holding cell for the next three days. The knife came back with my prints on it. Funny how it was the same steak knife I used that evening and of course the FBI had my credit card receipt verifying that I did eat there and had access to that knife. I was getting more furious the longer I was trapped in that cell over the holidays. Could not others see how I was being framed? Not only was I being framed but whoever was doing it made it look all too simple. As I sat there waiting for my attorney to arrive from New York the day after Christmas I knew I would be acquitted but then again if someone could frame me for murder so easily could they not fix a judge and jury as easily? It was the longest three days of my life.

Since the holidays were ruined for me despite my immediate trouble I didn't want my parents to know about this until after Christmas day. That did not happen. Somehow it was leaked that I was being detained in the death of a local author and college professor. Word spread quickly all throughout social networks as well as the general main stream media. My parents were escorted in to see me sit stoically across a table with a peering FBI agent watching from behind the glass window. I have little doubt all my words as well as my parents were being recorded for safe keeping.

My dad, being that sharp attorney he was, wanted to make sure I had not said anything to incriminate myself.

"There is nothing to tell Dad, I have replayed this over and over in my brain so many times and I see now how I was being set up for weeks now. This was an effort on more than one persons part to make sure anything I ever say in the future are tainted words and my political career would be over. That would be the least of my issues Dad, these people killed someone and don't seem to mind I can spend the rest of my life in jail for something I had nothing to do with at all."

"Who is your attorney son?"

"I called Carl Peterson and they are sending their top criminal attorney to represent me. He will be here first thing tomorrow morning. I didn't want to ruin his holiday. I know I am innocent. I am very scared right now but I have to believe in the system."

"Sit tight until tomorrow morning and don't say a thing to anyone. I know they have officially arrested and charged you with murder in the first degree. This is a very serious charge as you know so I am pleased that Peterson is watching over this for you. But keep your mouth shut till he arrives."

The Monday after Christmas my attorney William Pruitt arrived and spoke with the FBI about the charges and I was released after the arraignment. Someone was out to destroy not only my political career but my freedom. On the advice from Mr. Pruitt I returned to my condo in Florida. By the time I reached home my cell phone and email was flooded with people wanting to know what was going on. I stayed away from returning any calls except to Kristen. I explained all that had happened and asked her to make a few calls on my behalf. I could tell in her voice she was desperately attempting to believe my story but even she had a hint of doubt in her words. After all it was now a top story all over the country if not the world. A sitting United States Congressman murdered a poor defenseless elderly man in his sleep. I informed Kristen that my legal team would handle all media requests and she and the rest of my staff were to stay quiet.

By the next morning it was not fair for my neighbors with all the local media hounding the lobby and doors to our building. It was obvious I could not stay there. I spoke with Carl and it turns out that Dylan had an apartment in New York that was being renovated but I could stay there for the time being. I accepted the offer and told no one where I would be other than my legal team and parents. I had no idea who I could really trust now.

17

"**G**eorge, I have to be honest this is not good for you on the surface", stated my attorney. "You need to come clean and tell me all you know about this guy Danker. Why you were in contact with him, how do you know him, etcetera , etcetera."

We spent the next four hours locked in a room with five other attorneys assigned to my case. The firm even had a private investigator following up on how the knife could have left the restaurant as well as interviewing as much as possible anyone who knew Desmond Danker.

The odd part was that the Secret Service claimed to never having anyone with the name of Paula Green every working at the agency. They could not prove my story that she had tipped me off to spending habits from the account I had been researching. In fact they turned over all information about the account and it showed ordinary travel and operating expenses for a few agents and the agency around the country. It was very consistent in its intake and outflow of monies for the last twenty years which was all they claimed to still have without digging through old paper files stored in a warehouse. It was now obvious they were cleaning up anything that could lead back to anyone with authority higher than the Secret Service. The fix was in despite the fact that I had stopped investigating and attempted to be a "team player" that so many had begged me to become. I am not sure even my legal team believed all I told them. The other oddity was that the FBI arrested me and not the Capital Police. This was not their case and this was clearly a set up. When Pruitt questioned it, all he got was "He was under investigation for other crimes, this happened to fall to us as well."

I decided to pass along Danker's theory that the fund was being used by the President and possibly others to pay the expenses of children out of wedlock. It was imperative everyone believed that if anything I was assisting Danker. It was also vital I prove there was nothing to the claim he was blackmailing me.

It did not help that during that week the FBI discovered a small safe in Danker's home that he had notes with much of my personal financial information in it. After reviewing it, there really was nothing in his notes not found in public records since all my financial records were released when I ran for Congress.

It was now mid January and Congress was open again for business. One of the first documents brought to the floor of the House of Representatives was a censure against me. It seemed many in my so called party even voted to show displeasure with my conduct, yet only one Congressman contacted me since my arrest. Kristen told me that John had left a message that he "wished me all the best" but did not want me to contact him. Everyone was now in full protect mode not wanting to get close to me. My office stayed open but most calls were viscous attacks. I told Samantha it was ok to hang up immediately. It was the one time she didn't have to do her best with her phone skills.

I hated being essentially walled off from society for months other than my trips to the law office and an occasional walk down the streets of New York City. I missed not only sitting on the steps overlooking Mr. Lincoln but the give and take with votes. Oh, I learned quickly the majority of what the public sees on the House and Senate floors is for show but I missed the excitement of being in the middle of it all. I also took great pride in doing my best to place votes. I had one of the highest percentages of recorded votes. That was all being washed away since my legal team didn't want me anywhere near the Capitol building where the media would have access to me. I really didn't want to be side show walking around the halls of Congress either, so I stayed away. It was what was best for all concerned including the nation.

The government appointed Phillip Staerk as the prosecutor of the case. His conviction rate for capital crimes was higher than my attorney's was for acquittals. Here again this was not a coincidence the government had its toughest prosecutor and a hard nose judge appointed to the case.

My first visit back to Washington D.C in several months was to the E. Barrett Prettyman Federal Courthouse on Constitution Avenue to begin jury selection. It was imperative to find open minded people who would not rush to judgment or who were not already tainted with all the salacious reporting that had already been done. More and more had been leaked over time and it was obvious they wanted this trial to be over before it even could begin. My attorney did all he could to have the trial moved to Maryland or Virginia but every request was denied. It was not a fair fight and the jury had yet to be selected.

Selecting twelve men and women who did not seem already tainted somehow was not an easy task for our specialist. She grilled prospective jurors for three days until both sides could agree on the full jury with two alternates. I was not sure what was tougher, sitting and listening to people who I had never seen or met knowing my fate was in their hands or fighting the mad rush in and out of the court house each day. It was the first time I really did wish I had followed everyone's advice and not run for Congress after I had been appointed.

The trial began in mid May with some of my Congressional mates packed into the tiny courtroom. I would assume just to witness history and not as some kind of token of support on my behalf. Opening statements were as expected with Mr. Staerk slowly explaining how this was all as simple as someone blackmailing a Congressman with a bright political future who just snapped one evening and committed a heinous crime. If it was not so serious now it was almost funny, almost.

My attorney did his best to refute all that had been said by the prosecutor and introducing the idea that I was being framed because I had government secrets no one wanted exposed and so did Desmond Danker. This was all a conspiracy to protect high ranking government officials. Court was adjourned for the day after opening arguments. But not before Mr. Pruitt did his best to introduce reasonable doubt.

The media ran wild with speculation from reports that I knew we never landed on the moon to the idea that the President was not born in New Jersey but in Ireland and brought here as an infant. It was a frenzy that had not been seen in Washington in many years, if ever. Extra security had to be added for me and my lawyer to walk the few feet from the court house doors to a waiting vehicle. Questions from the media were being tossed at me in rapid fire as I entered and left each day but I did my best to pretend like no one was there. It was not an easy task. I wanted so badly to stop and just tell what I knew but it would not matter. It was already being reported that a murderer could not possibly be trusted with any possible defense. The court of public opinion was running against me but I had seen this all before.

The following morning the prosecution started to introduce the theory that Danker was attempting to extract money from me personally or perhaps even political favor. It was discovered during pre trial disclosures that Danker was accused at a young age of extortion but it was never proved in a courtroom. So the idea that he could attempt it again was possible.

The first witnesses were called more to show Danker was not always as ethical as he may have seemed to the uniformed public and the trial at first seemed more about him than about me. Judge Hook finally had heard enough and had the prosecution move on from that line of questioning though my defense team seemed to like it. They thought the more Danker seemed dishonest the more sympathetic a jury might be to me. Even if I had not committed any crimes, I kept imploring to anyone who could hear my plea.

The afternoon started with the prosecution calling the police and fire chiefs from my old town attempting to lead them into saying that I offered them favorable investment real estate deals in exchange for the time they altered the pension plans when I was in charge of turning around the city budget.

"Chief, we see from the tax records of Palm Beach County that you were involved in a real estate investment with Mr. McAdams that offered you a ten percent holding in a private corporation which by the tax returns are paying a pretty fair return on that same investment. We also know that a two short weeks after you entered into that venture your police force led by you reduced your pensions across the board. Is it possible that he did that so you would accept the cut in the pension?

"We did that to ensure the pensions would not go broke in the future."

"Of course Chief, I am not saying that you did anything with malice of thought but was it possible that Mr. McAdams was using his influence over you and it is only now that you can see this?

"Anything is possible but it was all done with the best intent."

"And whose best intent was it for Chief? Is it possible Mr. McAdams used you for his own gains, yes or no?"

"It is possible but.... "

"No more questions."

Mr. Pruitt did all he could to make all this sound like fairy tales which is what it all was in my mind. I mean was it possible I brought them into the investments to soften them up later in negotiations, I guess sure, it was possible but not for my personal political gain. The idea here that Danker was blackmailing me over pension deals from my past was ludicrous. However this went for two days of the prosecution calling people from my home town as well as locally attempting to paint a picture that I was some corrupt and immoral politician out to gain politically and financially in everything I touched.

When I questioned Mr. Pruitt about all of this he would only say "Relax the trial does not really start until the knife is brought into question. The rest of this is window dressing."

One of the first witnesses brought in by the prosecutor on day four of the trial was about the documents in the safe. He did not state much from the prosecution side other then it was in fact found in Danker's home. But then my attorney had his chance at questioning the witness.

"Mr. Hall, it is my understanding that you did forensics on the safe?"

"Yes."

"In your review did you find any finger prints on the safe?"

"What are you getting at counsel?"

"I am not suggesting anything. I am merely asking did you find anyone's finger prints on the safe, yes or no?"

"We never ran it for fingerprints."

"So, is it possible that was not even Danker's safe?"

"It was found in his bedroom closet, if not his safe then who did own it?"

"I only making certain that you can without question tell me the safe belonged to Desmond Danker? Did you research to find out if he even purchased a safe? After all, it seems all we have here is a safe found in a bedroom closet with a few meager documents easily obtained by anyone who knows how to work the system. All you have for me is that you found it in his closet? No finger prints, no real work done to see if it was not placed there after his murder?" Who knows, maybe someone gave it to Danker? And even if it was his, does any of the information incriminate the accused in anyway?"

"It was Danker's safe."

"And yet you say that with a quiver in your voice this time around as if maybe you are not as certain now. No more questions."

Two witnesses were called stating they had seen me in front of Danker's residence. My attorney stipulating I had in fact walked the area and sat on his steps. However when asked neither could say they actually saw me enter the steps through the outside door. Nor was there any sign that the door had been broken in any way. No one saw me run from the scene nor could anyone state they saw blood on me from the witnesses who claimed I seemed distraught on the streets after the time of the murder. The prosecution wanted the jury to believe it was too dark to see any blood splatter on my dark clothes and my attorney did a good job of cross examination making sure no one could prove with any certainty there was blood one me at any time. For me this entire case was circumstantial.

Recess came late Friday afternoon until Monday so I decided to head back to New York. The only reason I was able to come and go so freely was that my bail had been set high and I was wearing a small tracking device. It was not comfortable at all but it was much better than the alternative of sitting in a cell for even one more day. Those three long days would haunt me forever.

Monday started with testimony from the busboy who worked the table I sat at in the restaurant. He testified he was not certain that he collected my knife from the table but after listening to Steark weave his magic even I was convinced the place lost all its knives that night in my pockets. I guess I did learn that restaurants really do not know how many pieces of silverware they have on hand. Good thing to know should I ever need a spare spoon one day in the future.

Later that afternoon the lead forensic scientist in the investigation sat in the witness stand explaining the theory of how somehow someone managed to enter his building without damaging any doors, sneak into his bedroom and kill him with a knife in his sleep. I am not the largest man on the planet but the idea I could sneak up on anyone was yet another fairy tale to me. That was until he introduced testimony that the dead body was full of prescription sleeping pills and enough was still in his system to make believe it was possible someone could in fact do the crime while he was sleeping. All of this was getting far too serious for my liking even though I had absolutely nothing to do with the man's demise.

The one thing that my attorney did seem to make a dent into was the idea the dead body was not murdered in his bed as the experts wanted to explain away. There were unexplained traces of organic seaweed found in local rivers in the body's system as well.

Something did not seem right with the report but the forensics were only to state findings not assume innocence or guilt in the case.

"Mr. Harris in your testimony you stated that Mr. Danker was likely killed while sleeping in his bed, is that correct sir?"

"Yes, that is what I stated."

"Sir, how tall is the defendant?"

"I really do not know the exact size but by looking I would say he is approximately six feet tall."

"So, by that response am I to assume you have never measured the exact height of the defendant?"

"No, I never have."

"Assuming Mr. Danker was murdered as you say while sleeping, at what angle would the knife have had to strike his throat?"

"If you look at the photos counsel you can see it was about a one hundred and fifty seven degree angle."

"So in your estimation a man with a height of six feet would have to lean down pretty far and get pretty close to make such a strike with a knife of that size, is that true?"

"I would say so, yes."

"Explain to me then why there is no blood splatter on the wall near the bed or even on his bed stand. I mean if the murder happened as you suggest with someone leaning down to strike at that exact angle shown in your photos should some blood not have splattered above the head of whoever struck him if it really happened as you suggested?"

"I would think there would be some however since he was resting his blood was not pumping as quickly and that may have led to there not being as much splatter."

"Really Sir, are you trying to tell us intelligent people in this court room that someone could violently cut the throat of someone in his sleep and blood would not splatter on a wall not three feet away or even on the bed stand less than two feet away?"

"There was blood found in both places."

"Oh, maybe a spec here and there that could have happened while the body was being placed in the bed as I am suggesting and that would possibly explain why so little blood was found. And one more thing, if someone was that size and that close and the strike came from the side should there not have been blood on the killers clothes or face or hair?"

"Well of course some, but maybe your client washed."

"Move to strike Your Honor!"

"So moved, the jury will recognize that the witness was purely speculating with that last comment and was not based on fact."

"Last question for you Mr. Harris with all the evidence and blood spatter patterns found near the suspected crime area, is it possible the body was struck in one place then moved to the bed?"

"Yes, it is possible but in my estimation not likely."

After more than one week into the trial the prosecution came to my legal team with one last plea offer.

"We believe your client will be convicted however we are offering fifteen years and out in eight."

The shocking part to me was that my own attorney suggested that I should give it some serious consideration.

"Look George, it really does not matter what I think or you know, those twelve people are all that matters and right now I really do not know what way they will turn. You will still be a young man when you get out with your life still ahead of you. You could face life in prison otherwise."

"Mr. Pruitt with all due respect, for one if they think they are winning, why the plea? Also, why so short? Maybe the person or persons who have arranged this frame up is only trying to ruin me but not have me spend my life in prison since they know I am innocent."

"I can't think in those terms George. My job is to get you the best possible outcome and I am only informing you that this might be the best possible outcome of a horrible situation."

"Please inform Mr. Staerk my answer will always be a strong NO to any and all plea deals!"

The trial had a few days break before the strongest piece of evidence came into question with the knife. The prosecution went through all the boring details about how the wound matched perfectly with size and shape of the knife found at the crime scene. But once again Mr. Pruitt did all he could to introduce reasonable doubt with his cross examination. Once again the lead forensic scientist was on the stand.

My attorney handed Joel McCarthy a common steak knife and asked him to show the jury how he would cut a steak using the knife. His thumb print was on one side with a small portion of another finger on the other side of the knife. He then asked him to show the jury how he would hold the same knife if he were cutting someone's throat.

"I would not know how to hold a steak knife to butcher someone, I have never tried it."

"Oh come now Mr. McCarthy you must have some idea if you were about to strike a person sleeping in bed with that knife. Will you at least concede that the prints on this knife are more consistent with someone cutting steak than they would be if striking someone?"

"Here again, show the jury how you would hold the knife cutting a steak. Are the prints found on the knife in the same holding pattern as the way you are holding the knife right now?"

"Yes, they are but that does not…."

"You have answered the question Mr. McCarthy."

"Now, about the particular knife with the defendants prints on it, with the same pattern as you would find with someone cutting his meal and nothing more, were the wounds such that only that knife could have been used at the crime scene?"

"The marks are consistent with that type of knife, yes."

"Hold on sir, please repeat what you just said, that type of knife, not that exact knife."

"That is the murder weapon."

"No, what you just stated yourself was that it was that type of knife, not the exact knife. Are you telling me that you are one hundred percent positive that the knife in the evidence bag was the one used in the murder, or is it possible it was one that came from the same restaurant?"

"I am saying the marks are consistent with a knife such as the one in that bag."

"One more time so that we are all clear, could the wounds have come from another knife about the same age and the same kind from the same restaurant, yes or no?"

"Yes, but no other knife was found at the scene."

"Thank you Mr. McCarthy, no more questions."

The prosecution called a few more witnesses trying to show I had made financial gains from my political career but I do not think any of it really was strong evidence. I mean how could it be? It never happened. But there they were all on parade. That was the day I wanted to bring up the entire House and Senate members to tell the jury how so many enriched themselves with sweetheart deals with inside information they had obtained or political pay offs for votes. No, my career had barely begun I was not the one they needed to investigate over insider deals on Capitol Hill.

After what seemed like months to me but was actually two weeks of listening to expert after expert do their best to make me sound like a cold blooded monster or at least at times someone who could steal the last breathe from Mr. Desmond Danker, the prosecution rested. There would be a four day rest in the trial with the defense offering our side of the story starting the following Monday.

During the recess once again the prosecution came to Pruitt when it was leaked that I was likely going to take the stand on my behalf. The media went crazy on all the weekend talk shows speculating that I would tell the world the secret of Area 51, the remote patch of desert in Nevada, that some suspect the government is holding space aliens. Or was I really in some drug induced frenzy at the time of the murder and I would ask mercy on the court. It was all so laughable to me if not for it being my career and life in the balance.

"George, someone is scared to death you are going to get in that witness box and tell some dark secret. I know the press is already downplaying anything you will say as pure lies only to save your own ass but someone is afraid of something here. They are offering you eight years and out in three with the story that new evidence shows you were coerced into the murder or did not act alone. They will put you in a low security prison in the country with access to friends and relatives. It's a sweetheart deal, this time you really need to consider it. If not you could go to jail for a very long time."

"Mr. Pruitt, you have known me since I was a kid in college. Do you honestly believe I am capable of doing such an act of violence to another human being?"

"I have explained this once to you once my friend, it does not matter a damn what I know, believe to be true or have seen with my own eyes. It all comes down to those twelve strangers and before we put up our defense I put our odds at best at fifty fifty that you will walk out of that court room a free man. I know it does not seem fair to you at all, but three years in a low security prison is nothing."

"Nothing, you tell me! It may only be three years, I grant you that, but my reputation, my career, my entire being will be ruined."

"No, it's not George. Carl told me to let you know that even in prison he will make sure you have a place to land when you get out. He will hire you in some capacity. He believes in you."

"I need YOU to believe me in Mr. Pruitt and make sure I walk away from all of this with some dignity intact and my freedom."

"Once again, it is your choice George, but this time in my opinion, you might be making a mistake."

18

*T*he trial resumed with the defense bringing in a few people who would stand by me and tell the jurors in their estimation I was not the person the prosecution made me out to be during the past weeks. I think even the jurors enjoyed seeing Dylan James give it to the prosecutor during the cross examination.

"So I understand Mr. James that you played a concert in support of the defendant. Is that true?"

"Yea, so what, last I checked it was still a free country."

"Well, it is also true that you share in real estate investments with Mr. McAdams, is it possible he has promised you better deals in the future from his political connections?"

"Nope, maybe you need to look closer. I don't need crap from him or anyone else."

"Come now Mr. James, I realize you have a pretty secure life for yourself from your music but are you sure you are not branching out to make even more millions through your connections with a prominent politician and in return you raise money to keep him in office?"

"I don't consider him prominent, do you?"

"Ok Mr. James just answer the question, are you using each other to get what you want, just like he does with others, to build his power base and your personal wealth?"

"I don't think you answered my question about him being prominent enough to help anyone including me."

"I understand it has been reported you may have a possible mental disorder is this why you refuse to answer my questions?

"Well, I think it's been reported somewhere that you are an asshole but I guess we should not believe everything we read now can we?"

It was at that point Judge Hook stepped in and stopped all the frivolity but I know I enjoyed it. Dylan gave the jury a wink and wave as he parted the stand, always the showman. The judge gave Mr. Pruitt a stare like enough of that but it was not his fault, the prosecution was the one who didn't know how to deal with a pampered rock star.

The day ended with a few more people speaking on my behalf but nothing was really gained or lost in my estimation. There were only a few chuckles and a better understanding on my part about who my true friends were.

The following day was spent breaking down the theory that I was using my influence for political gains, which was the reason all along I wanted to murder Danker. To me it was such a weak argument but here again I was not one of the twelve sitting there day in and day out wanting to go home to their lives again. I was the one wanting to go back to being a Congressman even if Congress no longer wanted me. But for me there was only one person to call who could stop all this nonsense and that was my assistant since I worked for the city, Sue Juran.

"So, Miss Juran you have been the defendant's assistant for how many years now?"

"It has been about five or six years now I think."

"And in those many years, what exactly did you do for him?"

"Well, after every meeting he calls me and tells me what was said by everyone, or if he makes an investment, he tells me all the reasons why he did it and what he did so he knows in the future how to track his success and failures."

"And in what form do you keep this all in?"

"George calls it his personal history of life. All his thoughts and reasons for doing this are kept there."

"So he called you every day at the end of each day, almost like a diary?"

"Well not every day, and not exactly like a diary, but his thoughts and reasons for why he made certain decisions in work or with his investments are recorded."

"Are you the only one who has read this or even knows it exists?"

"Other than George and his other coworker from the days he worked for the city, Mali, probably, yes."

"Is it possible you are making this all up right now to find a way to show the defendant has an alibi for all his investments or political decisions?"

"No Sir."

"How can everyone here be so sure that you have not made this journal since he was arrested?"

"Because the sun is only in the same place in your yard once a year, that is why we have this record in such fine detail."

"Please explain more Miss Juran."

"Well you see George always said that if you keep very good track of the details you will always know when the sun will rise and when it will fall across your yard and in those details is your life. His life for many years now has been kept in such fine detail it would be hard to dispute why he did anything. However after he was arrested the one thing that was done was to pull out all the past phone records of the date and time he called me at night and we matched many to the date and times I logged in and out of his journal. He always asked me to track when we spoke. Some notes were even sent via emails or fax and they have time stamps on them. I don't think anyone is as detailed oriented as George so if you want to know anything about why he does what he does, it's all here."

Before it could be added into evidence the prosecution stated that it could not be added since they had no previous knowledge of its existence. My attorney spoke it all being a rebuttal to what had already been put into evidence and it was not necessary that it was brought into evidence before this time. Both sides huddled up close to Judge Hook for a few moments and when Pruitt turned with a smile on his face I knew he had won his argument with the judge.

Then it was Mr. Staerk's turn to question if the sudden entry of the personal journal. He wanted his chance to question if all the financial decisions were based on analytics not insider information obtained through political influence. Besides much of investing in the journal had been done long before I was even appointed to the Congress, so for me, the idea of blackmail was becoming less and less likely.

"Miss Juran, is the defendant your lover?"

"We have dated over time but to say we are now lovers would be inaccurate."

"But do admit to having a relationship beyond a working relationship."

"I admit that we have occasionally had dinner and enjoyed each other's company."

"So, because of your admitted emotional ties is it fair to assume you will do what you can to see your lover not go to jail, Miss Juran?"

"I don't want to see anyone go to jail for a crime they did not commit, especially someone I know personally to be a kind and gentle person, who was not being blackmailed nor is a killer."

I knew Sue was strong and true but I may have overlooked just how strong she was until she was put under the strain of her testimony. She had been forced to stay on the witness stand for a very long time proving it was very unlikely I was being blackmailed by anyone.

The next person to come forward was the librarian who put Danker in contact with me in the first place. She confirmed that she connected the two of us and we were acting more as allies than antagonists. Staerk did leave open the door since the librarian had no knowledge what happened after she gave Danker my name. She could only state that the two of us were looking at some of the same information at the Library of Congress and he connected the two of us. However, I did feel like my defense team showed considerable evidence that there was no reason for Danker to be blackmailing me. The knife however was still one piece of evidence that was hard to explain away. I knew someone must have put it there knowing they were there to execute Danker to frame me, but it was hard to be convinced the jurors felt the same way.

There was another day of testimony being set before closing arguments would begin. I had just returned to my hotel room from being prepared by my defense team as to what to expect with my testimony when my cell phone rang.

"George, its Tony, how are you hanging in there big guy?"

"I guess as well as can be expected, what's up?"

"I know this is going to sound crazy but I think I can get the charges dropped and you can walk out a free man tomorrow but I will need an answer quickly."

"What on earth are you talking about?"

"A week ago I received a strange call from someone who told me that you were innocent and that they thought I could help you. They were so upset you were being framed and it was all over something you were not even aware of. It was a very cryptic call but it sounded to me like you know that the monies you were researching are being used to protect the children of the President and other members of Congress who have children out of wedlock. Is this true?"

"I have to be honest with you Tony, this is what Danker suspected and what he told me the night he was murdered. It had nothing to do with him investigating me or anything like the prosecutor wants you to believe. I suspect now there is truth to it, but I have no hard evidence to prove it. And the worst part was that I had given my word to the leaders in the party that I was going to stop investigating and had stopped. When Danker first came to me I put him off, it was not until the day he was murdered I even made a call to see if there was any truth to his theory."

"Well, I am fairly certain I know who made the call and she told me she overheard a conversation that Danker was only to be roughed up and it got out of hand and they went to plan B. You must have used two knives that night. Someone took both from the restaurant. They have been following you for weeks extracting DNA in many forms in case they needed it. You have been being set up just in case you found out the truth and talked. I don't think you know how dangerous of a game you were really playing."

"I knew I was going against the grain big time Tony, it is one reason I backed off. I could sense for a while now that I was being followed. But I honestly don't know who is doing all this to me."

"Someone is feeling very guilty now and does not want to see you go to jail. Are you protecting anyone in all of this George?"

"I don't know if I am or not but either way I did not commit this crime."

"Here is the deal. Our bank holds all the notes on the properties that Lentz and his business associates own. We were also brought in as the lead bank to finance the construction loan on the new casino in the Bahamas. The balloon payment comes due next month. There are also other notes coming due very soon. I spoke with my father in law and despite the bank doing business with that company for many years we spoke with Lentz and told him that if he did not speak with the President and have your charges dropped the bank would not commit to continuing doing business with them. I can't tell you too much but not only does the President own stock using his brother as a front while he's in office many board members including Lentz do a lot of fundraising for him. Your guardian angel hinted to me that Lentz was the key to getting you released. Once I connected the dots, I found a small account was opened in his name where he receives government checks on a monthly basis. He only withdrawals cash from the account, but it is almost the same amount each month. I called our branch there and I was informed he sometimes has a young lady and child come with him into the lobby. You live in a small town, as you know George, and the teller recognized who collects the cash. I can only assume it's your guardian angel and the mother of the Presidents hidden child."

"All of this is too crazy to even think about Tony and why pin this all on me, I was being quiet?"

"Your guardian angel discovered that her cell phone was being tapped and when she did she went crazy on Lentz. It appears from here that Lentz knows all what is going on but does not really want to see you go to prison either. However when you called her cell phone and asked once again who the father was, people were listening on the other line. They already knew you spoke with Danker earlier in the day and well, things just got out control. They all panicked and you were set up for his murder. It cleaned up both sides of the mess."

"Ok, so if the President can make a call and have this all go away, he must know I am being set up."

"Yeah, and try to prove that one! I can assure you he is so far insulated from all of this there is no chance this could ever bounce back to him, no chance."

"Well, then how does this all go away?"

"All you have to do is sign a non disclosure agreement that you will never speak about your trial, why you were released or what it is you know about the monies being spent. The recording will say that you are admitting guilt and you will be imprisoned for twenty years if you ever breathe a word of this. However, if you sign it and never speak of that account again, you are a free man forever."

"That sucks big time Tony. Someone gets away with murder, the court of public opinion will likely always be against me, and I will have little chance to ever survive in politics."

"Wake up and see the big picture you idiot, you walk out a free man and I am sure you will land on your feet again and rebuild your reputation. Besides how long of a political career will have sitting in prison? Take the deal and learn to shut up. I know it sucks, but it's all I could for you."

"How much time do I have to think about this?"

"You have until the judge bangs the gavel in the morning. The prosecutor is not happy about this. He has been warned a deal is in the works. So don't take too long and for once swallow some pride and take the deal. I worked long and hard and there are people risking a lot of money here to win your freedom, a thank you would be nice as well."

"You are right Tony and I do thank you. I am just so shocked by all of this I had to digest it for a moment. I will call Pruitt right now and get his advice."

In speaking with Mr. Pruitt he was very skeptical but the legal documents were sent to him from the prosecutor just after my call with Tony. It all felt very unseemly and slimy to all involved with this scheme but then again how slimy was framing someone for murder? My legal team felt like they had done a good job of making a case for reasonable doubt but there was still no guarantee of an acquittal. Mr. Pruitt made sure I fully understood the consequences of signing that document and that it was in essence a gag order concerning all I knew. What I did now know was it was likely not one child but possibly several children were under the protection of the Secret Service. Not only did I know it, but others did as well. I was likely the only one remaining who would discuss it and my ability to tell was now once again being bought off. Only this time it was not for a potential Senate seat but save my butt from twenty years in prison.

I asked Mr. Pruitt to call Staerk to see if the three year prison term was still an option with no strings attached to my silence but it was no longer available to me. I think Mr. Staerk was more than mildly upset that his highest profile conviction was being bargained away and he was given no reason as to why.

All I could think about was what President Lincoln once stated in "Those who deny freedom to others deserve it not for themselves." This all started because I wanted to stop wasteful spending in a budget and now I had to decide between a possible prison term and my personal convictions. How much did I want to gamble my life with twelve strangers?

I took the offer after a few hours of gut wrenching thought back and forth. But this meant someone would walk away from murder and I was never going to be able to speak out about it. I had already been censured by my fellow House members with no shred of evidence that I had really committed a dastardly crime. But the alternative of potential prison time seemed all too real to me now. Since I turned down the previous offer I could be facing up to life in prison not a potential of only three years now. It was not something I wanted to risk no matter how wrong I knew all of this felt to me and would look to others.

When the news stories started to break the next morning that I was a free man through a plea agreement but not one of total vindication of innocence it really did not sit well with people who wanted to know the truth. I could not blame the public, it did all stink. I of course was forbidden to say a word as was my legal team. You can only say "no comment" so many times before the media suspected foul play. However the bottom line was that I was free to leave the court house the following morning and return home.

19

I decided to hide out in Hawaii on a small island where a Congressional friend of mine owned a small home on the beach. I am not sure he wanted to allow me to stay there for my own good or so he could ask me several times "Tell me how you got them to release you." There was no chance I was going to utter a word, especially this quickly.

Sitting on a quiet beach with a beautiful tropical breeze in my hair and the smell of native flowers at the edge of the sand I wanted to stay there and forget the about my entire political career. How could all of this be worth all the aggravation I had to endure not counting what would be next should I chose to return to finish out my term. After all, I was not tossed from Congress, only made to look like I had done something wrong when I was innocent. I did hear from Tracey and John sending best wishes but not too many others wanted to associate with me. Since Congress was on a short recess, my friend who had opened up his home to me was in town, and still asking too far many questions. After a few days of attempting to explain to him it was not possible for me to speak about the trial he relented. It was not until I went back to Florida did it occur to me that it was all a set up to see if I would leak some information.

Once back in Florida the media was relentless surrounding my home. I attempted to explain that there would be no statements or explanations coming from me or my office. It did not matter. The reporters all wanted to know why such a high profile murder trial would end with no explained plea deal and no conviction. The White House was now having their press secretary make a statement in the daily briefing, "There is no truth to the reports that the President was being blackmailed which led to the release of Congressman McAdams." That only led to more speculation from the media especially with such a carefully worded statement and no follow up. The constant need to fill content on the talk shows led to reporters now attempting to trace my paths and what my real connection was to the deceased Desmond Danker. It was the hardest thing I could ever imagine, sitting in my room not wanting to listen to any of the reporting, yet everywhere I turned it was on the television screen or radio. It got so bad that I went to the local video and music store and purchased several movies and music so that I didn't have to listen to it any longer.

The other issue I had to deal with was my office staff. They were not sure what my future held before the trial and even though I tried to assure them I would return they wanted to pursue different paths. Samantha had been working on a part time basis since she was away many days coaching with the ladies Olympic volleyball team. She pretended to want to remain part of the staff but it was clear she had moved on with her life. She didn't want to show disloyalty but her life was to be involved full time with her volleyball coaching and it was time for her to leave permanently and did.

Matthew knew he always wanted to eventually move into assisting others in home building for the less fortunate in some capacity and he applied for the regional director positions for Homes with Humanity. It was a missionary group that built homes all over North and Central America. He was going to be positioned in California with his main focus in Central America. He had not heard from them yet so he was still working in my office. However, it was only a matter of time before he moved on one way or the other.

Kristen was working with the Florida Governor's staff to start a drug prevention program for teenagers who abused prescription drugs. It was something close to her heart but the funding had yet to be passed by the Florida legislature. She was however committed to the project once the funds were approved. She was seeking private financing which kept her mostly in Florida.

Libby wanted to be a Congresswoman one day herself since she had a taste of working on Capitol Hill. She was becoming very familiar with all the bills and how the process worked, likely better than even myself. However since she was still very young and inexperienced it was decided that once Kristen left she would be my aide so she could deal directly with other members of Congress on my behalf and gain even more political experience.

I didn't want to hire anyone else until I could see what my future was going to hold after the election in the fall. With the House of Representatives having to run for election every two years it seemed like I had just been elected, but almost forty percent of my time was spent away from Congress or defending my honor with the trial. Even though I had lived up to my agreement with the Speaker about staying away from researching the budget item everyone assumed I had gone back on my word. There were rumblings I would not only have one person to contend with in November if I chose to run, but two with one coming from within my own party.

Recess was ending and it was time to return to Washington. Once I arrived and had time to meet with my two committee chairman, it seemed all the work was finished and there was nothing for me to do as far as the budget. Odd that they were the only two committees that had completed their work but I had to accept it and move on.

The Washington press corps was still not letting me walk around the area without someone sticking a microphone or camera in my face. I knew I could not comment but there was nothing stopping me from exercising my right to speak on the floor of the house. I spoke it over with Mr. Pruitt and he was not in favor of it, however he reluctantly agreed once I allowed him to approve my words. Something had to be done since very few would even say hello to me in the hallways. There was little doubt everyone wanted me wiped from these hallowed halls.

I asked for a speaking position which was still my right. It was granted but only at the end of the day's business and timed so that it was not possible to make the evening news. For one of the few times there were actual members sitting in the chamber to listen to what I might be inclined to deliver. I put on my best suit and tie yet again and delivered a very short remark.

"In every man and woman's life there comes a time to reflect on all the positives and negatives in their past. Despite my young age I have done nothing but that for several months now. What I have come to realize is that we live in the greatest country on earth. Yes, nothing is perfect other than our God. Our justice system though at times may not seem perfect or even fair, is still better than the alternative. Sometimes in that system, people are accused, yet are proven innocent of their crime. Yet at other times, some who may not be pure escape the halls of justice unscathed. In the end, it should remain to be a system based on innocence until proven guilty by a jury of our peers. It is not possible for it to be a perfect system since it was created and implemented by imperfect men. I arrived in Washington a very naïve young man and one day will leave knowing I may not have been as perfect as I would like, but will know I did my best every day to serve the hard working decent people who elected me. I did my job so well some might accuse me of doing it to too well, yet no one can ever accuse me of shirking my responsibilities. We also have a system where people of all races and personalities come from all over this great land with many wide eyed ideas and theories on how this town should be governed. Since we are all mere mortals none of the ideas are pure, yet we strive for perfection daily. I was and will remain one of those people with my imperfect ideas and theories striving for perfection. This form of government must not only survive but thrive so that we may pass our great blessings on to the next group of wide eyed individuals who want only the best for our systems we now have in place. President Lincoln once said that "A statesman is he who thinks in the future generations, and a politician is he who thinks about the next election." I surely don't lay claim to being a statesman but I strive daily never to be accused of a being purely a politician. Like most here I fail at times. However, what I have never failed at nor will I is to understand who I represent with my oath of office. I have not, nor will I ever, dishonor the promise I made when I took that solemn oath. Thank you and God Bless America."

My remarks were not delivered in time to reach the dinner time news watchers on the eastern seaboard but they were made in time to be printed in the morning papers. It was parsed and picked apart more than your average heady lyrics from Pink Floyd. I was accused of still dodging the truth but there was nothing more I could do. It was as close to the line as I could go without going to jail for a crime I did not commit.

With my committees having finished and a Presidential election within a few months, few wanted to attempt any major legislation. Sure, everyone would posture like they wanted to pass some magic pill that would fix all our ills of looming deficits and a social security in dire need of assistance to survive. I knew anything I dared to put forward would be blocked by the Speaker or his staff. The internal polls showed I was trailing badly in any reelection bid and not only would the President not step up for me as promised the Speaker made no effort to assist me either. I considered changing party affiliations back to an independent but that would look silly at this point. It seemed likely my political career was doomed.

The few people I could trust to offer sound advice all suggested that I not run for reelection and go home. Maybe regroup for an election cycle or two and attempt a comeback in the future. The majority opinion seemed to be, "This way you will still have never lost an election." It sounded like a defeatist attitude to me and a path I would not consider. I would win or lose on my own merits.

Before everyone wanted to run home and be seen in their own districts before the election, I offered up a bill that would create a national catastrophe insurance plan. I worked a way to take some money from the budgets of other disaster funds already in place and made it a benefit for all states if they wanted to participate. It really needed the majority of states to join to make it budget neutral and there would be a small premium to home and business owners though it was not mandatory. Most around the country would balk at it thinking they don't have natural disasters. They would only think of hurricanes but in fact many states have fires, tornadoes, mud slides, floods and so on which would all be covered under the plan.

There was a Senator from Kansas who was also working on a similar plan who I asked to cosponsor the bill. At first he agreed and we went around looking for support for the bill. After about two weeks his polling was taking a hit since his opponent in his election was running an ad back in Kansas about how the good Senator was working with criminals in the Congress. It was a very dirty advertisement and was not accurate at all. However when you are in a close election things like that matter and he quickly pulled his name off the bill.

"I am sorry George, I do believe in this piece of legislation so maybe after the election we can pick it up again."

"Thanks Senator but I am not sure my future here will continue after this November. It is unfortunate most can't see beyond the obvious but it is the world we live in it seems."

There was little left for me to do in Washington. The earlier budget committee I had been appointed to by the President would still meet on occasion but even that was wrapping up its work. The President wanted something on his desk so he could use it as something he would pretend to implement in a second term. I would offer a few words now and again and would still attempt to learn from others but it was not the same. Everyone was making it so difficult for me to function now.

Back home I was trailing by more than twenty points and the outlook was not looking bright. I was not going to quit but it was not easy to get in front of crowds as it was two years earlier. The people close to me wanted me to drop out of the election but I had done nothing wrong and even though it would have been easy to give up, it was not in me to be quitter.

The national polls for President were edging towards Morrison winning reelection. Many times the incumbent President loses some members of his party in Congress and this year looked to be the same. Personally I was trailing by double digits only sixty days out from the election. I would not even have won the primary battle except for the sadness that my opponent found out he was stricken with cancer and had to drop out. By the time he was diagnosed, it was too late to enter another candidate. So even though he dropped out I still only won by ten points. It all seemed humiliating but I had to wake up every day with the truth that I had not committed the crime that many still assumed I had.

Back home I walked the streets down the center of my home town the same way I had in the past election only this time only a few wanted to sit and chat with me. I was not going to go into a cocoon and act as if I had something to hide. Everyone of course wanted to know the truth but the closest I would dare to venture would be to say that our court systems do work. I was a free man and intended to stay that way. Even Mrs. K called me more than once trying to get the truth from me.

The last week in October a news report broke that the Speaker of the House may have a teenage son about to attend the University of Kansas who was born from an affair he had when he first stepped into public office in Kansas. I was unaware if the story was accurate or not nor did I care to poke my nose into the story. The Speaker had created enough enemies in recent years that if it were true someone would eventually find out. Before the report broke he was leading by almost thirty points so even though the story would hurt him and possibly even take away his leadership role he would survive his election.

For me, my opponent started to get increasingly negative with attack ads for no reason. He had a double digit lead but for reason that didn't stop him from running a horrible advertisement. He had a cartoon looking image of me moving from behind rock to rock as if the cartoon was hiding something. There were some words about hiding is no way to be a leader and ended with him and his family standing in the middle of a wide open field with the concept that he is out in the open about all. I could take a lot but this was starting to get out of bounds and a bit sickening. For the first time I woke not caring if I returned to Washington as an elected official or not.

20

*E*lection Day came and went but the fight in me was gone. I did all I could up until the last hour but once it was over I was relieved in a way. I lost by seventeen points. The election was never in doubt from the first returns to the last. I lost in every precinct including my own home town. I didn't have time to do much fundraising and I did my best to get in front of any audience that would have me but looking back it was inevitable. I had not gotten any endorsements of any real substance. I knew the Governor had to stay away from me this time since she was up for reelection as well. She was going to win easily but why risk standing by me. I understood it and was grateful for all she had done for me in the past. The only endorsement I received locally was from my friend Mayor Scharle who was still running the town as mayor. He was a very popular so endorsing me was not going to hurt him in the future. Besides, everyone knew we were close friends. It may have worked in the opposite direction in an odd way had he not stood by his close friend.

With now nothing to lose and no political future left in sight and a dead historian who died in vain, I decided to do more research without drawing attention to it. I was not going to report any findings and risk going to jail but I still wanted to find out what I could. I wanted to look for patterns in spending on the Secret

Service. After a day or so back in Washington, I realized there was nothing more I could find without drawing attention. I tried to follow the records in the Library of Congress and the Office of Management and Budget but there was nothing now to find. I suspect if there was a trail it was now destroyed or reclassified into other accounts. There was nothing more for me to do but finish out my term with dignity.

Matthew gave his notice and accepted his position as regional director Homes with Humanity. He was anxious to get started and since I really was not going to need media support I let him leave immediately. Kristen was going to leave at the first of the year no matter what now that her program was funded for two years. My friend Tracey was going to lose her aide since she became pregnant and wanted to be a stay at home mom. I recommended Libby to fill the role as her aide. She had met Libby a few times and they got along very well so the staff was all going to land on their feet quite nicely. Libby stayed with me until my last day in office as did Kristen. However I let Kristen come and go the last three weeks in December, since she wanted to get off to a fast start in her new position. Plus she needed to find a place to live and move to Tallahassee before the first of the year.

After the election my party still had a six member majority in the House with my loss and a few others. The other party lost some members to retirement and after it all shook out President Morrison still had a slim majority in the House of Representatives but he was seven members short of a majority in the Senate. I didn't see anything happening for another two years after I learned of the outcomes.

The only thing I could smile about was that Speaker Corbin was once again going to be challenged by Mr. Taylor. All signs pointed to Taylor beating him this time though with nine new members anything was possible. It would be interesting to me to see if Taylor did beat out Corbin would he remain Speaker or still continue to run for the Senate seat up for grabs in two years.

The last few votes I placed were meaningless as far as affecting anything nationally. They were making cosmetic changes to the IRS code and allowing veterans hospitals to allow for testing for more types of pulmonary diseases. After that it was time to go home for the holidays and the New Year. I moved what I had at John's home back to Florida.

Back home it was time to consider my future. It was nice to have dinner with friends without questions about what I might be doing with future votes or even introducing my own legislation. It had been a long time since I was able to sit and joke and just chill out. As much as it was a relief I still was already missing the prospect of remaining a member of only five hundred and thirty five members between the House and Senate. If you think about it, Congress is a very small fraternity.

The day after Christmas I went to visit with Nicole and her son. I had to drop off my gifts for him and one for Nicole. She seemed very sad especially considering having a child during the holidays is usually a happy time. She didn't want to say much other than "I am sorry for what you had to endure. I knew you were innocent and it was hard not to speak up. But there are things about all of this you don't know so let's put this behind us and look forward, please?"

"What is it that you think I don't know? I know who Michael's father is and I suspect, well really know, that you have been getting money from a fund from the Secret Service. After that I really don't know more and at this point I am not sure I want to."

"George, I was never going to let you go to jail, please know that. I feel terrible it had to get to the point it did, but I can't say I am unhappy you lost the election. It has nothing to do with you looking into where the money comes from but the people up there can be well, you know. I didn't want you dealing with them any longer."

"I appreciate all that Nicole but I really felt like I could make a difference there and now I am back to being just another guy on the street, only some now think I am a guy who got away with murder. A reputation is all someone has and mine is tarnished if not ruined. There are many nights I have thought about what might have happened if I let the jury decide my fate and not have this still hanging over my head. My dad always tells me that the truth wins out in the end but this time I am not so sure."

"You have your health and are a young man. You can comeback from this but please once and for all go back to doing what you are good at. I am sure Darcy will hire you back and we can work together again."

"Aww, you don't understand, to walk down the street and have people think you are something that you are not is not a comfortable place to be. I guess in time I will get used to it, but believe me, there are days I would rather have done my few years in prison and be able to tell my side even if no one believes it. At least I could speak my peace."

"Shh, let's just sit and listen to the waves now and forget about all the rest."

A few days later I stopped in to see Tom Darcy before returning to Washington to clean out my office and fill out my last few remaining days in as a member of a our representative government. He did not know I was coming over but I didn't think it was going to be such a big deal. After all he had offered me a position to work there in the past year.

"Hello George, what brings you by this morning?"

"Well Mr. Darcy as you may have read I am going to be unemployed in a couple of weeks, so I wanted to drop in and see if there was still an opening for me around here." I could see the expression on his face change almost immediately.

"George, step into my office where we can talk about all of this privately, please." His step was slower now as I could tell whatever was ailing him was having a debilitating effect on his body.

"George, after you decided to run for office over two years ago now, I assumed you had no desire to accept my offer and even though I will admit I left it open for some time, I had to look out for the future of our firm. I have been handing over more and more responsibilities to Terry Prindible. He has been with me for five years now and has been doing very well. I am sorry but I don't think it would be possible for you to work here now."

"Well I don't have to take over the position you had offered in the past, I can work as a broker again and prove to everyone that I can still be a valuable asset to the company. I am really just looking to get back on my feet."

"As much as I would like to help you, in all honesty, I am not so sure having you in our offices is what is best for us at this point in time. We go back a long way and maybe there is something you can do for us from your home behind the scenes, but I am not sure having you sit in the corner office is a good idea right now. I am sorry."

"Do you think I got away murder?"

"It really does not matter what I think now does it? It only matters what my clients would think and by judging by the election results I would think many would not trust you."

"You didn't answer my question. I asked you if you think I am guilty."

"I would like to believe you are still the same young kid I met when you came into my office fresh out of college but there are too many things that seem to be surrounding you now George, and quite frankly no matter how hard I want to believe you are innocent, the fact that you won't say so does concern me."

"I am forbidden from talking about my case. But I will tell you I am that same person only much wiser to the ways of the world. I would like to understand your position and maybe in time I will, but it is very hard to see how you would not believe in me. To not want me here in the office, ok, maybe I can see that part but for you to think I am remotely capable of such a horrific act of violence, well that does surprise me."

At that point, as I was turning to make my exit, Nicole who must have been listening intently by the door, came blasting in to almost knock me over.

"Mr. Darcy, if you don't hire George back, I quit! He is innocent of all the charges and this has to stop. He did nothing wrong here. He was doing his job in Washington and I know without a shadow of a doubt he did not kill anyone. He is a good man and he deserves his job back. If you don't give it to him, I quit."

Immediately both Darcy and I tried to convince her to retreat from her threat and calm down. She was covered in tears and as upset as I had ever seen her. I knew she was upset over how it was affecting my life but it was obvious now that it was bothering her far more than I had suspected. She was now seeing what I was up against in trying to reclaim my life.

"Nicole, look, I want to believe in George, I really do. But our business depends on people trusting us and placing their savings in our hands. We must keep our reputation with the public as clean as possible. Even if I knew for a fact that he was innocent that won't mean that others will see it my way. I am sorry he cannot work here right now. Maybe when things calm down we can let him work from home but for now I don't have a position for him with our firm. After you calm yourself I will take you to lunch. Hopefully you will understand I have a company to run and as hard as that is at times, I have to make difficult decisions that I think are in the best interest of my company."

"Funny that you would mention that Mr. Darcy, that was all I was trying to do in Washington. I was trying to do what I thought was best for our nation."

With that I parted with Nicole still sobbing in his leather chair and his beautiful office overlooking Worth Avenue on one side and the Atlantic Ocean on the other.

Returning to the nation's Capital was bittersweet. I had moved all my belongings back home other than a few items in my office. I decided to stay in a hotel for the last few remaining days despite John's insistence that I remain with him. I had caused him enough grief with reporters hovering around his residence. I didn't want to cause him any more interruptions.

Kristen was now gone as was the remainder of my staff other than Libby. She decided to stay with me until my last official day. She had prepared with Tracey to take over as her aide over the holidays and was all set up. A temp agency had sent over someone to answer the phones for a couple of weeks. My office back home was closed the first of the year and really I was only in town to say my last good bye.

I took the floor one last time only to say my last remarks to my constituents back home. I thanked them for their support and assured them one last time for anyone who would listen, that I never once broke my oath to represent them in a professional way.

As I was cleaning out my desk, the news was breaking that Speaker Corbin admitted to a child who was now eighteen and a freshman enrolling at the University of Kansas. Since it happened many years ago maybe it would have escaped the news cycle in a few days, however the report also mentioned money being funneled from his Congressional account into another account that was used to support his secret son for many years. There was also a story from an unconfirmed source from within the Secret Service that money had been transferred from an internal account from them to an account used for his reelection funds. I had to admit I had to chuckle at the report.

The town was now preparing for the inauguration and swearing in for President Morrison for a second time. I assumed my invitation was somehow lost in the mail but I had no desire to attend first hand. There was one invite to one of the balls being held around town but sitting at home relaxing to James Taylor or even The Overture seemed more appropriate. As bittersweet as it was, it was time to leave.

I took one last trip to the steps of the Lincoln Memorial and sat there on a cold overcast day which seemed fitting being it would possibly be my trip for some time. Many of the faces had changed though one or two of the vendors were familiar. There was no longer that mysterious looking man off in the distance watching what seemed to be my every move. In a strange way, this was the first time I felt like I was all alone on the cold grey steps. That feeling did not last much longer. Someone with what sounded like a female voice was behind me and started to speak.

"Congressman you don't know me and won't. Please don't turn around. We have a mutual friend who was devastated when the news broke the history teacher was killed. She knows it was not you who killed him and fears she knows what really happened. She is the one who gave Danker the information that likely started all this mess. She feared you were being followed by her agents and didn't want to get you or her, in trouble. She left her job soon after the news broke. She asked me to find you and tell you that she was sorry she could not be found for your trial but she feared what repercussions there might be against her if she came out in public and testified. She was not expecting this to get so out of hand over one small account. She has moved out west and has changed her name. It is not a coincidence that information is now leaking out, including news about Corbin. She feels at this point it may be the only way to make things right. She should not have called me but she wanted to apologize to you. I should go before anyone sees us talking for too long."

Would this never end? What was I to do with this information if anything? I decided nothing. I had no idea who this person was or if I was being set up somehow. I really didn't want to feel like there was a conspiracy under every tree but I now felt that way. Two days later, I packed my car and drove back to Florida without mentioning the conversation to anyone, including my attorney.

After being home for a couple of weeks I was lost as to what to do with the rest of my life. There were no offers banging down my door nor were too many calling me. The only person still attempting to get me to work was Carl Peterson. "George, I know you don't want to leave Florida but I would still like for you to help me find undervalued stocks. I know it's not what you want but it will keep your mind busy until you find what you really want to do again. It will also let some time pass and let people forget."

He was right. I needed something, anything to get my mind working again. I also knew he was hiding the fact that even though he knew I was innocent, he was not ready to turn over the real estate company for me to run, even if it was still relatively easy for me compared to my skill set. He had some very high profile people investing and he had to watch out for the reputation of the company. I took the offer and worked from home. It was not going to be enough long term to survive financially but mentally it was a beginning.

21

Josh Simpson was only three years removed from journalism school but somehow managed to not only dig up the story about now Congressman Corbin but work for the largest newspaper in the Washington area, the Washington Gazette. His reporting about Corbin's son swayed enough votes to allow Congressman Taylor to become Speaker. I would have loved to been in the room during the vote but I was many miles away relegated to looking for the next trend in the stock market.

My phone rang early one morning with young Josh Simpson on the other end of the call.

"Congressman, would you like to comment on my contention that the Secret Service has been protecting illegitimate children of high ranking politicians for a number of years and that was what you were researching?"

"Yes, I would. I don't consider any child illegitimate, do you?"

"You know what I am asking you Mr. McAdams, did you stumble across this along with Mr. Danker and now you are both silenced?"

"As much as I would like to be able to assist you Mr. Simpson, I am now a private citizen attempting to live a quiet life away from politics. Let me just tell you that your career is on the right path and I wish you all the best, but I have nothing more to add."

"One last thing if I might Mr. McAdams, did you know that no one bothered to investigate the fact that no one ever saw Danker's body removed from his apartment?"

"No, I was unaware of that but there were many photos shown during the trial. The fact that his body was never removed for others to see is of no concern of mine. My trial has ended and I am a private citizen never convicted of a crime."

"I have every intention to get to the entire story and get it right. I know you are hiding information. You may not know the entire story but I do believe it goes beyond Corbin and a few politicians from the recent past."

"Like I said, I wish you well in your investigation but I have nothing to add to your story."

I did my best to focus back on my work and besides who cares if no one actually saw Danker's body being removed from the building. There were so many photos from so many angles that it was likely hours before they removed him. After all, I was sure the media was scrambled outside of the crime scene, so they likely removed the body from the back of the building. That way they would draw less attention to the crime. Still, it was a curious question.

After a few hours I called Mr. Pruitt to see if he had known that Danker's body was not seen leaving the building in a body bag. "George, stop the nonsense right now. Did that reporter call you? He has called here asking questions too. Let it go. It's over, let him do his reporting but you stay as far away from it as you can and not give anyone any excuse to open up your case again. I ran into Staerk the other day and he is still fuming the case was dropped. He still believes he would have had a conviction and he does not particularly care about your innocence or guilt. He cares about his conviction rate and you were a big fish who got off the hook. Take my advice and do a good job for Carl and rehabilitate your reputation."

Three days later I received a call from Senator O'Hara who was on the co-chairman of the budget committee I was on briefly at the President's request. "George, the President has asked that we reconvene our committee. I fully admit there was some pushback to having you stay with us but you had your share of supporters as well. I am asking if you would like to remain on the committee. We meet again next month."

My first reaction was no way, but after a few moments and a surprisingly cordial conversation with the good Senator, I decided to stay on the committee. I despised it when I considered turning down good opportunities and acting as if I was guilty. I had nothing to hide even if I was silenced about it. Besides, this could be the start of rebuilding my reputation as Mr. Pruitt and others had suggested.

Later in the day Nicole asked if she could stop by on her way home from work. "Sure, it would be nice to see you, come on over." I was not sure why she wanted to stop by but it was something she did from time to time now that I was home again, so it was no big deal to me.

"George, I know you can't talk about your trial but I need your help. Do you know about any children the President might have with women other than with his wife?"

"Besides my godson you mean?" That was maybe not the best question after the stare I got but I could not help it. "I don't know if the President has any for certain, including Michael. Why do you ask?"

"Lentz has been acting really strange lately and he has reduced the amount of money I was receiving. He told me that the support money I get for Michael might stop for a while. He told me to stop whining about it because it was affecting more than just me. I don't know. I just got a very weird vibe about it all. I know some reporter is trying to break some story about politicians having kids all over the country. I am afraid he is going to find me. I talked it over with Lentz and he told me not to worry about it, but I don't think I can handle that kind of pressure."

"I wish I could help you but I really don't know if he has other kids or not. I never got that far with all of this. I think Danker had much more information than I did. I do think there was an account that was paying your bills and possibly others over many years but that's really all I know. You know I can't talk about any of this publically or I risk going to jail."

"Thanks, but I have been getting a weird vibe for many months now that I am starting to be abandoned by everyone including Lentz. I think it is time I move from where I am and find a smaller place that I can afford on my salary. What do you think?"

"I think that would be wise on your part."

Another story was being reported from Simpson that a source from inside the Secret Service confirmed that there was an account in the past that was used to funnel money to pay for expenses of relatives of politicians who were not already covered by the current law. This set off a firestorm on Capitol Hill of politicians wanting to get out in front of the story claiming no knowledge of funding such an account. The head of the Secret Service only released a short press release stating that "this matter was being investigated and will be dealt with internally." My attorney called to make sure I was not leaking any information. "I don't have to Mr. Pruitt, it seems someone else is doing a good job all on their own."

The next day I took my usual stroll down the center of town with not much fanfare. Only one person stopped me to say hello and I was not aware of any odd stares heading in my direction. I reached the part of the street where Lentz had his restaurant and was asked to step in and say hello. I was not sure why I should, but I did.

"How's it going Congressman?"

"You mean other than not being a Congressman any longer in large part I suspect due to you and your friends in high places?"

"It was not personal George, it was politics. You were warned many times to stay away from the Secret Service and were even given a nice position on that committee to stay away and you didn't."

"That's a lie Bob! After I gave my word to Morrison to stay away I did. I didn't ask any more questions nor did I press it in the budget talks after I told him I would back off and join the party. I did all I could to make peace but someone, whoever it was, would not accept that and leave me alone. We both know that trial was a sham and a complete set up."

"Yea, it was, but you should have stayed away from that book writer and kept your mouth shut."

"Hey, you need to get your facts straight pal. I didn't tell him a damn thing. He knew all he knew from sources other than me. I had nothing to offer to him and even if I did, I had given my word I would back off, which I did. It's why I didn't offer him any help and your pals killed him anyway and ruined my career."

"George, I know you think you know but in the end you were never going to jail for murder or any other crime. That's all I can tell you. Don't you think that if you exposed that the President has kids other than with his wife it would have been a major issue for him during the campaign? I am sorry you stumbled into what was going on but something had to be done. We had to protect him because if he went down it was likely so would our casino being constructed in the Bahamas as well as the one in the planning stages. Now, I assure you I had nothing to do with that messy trial business. That was all planned by others but I knew you were never going down for that murder. Don't' you think it was all so convenient for you that it was dropped so easily?"

"Of course I suspect there was more going on then maybe I will ever know about, but what is stopping me from going to the FBI today and telling all I know now?"

"Because if you do, I will deny everything I said as will others and you will go to jail for twenty years for a murder that was never committed."

"I don't know why you are telling me this Bob, but I really want to move on with my life."

"I am telling you this because I still think you have a bright future. The President won't be in office forever. I told you when we met that I collect friends in high places. Personally, I am a natural born survivor kid. I know you likely don't care for me right now and I guess I don't blame you. But the fact remains, you are not in jail. I will tell you only one or two of us made sure you stayed a free man walking down these streets. I don't know if the entire story will ever come out, in a way I sure hope not. But if it ever does you will see me as more valuable than you do at this present time."

"Let us both call it even then Mr. Lentz. I won't report what I know and you will leave me alone for now on. Besides, I don't think anyone would believe me right now but I do think your so called friends attempted to put me in that cold cell for a long time."

"You were never supposed to go to jail, only keep your mouth shut till after the election. It just happened to work out nicely that it's a more permanent solution."

"Yea, and let us all not forget about the guy in the ground eh Bob?"

229

"Things are not always what they seem Congressman, now go home and play with your computer, I will be here when the time arises that you need me."

Lincoln once said, "Public opinion in this country is everything." Now that the media was all over this story that funds were possibly being paid from tax payer money, the same people in Congress who I could not get to take thirty seconds to see what this budget item was, were now calling for hearings. I could only sit back and laugh at the hypocrisy and the butt covering that was now taking place.

One reporter even wrote that I knew about the money and that I was framed for murder to keep me from reporting it before the election. That not only prompted a call once again from Pruitt but also a personal visit from an employee working for the White House threatening to open my court case again. I assured him that I had not spoken a word with anyone and he needed to call that reporter and ask him his sources. The very next day the paper printed a small retraction stating that the previous story was merely conjecture on the part of the reporter and was not based on any factual information.

My phone was now ringing constantly to the point where I had to leave a recorded message on my cell phone that all questions regarding what was going on in Washington should be addressed to my attorney. As much as I wanted the story to break, I also didn't want to go to be the one accused of leaking information. Besides at this point, it did seem that the media knew much more of the story than I did. They were now connecting the dots to my murder trial and that Danker was investigating the secret funds before his murder as well. The media was starting to suggest publicly that it was possible Danker was not blackmailing me but working in tandem.

After about a week the story died down considerably. After all, no one really knew the true story and what the funds were really being used for anyway. It was all speculation since I was sure any record of that account was now so far buried into others that no one was ever going to get to the truth. And what account specifically where they talking about? The budget is so big and bloated that it could have been one of hundreds. I am not sure ten people knew the exact account in the budget.

The following week I was on my way back to D.C for the budget meetings. On my way I was invited to stay over with Dylan James and the family in North Carolina for a couple of days. I had been putting off that visit for over almost a year now. Once I got there Dylan showed me his new recording studio in his home as well as telling me all the news about his record label. For whatever reason, he and Carl were not agreeing with the direction of the record label, so Carl sold his interests. Carl had hinted to me several times he was going to do it but I did not know it was official until I arrived at Dylan's home.

"George I have big plans for this company but I am a musician. I will admit I enjoy learning about running this label and I think I did pretty well for myself being a band leader all these years but I would like to be able to rely on you for advice now and again. Are you willing to take a call from me now and again?"

"Of course Dylan, I don't have the slightest idea on how to judge the ability of a band but I can help with the financial side of the business."

"Thanks, I knew I could count on you."

I spent the next day taking a ride around the hills of North Carolina with Dylan and Lorenza, his wife. Later that evening we had dinner with his older daughter and her family and the younger daughter and her boy friend. I could sense some tension between Dylan and the younger daughter but when they decided to play the guitars all the tensions magically disappeared.

The following morning I was about to leave when Lorenza followed me to my car. "George, I need to ask you a favor please. Dylan, well his health needs to be watched and this record label business is stressing him out more than he realizes. He forgets things now and this is not so good for him. Please, please I beg you to help him. I am going to convince him to let someone help him more. I know he likes you and for me well, I can see into a person's soul. You have a good soul, so I am asking you to help him, please. He will never admit it but he does listen to me. If I tell him you are going to help, he will listen."

"Thank you for your trust Lorenza. It has been a long time since anyone other than a few close to me, has trusted me. I don't know anything about the music business but I will consider it."

"You are good man Mr. Congressperson. You make my heart full, ciao mio amico." With that I drove away with a smile not only because I was still filled from the previous night with pasta and good wine but her Italian accent and broken English always gave me a warm feeling.

The budget meeting seemed to me to be an exercise in futility. We had made our recommendations but since many involved huge budget cuts and the President ran on keeping all the entitlements in place with no cuts, he had to make it look like it was our responsibility to come up with fresh ideas. I had no idea why Congress was not taking on this issue but I guess it was more politically prudent to dump it all on some unelected committee to come up with ideas likely never to be implemented. Even though I did enjoy learning from others on the committee, all I could think about was that I could be watching spring training baseball back home and not sitting in this room filled with over inflated egos, most of which were suffering from diarrhea of the mouth.

After the second day of meeting as I was leaving the building, Josh Simpson once again approached me about Danker.

"Congressman, please give me just a moment of your time. I went by the morgue and it seems Danker's body was cremated only two days after the murder. Were you aware of that?"

"Yes that was all exposed in the trial, so what?"

"The coroner told me that the reason why it was done so quickly was for religious reasons and his family pressed for it to be done quickly. The investigators never objected. The thing is, the only family member I can find of his is a son in prison in California, convicted of drug trafficking. His son never signed that release, it was impossible the family asked for a quick cremation."

"Josh, I am sure you are doing a fine job with your investigation but let me give you some advice from someone who knows, this case is trouble, do us all a favor and let it drop."

"What the hell does that mean Congressman, trouble? One more thing, the same day of Danker's demise there was a boating accident on the Potomac River. The Harbor Police reported bringing in three drowning victims to the morgue yet only two bodies are on the record as having been recorded into the morgue. They were all illegal immigrants with little identification."

"Josh, one last time, none of this has anything to do with me. I am doing all I can to put this all behind me and move on with my life."

"I don't know what happened to you but I heard you were all about the truth and doing things right. You have been castrated. I will get to the bottom of this with or without you!"

"You really are not listening to me. Even if I wanted to help you, I don't know anything more than you seem to know. As far as I am concerned this case is in my rear view window."

"The coroner tells me off the record that not only was he pressured into claiming it was in fact Danker who was cremated but his finger tips were all destroyed. Why would his finger tips be destroyed? Did you notice if his hands seemed normal to you the day you met with him? I am convinced it was not Danker who was cremated. I am not even sure he was murdered. None of this matters to you?"

"Of course it matters to me but I was once told over and over to let it go, I suggest you now take that same advice."

"Can I quote you on that?"

"We never had this conversation Josh, now if you will excuse me."

I got right on the phone with Mr. Pruitt with all I had just learned from Simpson. "George, once and for all, the handling of the body and all surrounding I admit, it was atrocious. To a trained eye it there was fraud and deceit all over the investigation. If you think about it, I did all I could to expose these facts. Now, I don't know about drowned bodies in the river or burned off finger tips. I will look through the testimony if it will make you feel better but I do not have any recollection of the coroner suggesting foul play. How do you know that reporter talked with the same one who testified at the trial?"

"Mr. Pruitt, did you know that the sun only comes across your back yard in the same exact spot at the same time of day once a year? I can't dismiss Simpson completely. Plus, even you must see that if Danker is alive I can tell my side of the story and reclaim my life."

"Last I looked you were sitting on a high ranking committee appointed by the President of the United States sitting with captains of industry and working for a prestigious law firm in New York. You have your health and your freedom. I would suggest to you once again that your life though not perfect, is still better than most, let this go. Stop allowing that reporter to fill your head with innuendo and wild stories. I will do some checking but let it go, please."

I knew Mr. Pruitt was only protecting me and he really didn't have time to investigate some wild goose chase of a story. I also knew while in town with this story having been somewhat exposed, it was possible I was being watched again, so I needed to lay low and go home as quickly as possible without speaking with Simpson again.

Once back in Florida, I was settling into finding investments for Peterson and his clients. It had only been a couple of months so it was hard to tell if I was still doing as well as I had in the past. Josh Simpson was still reporting the occasional story about the three drowned immigrants but only two bodies were accounted for in the records. The records really did indicate that only two bodies were admitted to the morgue so there was no story as far as the morgue was concerned. The Harbor Police had records of three bodies taken from the water but the morgue had records of two bodies being delivered. Since the other bodies were here illegally it was hard to track the existence of a third body. It was a tough climb for Simpson and there was not much interest in an illegal immigrant drowning in the river. When Simpson contacted the police officer who signed the report of three drowning victims he had no recollection of the number he delivered. That only inspired him more since he knew the officer was lying. But his editor was growing weary of a story that was going nowhere and once again the reports ceased.

22

Nicole was feeling more and more abandoned. She would not tell me directly but I could tell if the President was Michael's father for sure, he was no longer in contact with her directly. She was no longer invited to the Bahamas with Lentz or the skiing trip in Aspen. Her monthly money had stopped and even Lentz was not talking with her as often. She was growing more and more frustrated with everyone but there was not much I could do for her.

"George, what am I supposed to do now? Michael's father does not seem to want to be involved which is ok I guess but I feel betrayed."

"How so?"

"Well, the guy told me he loved me and that one day when it all settled down we would be together one day but he has a bad way of showing it when I have not seen him in over nine months now and my support money stopped almost three months ago with no word on if it will continue again."

"First of all, you have to know the President was never going to divorce his wife while in office. You must know how insane that even sounds."

"Of course, but, hey wait, who says it's the President we are talking out here."

"Enough of the nonsense girl, if you want to come by and lean my shoulder it is time to come clean and stop the charade."

"You are right. It is even silly of me to think I can hide it from you. You have known for a while now who the father is. We did meet in the Bahamas a few times as well as here in Florida and once in Aspen. He is a kind person George and I am convinced he loves his son. I guess with all the reports going around about politicians having kids being protected by the Secret Service he has to be careful now. Maybe once his term is over he can spend more time with his son and me."

"I have no idea Nicole, I really don't but I would not sit around waiting for another three to four years to find out. I don't think the odds are in your favor that he will come to you one day. I am sorry but I don't see it happening."

"Maybe you are right George, but I don't really have any other options at this point."

"What are you crazy, you are still a young beautiful and smart woman get on with your life and stop throwing your daily pity parties."

"I guess you are right. It is time for me to start thinking about what is best for Michael and me and move on with my life. What about you? What do you think you are going to do?"

"I wish I knew. I can't pick investments for Carl forever. It is really a part time job that really does not pay much. Most of the big investment houses won't touch me, even now. I guess I could start my own business but I would not know what to do. Dylan calls me now and again about helping him but he really wants advice and does not really want to give up control. What I think I would like to do is run for that Senate seat but that's not a realistic goal right now. I know it's stupid to miss politics after what was done to me but I do miss it."

"What would it take for you to be able to run for Senate?"

"Having my reputation restored would be a start. That alone would not guarantee a thing since I am sure it would be a tough contest even with the best of reputations but that would certainly help. Maybe I could wait four years for the other seat to open up or even six when this one comes up again but it's a long shot. I think I am resigned to finding something in investments and working in that field forever. If the right private business opportunity came along I would jump on it if it meant I could never get back into politics."

"Never say never, don't give up your dream, you never know what can happen. What about us George, do you think it's possible we can try again?"

"I think I would like a family in the near future Nicole. Sue and I have been dating as you know. You and I have tried once and it didn't work."

"That was a long time ago now and I have changed with my child. I am starting to see what is important and what is stable and what is not. I would really like it if we could try again."

I didn't tell Nicole but the next day I went to see Bob Lentz about seeing if I could get some support payments made to her again.

"What are you kidding me, you ass! It's mostly your fault all this mess with the Secret Service came out in the news and that's why the payments had to be stopped. Like I have told that pain in the ass with a tight skirt, maybe in time we can get her some money again but not now. Besides, where do you think the money should come from now?"

"How about directly from the child's father for one."

"You really are a sick puppy aren't you? Do you really think he is going to admit to being the kid's father or send her money from any account with his name on it? If you care about her so much be a good boy and take her off everyone's hands. Now that would make some story, would it not?"

As I departed I could hear Lentz still laughing in the background. I knew it was a long shot but I had to see how much she really was being abandoned now that the election as over. I guess Morrison did not think Nicole would ever let this story leak out and one day tell her story to the media. To my thinking it was a big gamble for him to ignore her completely but I was not privy to what he had told her in the past or her true feelings for him. I also knew she didn't want her son to have to take the scrutiny of it all later in life.

I went home from seeing Lentz and took a nap. I didn't wake up until after dinner. When I did I was stunned to hear the teaser to the news being that there would be a story about my innocence. I made a call to the station to find out what it was all about. I was only told that someone had come forward to proclaim my side of the story. I called Pruitt but the office was closed and he was not answering his cell phone.

I was shocked even more to see Nicole on my television screen in what looked to be a quickly put together interview attempting to defend me. She was doing her best to explain to the well known local reporter that she knew I was innocent of any wrong doing but would not give any facts as to why. It got even more distorted when the reporter had her admit that we were at one time a couple and he slanted the report that I must have put her up to coming to the station because she had feelings for me. Of course the question was asked if I was the father of her child. He was not sympathetic to her story nor did it put me the best light. She would only repeat that she had evidence of my innocence of any crime but would not say what the evidence was. I was furious.

I called her immediately to see what she was thinking about when she decided to do that piece for the news. "I only wanted to make life easier for you so you can find a good job again. I want you to be able to be Senator and its all my fault you can't do that. I am so sorry, please forgive me."

What was I to do now? She really did try to do something with my best interest at heart but it only opened up history that I was desperately trying to bury. We talked for a few moments and I could tell she was still shaken from it all by the tone in her voice. I left a message for Pruitt then stayed up for hours worried about what might happen next on so many levels.

The next day the local newspaper called for a reaction and all I could do was give them my attorney's number and left it at that. I also received a visit from Lentz the next day at my home. "So what the hell was that all about? Was that your way of trying to shake some money from a stone? What is it going to take to get your leave this all alone and walk away?"

"Bob, I was as shocked as everyone to see her on my screen. She did not tell me anything about this nor did the station call to give me a heads up. I swear I was just as shocked as everyone else."

"You tell that girl friend of yours, no more stunts like that one or you are both going to wish you were never born. And yes that is a threat!"

Mr. Pruitt called the station and made sure they made a follow up on the story that I in no way had any idea the report was being done nor did I ask Nicole or suggest she do it. The station made no mention of it on any future reports.

A few days later Josh Simpson was on my cell phone sounding all giddy about something. "I have the smoking gun, the big one, and I don't mean the evidence about Danker. This is your last chance to come clean with your side of the story before I release mine. I will report what I know and you will be left behind on this one Congressman."

"Josh what on earth do you think you know now?"

"I know that pretty thing of yours was on local television proclaiming your innocence. It seems the local boys don't know how to do research, I do."

"What does that mean Josh?"

"It means I am calling you out of courtesy for you to give me what really happened in Washington, if not it will be front page news tomorrow from the evidence I did uncover."

"Good luck Josh."

I called Pruitt to warn him but at this point there was not much I could do. I also warned Nicole and Lentz about the reporter making claims but I was staying far away from it.

As promised by Simpson the story was front page news in the Washington Gazette only it was not accurate. The headline read, "Presidential Blackmail" with the story claiming I had knowledge of a child born to the President and was blackmailing him for political favor. The story then inferred that I was then charged with murder to gain my silence. Simpson was close but not totally accurate.

The report got instant attention from the White House press secretary claiming the story was pure fantasy. My attorneys were in front of every television station that would have them claiming no truth to the black mail story. The town now had a scandal of the highest degree. Reporters were camped in front of Nicole's and my apartments. The following day her son's birth certificate was printed on the front page all over the country with the name of the father being listed as J.M. Morrison. Stories were being written all over the place with none being one hundred percent accurate. Major news reporters were now covering Palm Beach County. There was no place to hide. I wanted to grab Nicole and get her out of town but it was too late. She had to stay in her apartment.

The story was breaking fast. It was now common knowledge her apartment was in the name of a company that the President's brother owned stock. The media was now connecting the dots. The President's spokespeople were all over the media claiming he had no knowledge of her living situation. That might have actually been accurate. He may not have personally known where she lived or in what name the apartment was listed.

Nicole called me the next day. "My lawyer tells me to stay in my apartment and say nothing, what do you think?"

"I think you should listen to your attorney."

"George, I only wanted to help you and now look at this mess. I got a call from someone in Colorado today claiming she has a daughter with the President too and we should go out in public and admit all we know. I told you I thought there was another child."

"That person can be anyone. You have no idea if she's telling the truth. I would listen to your attorney and let this all blow over."

"We both know this is too big of a story to blow over. I can't continue my life like this and neither can you. I need to tell the truth."

Twenty minutes later Nicole walked out front of her apartment with her attorney by her side and told the media that the President was the father of her son. They had met before he was President and it was a short term relationship. She also admitted that she did receive payments but did not know where the money came from and never asked. When asked about how she knew I was innocent she stated that I was looking into something in the national budget and because of it, it led to trouble for me. She continued that she knew I was not capable of murder nor did I ever blackmail anyone. All the cable news stations were on live with the story. I wept for her as I was watching her get throttled with questions for about ten minutes. The attorney then made a short statement and they quickly vanished.

Mr. Pruitt was on the line moments later discussing my options. He thought now with all the news breaking we could tell our side of the story and not risk going to jail but it was still a risk. I told him that my father was still reminding me that "the truth wins out in end no matter how far down its buried." I decided to sit tight. I was going crazy in my apartment for days and running out of food.

The next few days were a blur but I did manage to go out for a while to the grocery store. Granted I could have had someone do things like that for me but why? Josh Simpson was in town following me everywhere asking for an exclusive story.

"I'll tell you what Josh if I ever do speak, you will be my guy, how's that? But I will give you one bit of the story that everyone has wrong that you can quote me on. I was not investigating if the President had children out of wedlock nor was I aware about Nicole and the father of her son with any certainty until after the trial. That you can print. I was never blackmailing anyone. The White House press secretary is accurate in that statement."

"None of this makes sense Congressman. I don't think you killed anyone. I think Danker is alive and they cremated a drowned undocumented illegal. I think you know that. I think you knew all along. I think you are still protecting something or someone and I am not going to stop until I find out."

"You are wrong about Danker. I still believe he is dead. My life was on the line for his murder. I have an agreement never to speak about it and I intend to honor that agreement. Now I have told you all I know. If I ever decide to tell what I was looking for, which if you ask around you can easily find out, I will tell you. But in all sincerity, I want to move on with my life. Whatever happened with Danker, or Nicole and the President has nothing to do with me. I was living up to my responsibilities as an elected official, nothing more, and nothing less. Now, if you continue to follow me into every store I enter, I will renege on my word to tell you my story. But don't hold your breath waiting for that day to occur."

Josh let out a loud laugh, "Congressman this might be the biggest story that ever comes my way do you think I intend to let it go?" I watched him walk away so I could return to thumping a melon in the fruit section.

The following weeks were filled with stories of how Nicole seduced a powerful man for her own personal gain. It went way beyond ignorance and stupidity in my opinion but the President did have his allies in the press. Nicole was being made out to be someone she was not and tabloids from all over the world were offering substantial sums of money for photos of my godson. It had become overwhelming with the attention. The funny thing was how few reports went after the President for some kind of explanation, let alone his resignation. National polling showed that only fifty three percent of the people believed it was his child. It seemed that people had become so use to such improprieties now that this was twisted more about someone seeking a financial motive than an influential man taking advantage of a woman over twenty years his junior. Most stories were downright sickening to the point I had to avoid all the news casts and papers, so not to blow my blood pressure any higher.

Again Josh Simpson showed up at my door uninvited. "Come on Congressman, we both know the rest of the media is messing up this entire story. I know it is Morrison's kid. Come clean and let's get this story right."

"You might be correct Josh. It might be the President's child. But in reality, there is no proof. There has never been a blood test and I am only going by what everyone else knows. I do not think Nicole is lying, but concrete proof, I really can't help you."

"Congressman, one last time please tell me your story. I will tell you this time that I have a source telling me they have proof that Danker is indeed alive. In fact, he is in negotiations to turn himself in to the FBI."

I chuckled warmly before stating, "If anyone is ever going to get the complete and accurate story I know it will be you, but really you don't need me if Danker is still alive. Because if you can gain access to him, you can find out all I know and much more. And I will tell you one thing with certainty, if you can find Danker alive and prove I never should have been brought to trial for murder, I will tell you anything you want to know. But be warned there is no story beyond what you seem to know other than I didn't kill anyone and a few rumors about a President's wife from long ago."

"Oh, now I must find Danker and learn about the wife, that's the first I have heard about her in all of this."

"Tell me Josh why are you so certain that Danker is not pushing daisies?"

"I wish I could, but for now I am sworn to secrecy but it is from a very reliable source. It is my cousin who once worked at the Secret Service, that's all I will tell you for now. But keep an eye out for what I suspect to be true. Once it is, I will be back in touch for my exclusive story with you and Nicole."

"Hey I didn't say anything about Nicole's story, only mine."

We were both laughing pretty hard but he was of course serious about not only what I knew but insisting on an exclusive with Nicole as well. In a way I was starting to gain a little trust with Josh. He did seem sincere in getting the story correct even if he had been slightly wrong in his previous reports. I also gave him credit for one thing. He was the only reporter who kept following up on the Danker murder angle of the story and the drowned immigrants. His theory was starting to make sense to me.

A few days later a small story hit the Washington Gazette with Josh Simpson as the lead reporter with the headline, "FBI Spies Secret Service". Josh called me so that I could read the story over the internet. It was about how the FBI had information of faking a murder even within its own ranks. There were few details but he was again accurate in what was going to happen in the near future. It did not seem like a big story at the time to the uninformed public but I knew the implications of it all.

Later that day my attorney's office received a short note addressed to me that I asked them to open and read to me over the phone.

"I am sorry for the pain I had you endure. Family at times can make you do things you would never do for a stranger. I am not proud of what I did but I do intend to pay the price and make it right. I trust that now you will get your life back in order. I wish you all the best in the future. D.D."

I was surprised but at this point I can't say stunned. I think Mr. Pruitt was surprised but even he was starting to be a believer. He called the FBI to see what he could find out but they were being tight lipped about everything. No one would comment or even admit they were investigating the Secret Service and in house.

Nicole was still being harassed going back and forth from work. The White House press corps was asking the occasional question at the daily briefings but the story again seemed to go away as quickly as it started. There was even one story about how if the President was forced to resign over a scandal the Vice President who was not in the best of health with cancer treatments might not be able to assume the duties of the Presidency. The story went as far as to suggest replacing the current Vice President before they would have to travel down to the third in line to be President which would be the Speaker of the House, Dan Taylor. There were whispers from what I was being told from within the party the President was taking heat internally but no investigation was being planned. After all, being in the majority party in the House does have its advantages politically. Both major parties wanted this story to go away since I was convinced this went farther than Corbin and the President. I was certain both parties used that account for many years and that was one story no one wanted to see the light of day. So even though there may have been some who would bring down their own party for doing what was right, it was still the minority who would do it.

23

"George I am being offered a lot of money to tell my story. My attorney is listening to offers to be on television or maybe even a book deal. I was never in this for the money but this could help me start a college fund for little Michael, what do you think?'

"Oh, don't drag me into this decision. I mean what do you really plan on telling them? You have already seen how it can be twisted to make you look like the bad person here. Why do you still want to draw that kind of attention?"

"Because I can make two hundred thousand dollars for one interview, that's why."

"I don't know Nicole, I agree that is a lot of money but there are always consequences and I am not sure they will be good ones beyond a few bucks here. Can I ask you one question, it might sound silly but are you sure beyond a doubt Morrison is the father of Michael?"

After a long pause she calmly replied, "no, not really."

"Are you kidding me? You really don't know one hundred percent for sure?"

"Well, I think he is but you and I were still going out when I met him and if you remember you did stay overnight one time a week or so before I met Jeff. I mean I know I was stupid and things got out of control for a few days after I met him. I didn't know where to turn and I happen to mention it to Bob Lentz I was pregnant and I had slept with Jeff and everyone was so intent on getting him elected they just paid me to stay quiet. I never asked for the money. I mean, like one day Bob Lentz showed up with a handful of money and told me I would be cared for if I stayed quiet about it all. I was so scared to tell you because we had been fighting and really were not seeing each other anymore. I was scared and had no place to turn."

"Does anyone else know what you just told me?"

"No."

"What on earth do you think you would say in the interview then? Did it ever occur to you that these people are very good at what they do and they would drag that information out of you?"

"No, I guess not, maybe I should just stay quiet then huh?"

"I am at a loss for words Nicole, all this time Michael could be my son?"

"Maybe but I really don't think so George. However it is why I made you the godfather."

Was it possible my day could get even stranger? I think not. I went home and for the first time in a long time had a few drinks to calm my nerves. Later that night my cell phone would not stop ringing so I finally picked it up.

"Congressman, the FBI has Danker in protective custody. He has told them it was all a set up and turned over the name Agent Fenton to them"

"Who's this?"

"It's Josh... Josh Simpson, isn't this Congressman McAdams?"

"Congressman? Me? Nah, I used to be one but they kicked me out, who is this?"

"Are you drunk or something, it's Josh, I am trying to tell you that Danker is alive and he handed all over all the evidence to clear you, so now I want your story and Nicole's."

"Who is this on my phone, is it you Desmond?"

"Go sleep it off, I will contact you tomorrow."

I woke up the next morning with a splitting headache since I rarely drank. My phone rang again with ole Josh laughing in my ear. "So did you have fun last night Congressman?"

"What do you mean, did I have fun?"

Again another roar of laughter came through my splitting headache. "You don't even remember talking with me last night do you?"

"You called me last night?"

"Yeah I told that the FBI had Danker in custody and that he admitted to them you were set up, you don't remember any of that?"

"Sorry, I guess not, what time was all that?"

"I don't know it was late, maybe even past midnight. So when do I get my interview?"

Now it was my turn to laugh, "How do I know any of this is true?"

"Give it up pal, we both know now it's true and there will be story about it all very soon, we are double checking a few facts before we release all the information."

"Josh, ok if all of this is true I will give you my side of the story as promised but how did you know about all of this and the drowned bodies and that Danker was still alive, the whole thing? I mean you even found me sitting at the Lincoln Memorial, how did you know to find me there?"

"Oh please George, most people around Washington worth a darn knew you sat there all the time, but you know my cousin, Paula Green. As you know she worked for the Secret Service. She gave Danker a lot of information, the same that you were looking for, so to some degree I do know what you were looking for. I know it was a budget thing, I know you and Danker were both getting close to the truth and someone found a way to silence the both of you. I think I know how they got to Danker but I am still somewhat confused as to why they let you off the hook so easily."

"Where is Paula now?"

"She went into the witness protection program after she felt like people were following her. If they knew she was calling me they would be really pissed off with her. She knew it was all a set up and went to the FBI long ago and they have been quietly investigating her story. The problem was they didn't have enough evidence until Danker was found. She somehow knew Danker was going to turn himself in. I think she had stayed in contact with him, even after she went into seclusion out west."

"Ok, Josh, if all of this turns out to be accurate, I will sit down and tell you what you want to know. But I warn you, you are going to be disappointed. You seem to know all I know now and more just like Danker did."

"Oh there are other things I am sure. I will talk with you soon, go take some aspirin. You sound like crap."

A few days later, there was a press release from the Federal Bureau of Investigations with a carefully worded statement.

"There is a pending investigation concerning the murder of Desmond Danker. There is undeniable evidence that Congressman George McAdams never committed or attempted the murder of Mr. Desmond Danker. We will release more information once the investigation has been completed."

I knew a few hours before hand what the statement would say since the lead investigator informed Mr. Pruitt that Mr. Danker would not give up any evidence unless it was released to the media that I had not committed his murder. It was part of his plea agreement.

Many of the cable news shows started to call me later that evening to set up interviews but I was going to keep my word to Josh Simpson. Mr. Pruitt released a statement that we were all very relieved that this incident was now behind us and it was time to move forward. There would a full statement at a later date.

24

The calls were flooding in from people who now wanted to be friends again. It was like a bulls eye was taken off my back but I was very wary about who I could trust and who not. This experience was not only a large eye opener but changed me personally. I grew a harder exterior now and was not as naïve as I was only a few years previous.

Nicole came over to see me since she could not get me on the phone, "Hey, Oprah called she wants us on the show this week."

"Are you crazy, you want me to get on that couch with Oprah and cry my eyes out? No way, you go alone."

It was not the reaction she had expected but I did not want this to turn into a tabloid story. I wanted it to all go away so I could adjust my life and decide where I could go from here. I did enjoy my call from Tom Darcy however.

"George, I trust one day you will forgive me for the way I treated you the last time we were together but I had to think about my company first and foremost. I hope you understand. I wanted to believe in you, I really did. If you will accept my apology I am sure we can find an appropriate office for you."

"Thanks Mr. Darcy, I will keep that in mind but right now I am going to keep all my options open, but I thank you for the call."

Soon after the call from Darcy, Bob Lentz's shadow was in my door way. "May I come in? We need to get started George, I know it seems like a long time but four years will go by fast."

"Get started on what?"

"Raising money and getting you back in the public eye for the Senate seat that's open in four years. I don't think we have enough time for this next election and besides it looks like Taylor is going to give up the Speaker post and run. He owns the northern part of the state so let's let that go and you focus on the southern part of the state and the other Senate seat."

"Lentz, you are too much. I could contact the FBI and have you put in jail why on earth would I have you help me rather than see you rot in jail?"

"Rot in jail, are you crazy, there is not a damn thing you can do to incriminate me. Now are you going to let me help you or not?"

"Slow down, what about all the payments given to Nicole from the US Treasury, that only for starters."

He gave me a very evil stare and proceeded to either an offer a lecture or a warning my way. I guess I will never be sure. "What payments do you mean? You mean the payments for rent on the apartment that my company partially owns that we were gracious enough to allow Ms. Hunter to work as property manager? She was allowed reduced rents for her work as property manager, just ask her George. Or the payments I received for all the catering I did at government functions in my establishment? You still have no idea how all this works do you Mr. Senator?"

I was amazed at his brash behavior and nature but then again I guess I should have been use to it by now.

"George, the public is going to love you once we get done with you. I mean a man willing to go to jail to protect his integrity and his principles. No, you don't see the big picture yet like I do. The party will have you pegged very soon and promote you straight to the top, you watch. No, I have seen it in your eyes. That look that someone get's after they have felt the political power Washington affords someone. Don't you dare insult me and tell me it's not in your blood now despite what politics did to you. I am a kingmaker, you are my next king."

"That's not exactly what happened, Bob. I was set up for murder to keep my mouth shut."

"No, you were set up for murder because of your relentless search for the truth and to stand up for all those poor taxpayers who still think a million dollars is a lot of money. You did all that even after the media tore you to shreds. You honored your agreement and kept quiet about it all. That's true courage and leadership Mr. Future President."

"Oh please, I kept my mouth shut so I would not go to jail for murder for a guy who was apparently laying on a beach with a margarita somewhere."

"George, wake up and realize after a short run of being a Senator, we can push you into the White House. It will be all about public perception and very soon you are will be as hot as they come. Now, I have the connections to get you the cash you will need, give me a call when you are ready. And don't do anything stupid like inform the FBI about some payments you think you know about. You will only look the fool."

Once I thought about it, I knew he was likely right in that I would never be able to get him connected to payments used for hush money now and besides that would only hurt Nicole and Michael in the long run.

My head was spinning with all the calls and offers coming for interviews and even job offers. One was from Carl Peterson who I had to admit along with Dylan James were two people who never wavered from my defense. I knew when Carl offered to take me to lunch I had to find the time.

"I have a really good opportunity for you George, one I want you to put some real thought into before you say yes or no. The entertainment management side of our business has gone so well the law firm wants to make it a separate entity. Some feel it is hurting the trial and defense side of our business. I think it only enhances it, but our firm was founded as a criminal defense legal team and some feel that is being lost. We are considering very carefully the idea of moving the entertainment agency part of the business to Palm Beach or Orlando. We have more and more clients now who live in Florida for tax reasons and it seems I spend a good part of my time in your area now. We would keep a small office in our offices in New York for show but we would move a large majority of it to Florida. You would still help me with investments but you would work directly for me as the manager of all our investments. You will meet with me and our clients and explain to them all their security and investment options. Think about it George, you will be hanging out with the some of the top ball players, musicians and movie stars from all over the country. It is a very good opportunity for you, take your time and think about. I won't say that you owe me one, but you owe me one. We handled your trial at a fraction of our usual fees and the other guys took a chunk of it from my profits last year. You think on this one, it will be the best offer you get."

He was right, it was an incredible offer and I did owe him. It was one I really had to consider. But I also knew that was not a job where you go home at five and sip a wine cooler. This was going to be an exhausting job with high profile people for big dollars. Was it something I really wanted to do? I was not sure but it sure was something to think about.

At the press briefing inside the White House the press secretary, Stefan Carney made a remark about how pleased the President and the entire administration was that Congressman McAdams was exonerated of all charges. He continued on how the President knew his faith in me was on target all along. That was why I had been appointed to his special committee. I knew that was code to me to stay quiet, please.

Later in the week Josh gave me another call. "Congressman, I will ask for more of a story later but for now tell me, do you think you were being set up because you were investigating too close to the Secret Service and did you believe they were using the funds to hide children of politicians?"

"On the record, yes I was searching for where the money was going. Off the record, Danker only told me about the connection to the kids the day he was murdered, well not murdered, well you know. I cannot verify that the money was being used to harbor kids of any politician though I would not rule out that angle if I were you."

"You have to do better than that dude, you know if your girl friend Nicole was collecting cash or not."

"Where her funds come from is not my concern now. If you speak with Danker he will fill you in, or your cousin. Honest and truly they know more than me."

"I get it, you are going to protect your girl but you owe me more."

"I seems like I am hearing that a lot these days" I said laughing as I hung up the phone.

The next day in the Gazette a story was printed by Josh Simpson of how it all started with a low level Congressman looking into a small budget item and he was eventually set up for murder. The story went on to tell about how the Secret Service was protecting children of politician's born out of wedlock. It continued with how when that Congressman got too close to discovering it all and blowing the whistle, there was a major cover up and a murder scheme. It told about how Desmond Danker was investigating a story for an upcoming book and stumbled across the same story about the same time the Congressman did. When all this happened at the same time the Secret Service plotted to protect those they are in charge of protecting and decided to eliminate both people by setting up a Congressman for murder. It talked about the drowned immigrants and how one of the bodies was likely used as Danker's body for cremation. Danker went along with the idea only because he was promised from the Justice Department that his son would be released from jail for a crime for which a grieving father never wanted to believe was possible. He would also have to remain silent on what he had uncovered at the Secret Service and stay out of the public eye. It made mention of how promises were made at high levels in the Justice Department but did not go as far as accusing President Morrison of approving such a release. It mentioned Nicole Hunter and how she and her son received payoffs from the Secret Service. It explained how the Congressman knew at one point and backed off pointing a finger at Nicole since he is the godfather of her child. The story was still not completely accurate but it did once again start the firestorm of a scandal in Washington.

Stefan Carney was in the press room in the White House denouncing the story again as pure fantasy. My attorney released a statement claiming at no time did I know of any payments and that I was only investigating a budget item as part of my daily responsibilities. The Justice Department released a strongly worded statement that at no time did anyone from within Justice ever promise or meet with Danker. The FBI again continued its silence because of a pending investigation.

The scandal was swirling around Washington but it really was not my concern now. I knew one day soon I would have to sit down with Josh as promised. There were still a few holes in his story.

Libby called and wanted to let me know that she enjoyed working for Tracey but when I was ready to make a run for the Senate seat she would be ready to come back as my aide. Kristen didn't mind since she was now entrenched back home in Florida with her ever expanding drug prevention program. Matthew was doing well with his home building company and Samantha well, I saw her on ESPN the other night screaming at the officials from the bench for her girl's team. She was now the head coach at a large university and well some things never change. Mrs. Klienberg still calls me when her pipes are backed up or her lawn is not cut properly and invites me thinking I can still help her but really I know it's an invitation for a home cooked meal. "Bring a date this time, you need to be married with children and soon." I go because I do enjoy her and hey, you never know when I will need votes again.

Dylan James called and told me that his wife is in his ear way too much now about turning over the record label to someone else to run full time. "The job is yours, you will get to work from home and travel with me around the world looking for new talent to sign and develop. You get to use your marketing skills, your financial skills and you get to eat Lorenza's pasta from time to time. Think about it."

I certainly have a lot to think about, that's for sure. I guess I will have to do that while I sit in the Doctor's office getting a blood test to see if Nicole is right or not. I can only think about what President Lincoln once said, "I walk slowly but I never walk backwards."

ABOUT THE AUTHOR

I was told that in this section for my first novel "A Beautiful Song" it made me sound like a boring person. But I am who I am and at times I guess I can be boring but I am ok with that. I reside in Florida with my wife and kids who are not boring and are all exceptional people. I have a few friends who sometimes are boring but they we don't seem to mind either. When not writing I attempt to do commercial real estate, enjoy photography and find spare time to play a game of chess. I am big sports fan and can be found taking photos at spring training baseball games. I also will spend hours walking around our local lake enjoying what mother nature has to offer. I use writing as an outlet to relieve my stress from real estate deals gone bad which are all too common now. Sometimes when no one is around I will pretend to be Dylan James from the first novel and play the guitar but I can assure never as successfully as him.

I have no idea how many more books or short stories I will write. I guess it depends on the real estate market and how many of my non boring friends and others honor me with reading my works. I take it as a great honor when someone reads my stories and never take that for granted. I thank you all for your support. So until the next time, I am going to try not to be boring and start to think about the next story. Till then, I wish you all the best and living the life you want to live even if it tends to be boring at times, like me.

Mike Cantwell